"*You* cannot sleep here," she insisted.

She pushed against his naked chest with both hands, trying to put distance between them, but Ash was as unmovable as a granite wall.

"Stop squirming," he said.

"Get out of my bed!"

"Wrestler said he'd make you first wife. You might want to consider it."

The suggestion shocked her nearly as much as having this naked bounty hunter wrapped around her. "Marry him? I'd sooner wed you."

"I haven't proposed," he reminded her.

"I should have said I'd sooner wed the devil."

He chuckled. "I make it a practice never to marry a woman who's likely to shoot me."

"I don't think this is funny."

He cut her off with a kiss, a caress so sweet and tender that her resistance crumbled. . . .

By Judith E. French:

FORTUNE'S BRIDE
FORTUNE'S FLAME
FORTUNE'S MISTRESS
SHAWNEE MOON
SUNDANCER'S WOMAN
THIS FIERCE LOVING
McKENNA'S BRIDE*
RACHEL'S CHOICE*
MORGAN'S WOMAN*

*Published by Ballantine Books

MORGAN'S WOMAN

Judith E. French

BALLANTINE BOOKS • NEW YORK

A Ballantine Book
Published by The Ballantine Publishing Group
Copyright © 1999 by Judith E. French

All rights reserved under International and Pan-American Copyright Conventions. Published in the United States by The Ballantine Publishing Group, a division of Random House, Inc., New York, and simultaneously in Canada by Random House of Canada Limited, Toronto.

Ballantine and colophon are registered trademarks of Random House, Inc.

www.randomhouse.com/BB/

Library of Congress Catalog Card Number: 99-90434

ISBN 0-345-40875-6

Manufactured in the United States of America

First Edition: December 1999

10   9   8   7   6   5   4   3   2   1

For my mother,
Mildred E. Faulkner Bennett,
the bravest woman I'll ever know

The light that lies
In woman's eyes,
Has been my heart's undoing.
— THOMAS MOORE

Prologue

Autumn 1865

"Two horses? What do you mean, two horses?" Tamsin MacGreggor pushed back the black netting of her widow's veil and stared in shock at the lawyer.

"Best you sit, Mrs. MacGreggor," Randolph Crawshaw advised. "It's understandable that a lady in your circumstances—"

Tamsin found it hard to breathe. "You knew what my grandfather left me," she managed. "Four hundred acres of prime farmland, a mill, two houses, barns, over forty head of breeding horses—"

He shook his head. "Unfortunately, your husband—"

"Was a fool!" She struggled to regain her composure. "Surely our investments, the railroad stocks—"

"All gone." The lawyer mopped his bald head. "It grieves me to bring you such terrible financial news on top of your loss."

"Loss? Atwood MacGreggor?" She pressed her lips tightly together and stood up. "The only good thing my husband ever did for me was to save me the trouble of shooting him."

1

Chapter 1

Tamsin MacGreggor rose at first light and tiptoed across the bare, splintery floorboards to the washstand. The room was unheated and smelled of lye soap and tobacco. Shivering, she poured water from a pitcher into the cracked crockery basin.

Sweetwater, Colorado, hadn't impressed her very much, but it was farther west than Denver. And the ugly boardinghouse room was cleaner and cheaper than the hotel in Wheaton, Nebraska, where she'd worked in a general store for two months. Best of all, she'd left Jack Cannon behind her.

Tamsin scrubbed her face, then rubbed her aching back. She was still tired, despite ten hours' sleep. Sometimes it seemed as though she'd been weary since she left her home in Three Forks, Tennessee. There'd been so many small towns she couldn't remember them all, most cold and muddy. She'd traveled by train when she could manage the expense of shipping her horses. The rest of the time she'd ridden them, stopping only when her funds ran low or the weather was too awful.

She'd have made faster progress if she hadn't had to work her way across the country. Lawyer Crawshaw had been right when he'd said that Atwood had left her nothing but the two animals. She'd sold her mother's jewelry and most of her own clothing and personal items for what little money she could get.

Now she was down to ninety-two dollars and sixty-three cents. There would be no more trains. From here to California, across desert, mountain, and plains, she would ride her horses. Heaven help them all if one of the animals broke a leg or pulled a tendon.

Randolph Crawshaw had laughed at her when she'd told him that she intended to take the mare and stallion to California to start a new life. The lawyer had scoffed that a gentlewoman, alone, in these lawless times since the war had ended, wouldn't get as far as the Tennessee line with such valuable horseflesh.

"I guess I showed you, didn't I, Randolph?" she declared as she twisted her carrot-colored hair into a sensible braid and tied her hat strings under her chin. One thing she hadn't sold was her grandfather's Navy Colt. And any man who tried to take Fancy or Dancer from her would have to come through a hail of lead to get them.

The small looking glass over the washstand was blackened with age. Tamsin didn't bother to glance into it as she dressed. Years of rushing out in the darkness to aid a horse in distress had taught her to find her clothing and plait her thick hair by touch. Besides, a twenty-six-year-old woman, as tall and sturdy as she was, had no need of mirrors.

Tamsin had left her black widow's garments behind in Tennessee. Her clothing was as sensible as her plain freckled face: a dark green wool skirt, divided for riding astride, a neat white shirt, and a short green jacket to match the skirt. Her russet boots were old but crafted of the finest leather with heels high enough for riding and low enough for comfortable walking.

She gathered her few belongings and stowed them in the saddlebags, then slid the heavy pistol into the holster hidden beneath her skirt. It was amazing how little a woman could get by with when it had to be carried on two horses. Her entire future, all her hopes and dreams, was wrapped up in those animals.

Thoroughbreds both, the stallion and mare were the results of her grandfather's life as a breeder of champion racing stock. Surely, such speed and noble lines would be appreciated in California. And with luck and hard work, she intended to build another stable of purebred horses, one that no spendthrift husband would ever wrest away from her.

She hurried through breakfast, paid for her accommodations. Pausing for a moment on the uneven wooden walkway outside of the boardinghouse, she swung the saddlebags over one shoulder and looked carefully around.

Except for a farmer leading a workhorse into the smithy and a boy washing the window in front of a dry goods store, the muddy street was nearly deserted. A block down, she could see someone raking the dirt in front of the livery stable where she'd left Fancy and Dancer for the night.

It had rained sometime after midnight. Tamsin remembered hearing the rhythmic downpour against the tin roof. Yesterday's choking dust was gone, replaced with brisk, fresh air. Fingers of fog hung over the town, but the golden rays piercing the clouds promised a fair day.

Then, to her left, she heard the creak of saddle leather. She glanced at the tall rider coming around the corner and quickly looked away when their eyes met.

"Morning, ma'am," the big man said. He shifted his rifle to his other arm and touched his hat with one gloved finger.

Tamsin gasped as she took in the stranger and the two horses trailing behind him. Each animal carried a gruesome cargo, a dead man slung over the bloodstained saddle.

Muffling a cry of distress, she seized the doorknob, preparing to rush back into the boardinghouse. The quick glimpse she'd had of the ruffian was enough to convince her she didn't wish to be on the same street with him.

A wide-brimmed hat had shaded stark features bronzed by sun and wind. His sensual mouth was a thin line, his sharply chiseled jawline unshaven. The broad shoulders, long legs, hard-muscled arms were barely concealed by the black calf-length leather coat.

Tamsin had seen her share of desperate men since she started traveling west. This one reminded her of Jack Cannon. The polished rifle, and the gun belt visible where the stranger's duster hung open, didn't belong to a cowhand who had innocently stumbled upon two bodies.

The boardinghouse door opened and the widow Fremont peered into Tamsin's face suspiciously. "You forget something?"

"No, no," Tamsin assured her. "I just . . ." She motioned toward the horseman. "That man—He's . . . He has two dead—"

"More business for the undertaker?" The widow sniffed. "Best you steer clear of him, Mrs. MacGreggor." She emphasized the word *Mrs.* in an irritating manner. "That's Ash Morgan. He's a bounty hunter, a pistolero. If he's bringing in dead men, like as not he made them that way. Morgan hunts outlaws for a living. He's not to be trifled with."

Tamsin suppressed a shiver, hoping California would prove more civilized than Nebraska and Colorado. "I assure you, Mrs. Fremont, I have no intention of trifling with this gun shark or any other gentleman in Sweetwater. I was startled by . . . by the bodies. I thought perhaps he might be a desperado."

Mrs. Fremont sniffed again. "He claims to be on the side of law and order, but I'm not the judge of that." She frowned. "Decent women don't associate with his kind. Be seen with Ash Morgan and people will think you're one of Maudine's fancy pieces."

"I wasn't with him," Tamsin replied. "I was standing on your boardwalk when he rode by and spoke to me. I don't know him. I don't care to know him. As I explained, I'm leaving town this morning."

"Just as well. I run a decent place here. You be sure and tell any travelers you meet that I serve good grub and my beds are free of vermin."

"I will certainly do that." Seeing that the bounty hunter had turned off at the next corner, Tamsin lifted her skirts ankle high and stepped off the walk into the oozing wagon ruts. She was still unnerved by the terrible sight, but she'd not be deterred from her departure by a man like Morgan. Detouring around livestock droppings and mud puddles, she made it safely to the far side of the street.

The widow Fremont did provide excellent room and board for the cost, but her superior Philadelphia airs were infuriating. Mrs. Fremont might pass herself off as a lady here on the frontier, but she was obviously an uneducated, ill-bred woman. What made her assume that Tamsin intended to make the acquaintance of a gunfighter when she'd obviously been entering the boardinghouse to avoid him?

A small black terrier yipped loudly and ran behind an olive-skinned boy raking soiled straw away from the livery door. Tamsin smiled and bid the lad a good morning.

His dark, liquid eyes widened in surprise. For an instant, an odd expression flashed across his thin face. Then he darted away, followed by the still-barking dog.

Tamsin stepped inside the stable, taking a minute to let her eyes grow accustomed to the semidarkness. The air was heavy with the pungent scent of animals, fresh manure, and hay. Most women, she supposed, found such a place offensive. But she'd always felt at home amid the earthy smells and the familiar sounds of horses and the men who cared for them.

"Mr. Edwards," she called. "I've come for—" She broke off in midsentence as she saw the empty stall where she'd tied Fancy and Dancer the night before.

Hope of heaven! Her stomach turned over as she went suddenly cold. Where were her animals? She ran to the box stall and stared at it as if she expected them to magically reappear.

"Mr. Edwards!" she shouted. "Where are my horses?"

She paced the length of the barn looking into each space. Where could they be? She'd given distinct orders that no one was to approach her animals. Fancy was sweet-natured enough, but Dancer—Dancer had nearly killed a groom who tried to put a saddle on him.

"Miz MacGreggor?"

Tamsin turned to face the stable owner. Edwards was bull-necked, shorter than she was, and heavily bearded. A middle-aged man wearing a battered star on his vest strode shoulder to shoulder beside Edwards.

"Where are my animals?" Tamsin demanded.

Edwards grimaced and shook his head. "Gone." He shrugged and scratched his unwashed neck. "No idee where they could have got to," he drawled. "Hoped maybe you'd come in early and picked them up."

"Stolen?" She swallowed hard. "My horses have been stolen?" She glanced at the second man, noting his shoulder-length white-blond hair and handlebar mustache. "Are you the county sheriff? I need to—"

"That would be me," he answered. "Sheriff Roy Walker."

His pale eyes were bloodshot and slightly crossed, hardly a recommendation for an upholder of justice. Neither he nor Edwards smelled as though they had bathed in the last month. She barely conquered an urge to back away from them. Instead, she held her ground and tried to keep her emotions in check. "You've got to find my horses, Sheriff," she urged. "They're worth a fortune."

Walker rocked back on his heels and peered down his long nose at her as if she were a suspicious character. "Not so fast, Miss MacGreggor. Got some questions of my own. You want to come down to the office and fill out a report?"

Tamsin drew herself up to her full height. "No, I do not. I want you to start looking for my animals. A bay thoroughbred stallion with black points, sixteen and a half hands, a chestnut mare with a white star on her forehead and one white stocking. She's a thoroughbred as well, and she's sixteen hands high. How many horses can there be that match that description?" She paused for breath and added, "It's Mrs. MacGreggor, sir, not miss."

"Mr. MacGreggor with you, is he?"

"No. He's not. What of it?" She'd not tell them that Atwood was dead, drowned in a drunken stupor in four inches of water behind a house of ill repute.

The sheriff spat a wad of tobacco into the straw near her foot. "Not usual for a *lady* of means to be traveling these parts alone. 'Specially not with horses like you claim you lost."

Tamsin knotted her gloved hands into fists and tried to hold her temper. "Not lost, Sheriff, stolen. Stolen from that stall—" She pointed. "Late last night or early this morning. And I want them back. It's your job to—"

"Don't be telling me my job, lady. You say you been robbed; there's procedure to be followed. Things got to be done proper like. Don't know how things is back where you come from but—"

"While you're wasting time interrogating me, Sheriff, you're letting the thief get farther and farther away." Dismissing him with a withering glare, Tamsin turned her ire on Edwards. "As for you—I hold you responsible for this theft."

The stableman shifted from one foot to the other and twisted his battered hat in his hand.

"Is this common?" she continued. "Do animals in your care regularly vanish?"

"Matter o' fact, this ain't the first time it happened," Edwards admitted.

"No need to take on so," the sheriff said. "You mind your manners and leave me to get to the bottom of this."

She glanced from one to the other as a bad feeling washed through her. Something was wrong here, dreadfully wrong. Was it possible that Edwards and Walker had conspired to steal her horses? "Please," she said, no longer caring what they thought of her. "I've got to get those animals back."

Roy Walker tucked another plug of tobacco under his lip. "Do what we can for you," he offered. "Soon as you fill out them papers."

"Don't get your hopes up," Edwards said. "If they was stole, likely the horse thief is to hell and gone from here by now. Some bad hombres around, that's certain, and old Roy here . . ." The livery owner gestured toward the sheriff. "He don't have the greatest record for catching 'em."

Studying the sorry pair, Tamsin's intuition told her that this sheriff wasn't to be trusted any more than Edwards. It was obvious that waiting for them to do something was a waste of time. If she was going to recover her horses, she'd have to find them herself.

Tamsin stepped back, lowered her eyes, and tried to look flustered. "Forgive me," she said. "It's just the shock of finding my mare and stallion gone. Naturally, I'll cooperate in any way I can. Could I meet you in your office? Say, in an hour? I need to go back to the boardinghouse and . . ." She fumbled for some excuse. "I'm feeling a little faint, sir. I think I'd best lie down."

"Good idee," Edwards agreed.

Sheriff Walker nodded. "An hour, little lady. I'll look over your bill of sale on them animals, and we'll see what we can do for you."

"I have every faith that you will," she murmured. Lying son of a goat! If Walker wasn't in on the thieving, she'd swallow his sack of chewing tobacco whole. With a small sound of distress and a foolish simper, she backed out of the stable.

Once out of the men's sight, she shouldered her saddlebags and followed the alley to the back of the barn. As she'd hoped, the boy was there, leaning against a rail fence. He looked up warily as she approached him.

"My horses have been stolen," she said.

He pretended not to hear. Instead, he crouched down and tossed a stick to the dog.

Tamsin fumbled in her skirt pocket and came up with a ten-dollar gold piece. She tilted the coin so that it gleamed in the sunlight. "You can have this if you tell me where they are."

He ruffled the fur on the terrier's back.

"I won't say anything," she promised. "Please help me."

He reached for the money with a dirty hand. "Sam

Steele trades in horses," he whispered. "Some people say he don't care whose."

"Where?"

Sweat ran down the boy's pockmarked face. "They'll kill me if they find out I told."

She held the coin just out of reach. "Where?" she repeated. "You can trust me."

" 'Bout four mile out of town. The Lazy S, first place on the right. You kin see the house from the road. But—" He licked his lower lip and glanced over his shoulder nervously. "Sam Steele's a brother to Judge Henry Steele. Best you forget yer hosses and get away from here, ma'am. Worse kin happen to ya than get yer cayuses stole."

She tucked the ten dollars into his hand. "Thank you."

"Yeah," he said, flashing ebony eyes that seemed far too old for his face. "But I ain't done you no favors, lady."

Maybe not, she thought as he dashed away. She hoped he'd told the truth. If he hadn't, she wouldn't know where to start looking.

She retraced her steps to the front of the stable and was relieved to hear the murmur of voices inside. She couldn't tell what they were saying, but she recognized Walker's voice.

She'd told them she meant to return to the boarding-house. Now she did just that. But when she reached the side street that the building was on, she kept going, circling around until she was once more behind the livery. The muddy ground was covered with horse tracks, far too many to make sense of until she saw one perfect impression.

In Nebraska, Tamsin had paid a smith to fit both animals with special shoes, studded to give them better footing on rocky ground. This print wasn't large enough to belong to Dancer. It had to be Fancy's trail. And where the mare went, the stud followed. Someone might have been tough enough to get him out of the barn, but they couldn't stop him from going after his mate—not without killing him.

Tamsin took a deep breath and started down the road. Her belongings were heavy, but she had no intentions of leaving them behind. Once she got Fancy and Dancer back, she'd put Sweetwater behind her.

Tamsin guessed that she'd been walking for more than an hour when she reached the wooden gate with an oxbow suspended overhead. A large letter *S*, not upright but turned on its back, was burned into the weathered wood. Beneath the brand were the words SAMUEL STEELE, LAZY S.

Not certain of what she would find or what she would do if these people did have her missing animals, she backtracked a few hundred yards and hid her saddlebags in the bushes just off the road.

She was halfway up the lane to the sprawling log ranch house when a grizzled cowboy loped toward her on a black-and-white horse.

The man pulled in his mount, touching the brim of his slouch hat with a forefinger in greeting, but he didn't smile. What she could see of his hair was sandy, streaked with gray. One cheek was covered with a purple birthmark. It was not a face to inspire confidence.

"You must be lost, woman. This here's private property. You're trespassin'." He reined the piebald around so that they blocked her way. She noticed that the rawboned gelding had one blue eye ringed in white, a feature she'd found linked to a nasty disposition in horses.

"Are you Mr. Steele?" she demanded with more courage than she felt. "I've important business with him."

The cowboy scowled. "He expectin' you?"

"Not exactly, but if you tell him that Mrs. MacGreggor is here, I know he'll see me."

"Nobody but Injuns and sodbusters walks out here, lady." The horse bared his yellow teeth and chewed at the bit.

Tamsin caught the animal's bridle by the headstall and ran an exploring hand over his neck. "Easy, easy boy," she crooned. "There's an infection here," she said, glancing up at the rider. "It may be a splinter of wood or a thorn. You can feel the heat around the swelling. You'd best cut it out before it becomes serious."

The cowboy's eyes widened questioningly. "You think that's what it is? I figured it for a bee sting."

She shook her head and scratched under the piebald's chin. The horse blew noisily through his lips but then visibly calmed under her touch. "I know horses." She glanced toward the house. "I really need to talk with Mr. Steele."

He shrugged. "Guess he can't do no more than run you off. Ma'am," he added respectfully. She let go of the bridle. He tapped the horse's rump with the end of the reins and continued on down the rutted lane.

Tamsin hadn't gone another hundred feet before she heard the screaming whinny and the thud of iron-shod hooves against a barn wall. Dancer! She would recognize his angry bellow anywhere. And if her stallion was there, Fancy must be with him.

Tamsin broke into a run, but as she neared the stables, she saw several men repairing a railing on the corral. One turned to stare at her, and she slowed to a dignified walk.

"Hey!" the cowboy shouted.

She ignored him and turned toward the house. A black gelding, hitched to a piano-box buggy with yellow wheels, stood near the front porch. The animal's sides were streaked with sweat, and foam dripped from his mouth.

Tamsin circled the horse and carriage, stepped over a sleeping cat, and climbed the steps to the front porch. The door stood open. From inside came the sound of a man's swearing.

"It's not what you think, Sam," a woman pleaded. "Henry—"

"Henry's my brother and you're my wife! You've been whoring with him behind my back!"

Tamsin heard a second man's voice, an older man. "I warn you, Sam. It isn't like that. Don't do anything you'll regret!"

A woman's scream was followed by the crack of a gunshot. Glass shattered and the woman began to sob. "No! No! No!"

Tamsin stood motionless, not sure if she should go inside or turn and run. Then the three burst through the door onto the porch.

The woman, a petite blonde in her mid-thirties, bore the imprint of a man's hand across her cheek. Her eyes were swollen with tears, and her elaborately coiffured hair was disheveled. She clung to the arm of a muscular man with shoulder-length brown hair and a drooping mustache.

"Sam, please," she begged. "It's not true."

Cursing, he backhanded his wife and drove a clenched fist into the belly of the man Tamsin supposed must be Henry.

The blow rocked the middle-aged gentleman in white shirt and waistcoat, and he doubled up, clutching his stomach. Blood trickled from the corner of his mouth.

"Get the hell off my place, Henry! If I ever lay eyes on you again, I'll blow you to hell!"

Henry staggered back and steadied himself against a porch post. "Come with me, Sarah," he urged. "It's over. You don't need to stay with him anymore."

"I warn you, I'll kill you." Sam's face darkened with rage. "I'll kill the both of—"

"Not if I kill you first!" Henry flung back.

Then, for the first time, Sam caught sight of Tamsin. "Who are you?" he demanded. "What the hell are you doing on my spread?"

She blanched. "I'm Tamsin MacGreggor," she managed. "And I've come for my horses. A mare and a stallion, thoroughbreds, stolen last night from the livery in Sweetwater."

"You're out of your mind," Sam grated.

"Am I?" she dared. "Let's take a look in your barn."

Henry wiped the blood from his chin and stared at Tamsin. She caught a whiff of hair lotion from his too black, obviously dyed hair.

"I've got two thoroughbreds in my stable," Sam admitted. "Bought and paid for from a dealer yesterday. I don't know who the hell you are, woman, or what your game is. But if you're calling me a horse thief, you belong in a madhouse."

"No! They're mine," Tamsin insisted. "I bred them both, back in Tennessee. I—"

"Get the hell off the Lazy S," Sam ordered. "Broom! Willy!"

The two cowboys, who'd been mending the fence, came on the run. A third man in a farrier's apron followed, still carrying his hammer. "Yeah, boss?" the first man said.

"See these two off my land," Sam ordered. "If they come back, you're fired."

"The judge, too?" The tall cowboy who had spoken first looked uncertain.

Sam nodded. "You heard me, Broom." Sam seized his wife by the shoulders and pushed her roughly back inside the house.

"Keep your hands off her," Henry said.

"She's mine, brother. I'll do with her as I please."

Tamsin turned toward Henry. "If you're a judge, you've got to help me."

He scowled at her. "I'd advise you to get back where you came from. Accusing a man like Sam of stealing can get you in more trouble than you can imagine."

The man Sam had called Broom held up his hands. "I'm havin' no part of this, boss. You want Judge Henry throwed out of here, you do it yerself."

"Damn you, Broom," Sam snapped. "You can get off the Lazy S as well."

The tall cowboy's weathered tan flushed beet-red. "You can't do that, Mr. Steele. I worked for your father since you were both mites. Who else is gonna hire me with my gimpy leg?"

"You heard me," the rancher replied. "You haven't been worth your keep in years. Get the hell off this spread."

"Not without my pay," Broom said. "I'm owed—"

"You're owed shit. You don't follow my orders, you're fired!" Sam advanced on Tamsin with a clenched fist. "I warned you to git off the Lazy S, woman."

She took a step backward. "I'm going."

Broom took a swing at Sam, and the rancher hit him hard in the face. The cowboy got in a weak punch to Sam's chest, but the younger man's return blow caught him full on the nose. Blood spurted as Broom went down on one knee. Sam followed up with a vicious kick to the midsection.

Broom groaned and sank to the ground. "You bastard," he managed. "I'll get you for this."

Sam kicked him once more before glancing at the second cowhand and the man with the hammer. Swiftly, they moved toward Henry.

Swearing, the judge retreated to his buggy. "You'll regret this, Sam," he warned. "I'll be back, and we'll settle this for once and all."

Tamsin touched Henry's arm. "I'm on foot," she said. "Could you at least give me a ride back to town?"

He scowled at her. "Get back the same way you got here." The judge slapped his lines over the horse's rump and drove away without looking back.

Sam gave Tamsin a shove. "Get moving," he warned.

She winced as she heard Dancer's angry whinny from the barn. "I'm going," she repeated. But I'll be back, too, she vowed silently. You can count on it.

Chapter 2

By Tamsin's reckoning, it was close to midnight when she crept close to Steele's barn. She'd thought long and hard about what she meant to do, and it seemed that there was only one answer to her dilemma.

She had to steal her horses back.

The night was dark, the low, heavy clouds split by flashes of lightning. Heavy drops of rain were beginning to fall.

If the lane to the ranch house hadn't been lined with pines, she doubted if she could see well enough to find her way to the stable. As it was, she wandered blindly until a jagged bolt illuminated the corral.

She followed the split-rail fence to the barn door. Once inside, she threw caution to the wind and lit the small lantern she'd purchased in town. Then she lifted the lamp high and looked around nervously. Fancy would answer to her name, but Tamsin was afraid to call out to the mare for fear of alerting one of the cowhands.

Outside, the wind was rising, blowing in gusts against the north side of the building. Common sense told her that she could stand in the middle of the barn and shout and not be heard above the coming storm. But she moved silently, placing one foot and then the other as though she were stepping on ice rather than hard-packed dirt.

The first two stalls were empty. A third held a spotted

pony. Beyond that, nearly out of the pale circle of flickering light was a high-walled enclosure. Tamsin hung the lantern on a post and had started for the gate when a loud peal of thunder vibrated through the stable.

She jumped and clamped her hand over her mouth to keep from crying out. Another ear-splitting rumble rolled overhead, and waves of rain began pelting the tin roof. The paint snorted and paced anxiously. From inside the closed box stall came a high-pitched nicker.

"Dancer?" Heart thudding, Tamsin hurried toward the familiar sound, then noticed the dark object lying on the floor. It looked like . . .

"Sweet hope of heaven!" She uttered a startled gasp and dropped to her knees beside the crumpled form of a man. "What's wrong?" she asked. Then the sickly sweet scent of blood filled her head, and her fingers touched the soaked back of his rawhide vest. "Oh, no . . ."

She drew back as though she'd been stung, and stared at her hand. Red smeared her palm. Horrified, she rubbed her hand in a heap of straw, trying to clean away the gore.

Then, hesitantly, she touched his cheek.

His flesh was warm, but he lay too still for a living man. She rolled him over and leaned close to see if she could detect any breathing.

Sam Steele's eyes were open, staring.

Tamsin stood, numb with fear, a dead man sprawled at her feet. For a long minute, she didn't move; then slowly, woodenly, she circled around the body and slid back the bar on the stall door.

A horse's head nudged through the opening, a splendidly shaped head with black ears and nose and intelligent brown eyes. "Dancer!" she cried. She threw her arms around the horse's neck.

Behind him, Fancy blew through her lips and pawed the bedding, jealously waiting to be noticed.

"I see you," Tamsin murmured. She blinked back tears and stepped out of the stall. There was no time for a reunion. She had to get her animals away from here as quickly as she could.

Deliberately, she kept her gaze away from the spot where Sam Steele lay. She'd noticed a tack area near the entrance to the barn and wasn't surprised when she recognized her own saddles and bridles among the others. "Thieving blackguards," she muttered. "If you steal horses, why not their gear?"

As she saddled Dancer and Fancy with shaking hands, she couldn't help wondering who had killed the ill-tempered rancher and why. Doubtless, a horse thief had plenty of enemies, but it took a special evil to shoot a man in the back. By rights she should call out for help—tell someone that he was dead. But if she was caught here, who would believe her story?

She swung up onto the mare's back and guided her toward the door with Dancer tied securely to a lead rope. Then she remembered the lantern. Even now it wouldn't do to leave it burning, for fear of fire in the barn.

Tamsin backed Fancy until the lamp was in easy reach. She'd just taken hold of the handle when the barn door swung open.

"What the hell?" a gruff male voice shouted.

Startled, Fancy reared. Tamsin reined her in with one hand and leaned forward to bring the horse down on all four feet. The lantern wavered, and for an instant the light shone full in Henry Steele's face.

"You!" Tamsin said. She didn't have to ask why he was here in his brother's barn at midnight. The answer was all too clear.

The judge had kept his word. He'd come back to settle

the score with his brother, and he'd put a bullet through his heart.

Henry grabbed at Fancy's bridle, but the chestnut tossed her head and backed away. "Get off that horse!" the judge ordered.

"You get out of my way!" Tamsin replied. "Murderer!"

"What are you talking about?" He pushed back his hat and stood in front of her with water streaming off his face and rain slicker.

Rain and wind battered the building. The storm was so loud that she could barely hear what Henry was saying. She pointed to Sam's body. "I saw what you did!"

The judge ran to Sam and looked down at him. "He's dead," he said. "Shot in the back." Then he twisted and stared at her. "You killed him for those damned horses."

Tamsin raised the lantern to her lips and blew out the flame.

"I'm the law in this part of Colorado!" Henry's voice echoed through the pitch darkness. "Woman or not, I'll see you hanged!"

"I didn't kill him," she protested.

"Tell it to the jury."

Tamsin ducked and urged Fancy forward through the open door. A pistol roared and wood splintered over Tamsin's head. She stifled a cry as Dancer plunged after them.

A blast of wind and driving rain made it impossible to see. Tamsin pulled hard on the reins to avoid the corner of the barn, loosened the reins, and gave Fancy her head. The mare stretched out her long legs and broke into a gallop.

"You won't get away!" Henry roared, firing a second time. "You'll never get away!"

Tamsin guided Fancy along the line of trees until they reached the road and then pulled her to the right, in the direction of Sweetwater. The mare slid in the slick mud and nearly went to her knees, but Tamsin stayed in the saddle.

Her only safety lay in putting distance between her and Sweetwater, but she couldn't go without her saddlebags. Her slicker was there, her blanket, her maps, and all her supplies. Only a fool would ride into the wilderness with empty hands. Teeth chattering from the cold, Tamsin soothed the frightened chestnut and rode on toward the spot where she'd hidden her things.

Lightning shattered a tree a few hundred yards away, momentarily blinding Tamsin and sending both horses into a frenzy. Dancer reared, snapping the lead line, and Fancy began to buck. Tamsin clung to Fancy's mane and fought to keep her from bolting as the acrid scent of sulfur filled the air.

"Whoa, whoa!" Tamsin cried. "Easy, girl!"

Dancer lunged past them, brushing so close to the mare that Tamsin's leg was squeezed between the two animals. She gasped in pain and reined hard to the left, turning Fancy in an ever-tightening circle.

Tamsin's boot slipped out of the right stirrup, causing her to lose her balance. She hung on, knowing that if she fell she could be crushed under Fancy's hooves. Finally, the mare's trusting nature won out over panic, and the animal came to a trembling halt.

Tamsin dismounted, but her knees were almost too weak to hold her up. Whispering the mare's name, Tamsin closed her eyes and leaned against the animal's side.

"What am I doing?" She was too scared to cry and too shaken to stand. She was drenched and freezing. Any minute, men with guns would be coming after her, and she was clinging to her horse paralyzed with fear.

"Where's your backbone, girl?" she heard an inner voice demand. Her grandfather had asked her that question since she was a small child, and it had never failed to raise her temper.

"I hear you," she muttered. It wasn't really her grandfather's voice; at least she hoped it wasn't. What she heard inside her was the echo of a personality too big to die when his old body gave out.

With a sigh, she stood up, took Fancy firmly by the bridle, and started down the road. It was too dark to see Dancer, but he wouldn't go too far from his mate. She prayed that the dangling rope wouldn't trip him up.

Another jagged illumination flashed, lighting the lane enough for Tamsin to get her bearings and to catch sight of her stallion a short ways ahead. There was no use in trying to catch him. Dancer would follow her, but he wouldn't be captured until he was good and ready.

With a little searching, Tamsin found her saddlebags and donned her rain slicker. It was impossible to get any wetter, but at least the coat would cut some of the wind. In an outside pocket, stashed for just such emergencies, she found a shriveled carrot. She snapped it in half and offered one piece to Fancy.

The mare took it gently from Tamsin's fingers. "Good girl," she murmured. "Good Fancy."

Then something nudged Tamsin in the center of her back. "No carrot for you," she said. "You don't deserve any." But when the stallion nuzzled her neck, she relented and gave him the treat.

She took hold of his trailing rope and snubbed it tightly to Fancy's saddle while she strapped her possessions onto his back. All the while, Dancer stood motionless in the driving rain, as docile as a lamb.

"You're impossible," she said to the big horse. "I'll trade you for a mule, first chance I get."

Then she swung up into the mare's saddle and turned her back toward the town. She didn't think that anyone would expect her to run back to Sweetwater, and she remembered a half-built church about a mile beyond the settlement. If she could get there, she could change her wet clothing and plan a route of escape.

She'd have to leave the trail and head directly into the foothills. Henry Steele would have the sheriff after her. She didn't think the judge was the type of man to let a witness walk away, not when she knew he'd shot his brother in the back . . .

. . . as he'd tried to shoot her.

Tamsin shivered violently. Henry Steele had nearly killed her. He wouldn't hesitate if he got her in his gunsight again.

She'd just have to make certain he never did.

The wind-driven rain swept over Sweetwater, ripping at the shingles of Maudine's Social Club and rattling the glass windows. Thunder rolled in deafening volleys, making the hostesses of the bawdy establishment squeal and clutch at their customers and the piano player play louder.

Raucous sounds of laughter drifted through the thin walls and added to the contentment of the solitary big man in Maudine's infamous bathroom.

Ash Morgan groaned and settled back into the oversize tub, letting himself sink until only his nose and mouth were above the surface. Damn, but it felt good to soak his weary body in hot water.

He submerged, then sat up sputtering and reached for the mug of warm milk on the stool beside him. He'd scrubbed himself with soft lye soap and rinsed under the shower before climbing into the bath, and he'd even paid Maudine extra to have the tub drained and filled with fresh water before he'd gotten in.

Shelly, the black-haired lass who always welcomed

him to the Social Club, had teased him about his desire for clean water and towels.

"You're wastin' good money, Ash," Shelly said. "Maudine charges you four times the goin' rate for a bath. And there ain't nothin' wrong with them towels." She pointed to a heap of used ones in the corner. "A man what's washed already ain't so dirty."

Nevertheless, he'd had his way. He liked his bathing alone, door barred, heavy wooden shutters closed and bolted, and plenty of good food and drink within reach.

He rubbed a hand over his six-day beard. Hell's bells but he must look a sight. He'd trailed Dave Johnson and Nate Sánchez for three weeks, but the last one had been fierce.

"Wonder if I'm getting a little old for this work?" he muttered to himself. It was a question he asked a lot lately.

Lighting struck somewhere close, and the eerie glow illuminated cracks around the window shutters. It was a good night to be inside, he thought. And a bad night to be camped under the open sky as he'd done for the past month.

A rap at the door caused him to bolt upright and reach for the loaded rifle propped alongside the tub. "Who is it?" he called.

"Ain't you done in there yet?" Shelly pleaded. "There's two customers waitin' for a bath out here."

Ash grinned and lay back in the water. A potbellied stove in the corner heated the rocks that made up the floor of Maudine's bathroom and kept the temperature pleasantly warm, no matter how cold it was outside. Ash had ridden thirty miles to get here today, and he wasn't about to be rushed.

"Ash, please!"

"Entertain them," he answered. "I paid for two hours, and I'm going to enjoy every minute of it."

He scooped up a little soap and scrubbed his long hair for the second time. He needed a haircut and that was certain. He'd always worn his hair shoulder length, but now it was getting out of hand. If he didn't get to a barber soon, someone was likely to take him for an Indian and take a shot at him.

He didn't need that.

A bounty hunter had enough enemies. No reasonable man would go out of his way to make more. And Ash had always considered himself a reasonable man.

If Johnson and Sánchez had understood that, they might both be alive tonight, instead of lying stiff as logs in the undertaker's shed. Big Nose Johnson was a common bushwacker. He'd ridden with Texas Jack Cannon since the war, but Sánchez was hardly more than a boy. Sadly, he'd taken up with the wrong sort and paid for it with his life. Bank robbery was bad business, and Texas Jack Cannon's gang had cut a swath from Missouri west.

"Those that live by the gun . . ." Ash murmured under his breath. He hadn't wanted to kill either of them, especially not Sánchez. In the end, it was that or go under himself. A sensible man had to look out for his own skin, but he had two more deaths to explain to the Almighty on Judgment Day.

Most of the road agents he was hired to hunt down were the scum of the earth, and somehow he'd gotten the reputation of being as bloodthirsty as his prey. It wasn't true, not by a long sight. Ash didn't like putting a bullet through a man and watching the light in his eyes fade. He believed in the law. No matter how high the reward, it always made him feel better inside to bring a desperado to justice. Unfortunately, most of them would rather be dead than face a judge and jury.

"Come on, Ash," Shelly called through the door. "Come up to my room with me. The night's still young, and I'll treat you real good."

"I know you would, sweetheart," he replied. Once, he had been desperate enough for a woman's soft embrace to go upstairs with her. The sex had been quick and hot. Shelly knew her trade well. But he'd caught the scent of other men on her body, and her laughter had been a shade too forced. He had paid her fairly, but he hadn't felt so good about himself the next day. And he hadn't purchased the services of Shelly or any other lady of the night since.

An animal will rut with any female that takes his fancy, he thought. But when a man takes a woman, there should be more between them than just the physical act.

He couldn't stop his thoughts from drifting back to this morning when he'd caught sight of Jack Cannon's woman. He'd been trailing her when his path had crossed that of Johnson and Sánchez.

Tamsin MacGreggor looked too innocent to be with Jack Cannon, but there couldn't be two women in Colorado that fit that description. A fine-looking filly, tall as most men, with hair like molten copper, the Wheaton sheriff had said. And that's what had proved her undoing. Sunlight sparkling off those red tresses had nearly stopped Ash dead in his tracks.

She looked as wholesome as a ripe apple, but her heart was probably as rotten as hell. It proved that you just couldn't tell what went on inside a female's head by her appearance. Aunt Jane had always said that a bad woman was worse than a bad man. Maybe she was right. Some women were drawn to ice-cold killers. Still, he wondered how Tamsin MacGreggor had fallen low enough to trail after a murdering coyote like Cannon.

The bank trustees had sent for Ash the day after the robbery, and it had taken ten more days for him to get the message and arrive in Wheaton. The sheriff had told him that Tamsin MacGreggor had ridden out of town on a Monday morning. Texas Jack's gang had held up the First Nebraska Savings and Loan the following Friday, killing two innocent bystanders and the town deputy. Then, the way Ash figured it, the outlaws had divided the loot and split up.

Sánchez and Johnson had nearly four hundred dollars on them in fresh bills, money Ash was certain they hadn't come by honestly. He'd deposited that here in Sweetwater, in Maudine's safe. First he'd pay for their burial; the rest he'd hold on to as a down payment on the reward offered for Cannon's gang.

Texas Jack had vanished without a trace, as he'd done a dozen times before. But this time would be different. This time, Ash meant to watch Jack's lady. Sooner or later, he'd show up to claim her. And Ash meant to take him then.

The impatient rapping came again.

"Go away, Shelly," he said, beginning to be a little annoyed. "I'll take the room for the night, but I want clean sheets."

"Good," she answered.

"I'll pay your fee, prairie flower, but you'll have to find another place to sleep."

"What?"

He laughed. "You heard me, Shelly. I'll take your bed, but all by myself. I want twelve hours of uninterrupted sleep, and you're just pretty enough to be a powerful distraction to any man's rest."

Truth was, he couldn't think about black-haired Shelly just now. His head was too full of questions about the redheaded armful that he'd seen outside of Mrs. Fremont's boardinghouse.

Chapter 3

The following afternoon, Ash Morgan faced Henry Steele and Roy Walker across a table in the Sweetwater sheriff's office. "Are you certain that there wasn't a man there with her?" Ash asked. "I can't see this MacGreggor woman committing murder and horse thievery on her own. Jack Cannon or some of his boys had to be in on this."

Sheriff Walker scowled. "What do you take me for, Morgan? The woman killed Sam. That's plain enough. She went there to steal those horses, got caught, and shot her way out."

Ash arched a dark eyebrow skeptically. "If Sam happened on the robbery, wouldn't he have been facing Tamsin MacGreggor? Either that or he was running from her, and I don't buy that. She may well have done the shooting, but if she did, Sam's attention was on someone else."

"But Henry arrived right after—"

The judge silenced Walker with an impatient wave of his hand. "How long have we known each other, Ash? Since before the war, right?"

Morgan nodded. Henry Steele was no educated fool. He was shrewd, tough, and honest. If the judge hadn't seen anyone else there in the barn, they must have ridden out before he got there. Trouble was, the storm

30

had washed away all the tracks. A cavalry regiment could have ridden through that barnyard during that downpour without leaving clear sign.

"I saw Tamsin MacGreggor covered in my brother's blood and ready to ride out of his barn. She murdered Sam in cold blood." Henry stubbed out the cigar he'd lit and hardly bothered to take a puff on. He looked as though he hadn't slept. His eyes were bloodshot and sunk back in his head. "You know that there's been hard feelings between me and Sam for years. It's common knowledge that Sarah and I were keeping company before she married my brother."

Ash nodded. "I heard as much."

"What's that got to do with this woman being a murderin' horse thief?" the sheriff demanded as he slapped a warrant down in front of Ash. "Bring her in dead or alive and you'll get your reward. That's all you care about, isn't it, Morgan?"

"Shut up, Walker," Henry said. "Whether I'm telling the truth or not has everything to do the murder. I'm the only witness. I fought with Sam the day before. I'm a logical suspect in his death." He fixed Ash with a steady gaze. "I didn't kill my brother. The MacGreggor woman did, and I'm offering a reward for her capture."

Ash glanced from one man to another. He didn't know Walker well, but as far as he was concerned the sheriff was lazy, stupid, and worthless as a lawman. He wondered how such a fool had managed to get himself elected.

"I've never been given a contract on a woman before," Ash said as he picked up the paper and scanned it quickly. "You say Sam was killed sometime before midnight."

"That's right," Henry agreed. "I roused his cowhands and sent them after her, but they didn't find a trace."

Ash glanced out the dirty window and mulled the information over in his head. Walker's office smelled of stale tobacco and unwashed bodies. The floor couldn't have been swept out since Noah was a pup.

He knew that Jack Cannon had relatives not far from Sweetwater. It was possible that he'd find MacGreggor there, and more important, he'd probably find Jack and the remainder of his gang.

"What's the matter?" Walker leaned over the table. "Ain't got the stones for this job? Don't tell me a big hombre like you is scared of a little ole gal?"

Ignoring Walker's insult, Ash turned his gaze on Henry. "I trailed her here from Nebraska, but yesterday was the first glimpse I had of her. Tell me whatever you know about the woman."

He didn't interrupt as Steele told him what he had on MacGreggor, hardly more than a description and the fact that she claimed to be from Tennessee.

"Mrs. Fremont over at the boardinghouse might tell you something," the judge finished.

"I'll talk to her and her guests," Ash replied. "I want to stop by the livery as well."

"And all the while you're jabberin', she's getting farther away," Walker grumbled.

Ash rose to his feet. He towered a good six inches over the ashen-haired sheriff. "I don't like you much, Walker. Unless you've got something solid to contribute to this conversation, I'd appreciate it if you'd keep your opinions to yourself . . . before we have a serious disagreement," he added quietly.

Steele pulled a roll of bills from his pocket. "You'll need this for expenses."

"Nope." Ash shook his head. "I expect my pay when the job's complete. If I don't bring her back, you don't owe me two bits."

"Not much chance of you failing, is there?" Steele said. "Ash Morgan always gets his man."

Ash didn't comment. He wasn't infallible. He hadn't brought in Texas Jack Cannon yet. Jack and his boys were human rattlesnakes that Ash meant to send straight to hell the first time he had them in his gunsight.

For a few seconds, the flames of hate deep inside Ash's soul flared stronger than his present company. Jack Cannon's image—all yellow curls and pretty-boy features—flashed back to haunt him.

Then Walker broke through Ash's musings with a foul curse. "Morgan brings in more prisoners dead than alive."

Ash stiffened. Maybe the sheriff's drooping mustache and fancy haircut reminded him of Cannon, but there the similarity ended. Texas Jack's eyes were gray and flat, as empty as shards of glass. His were killer's eyes, the kind that stalked a man's dreams. Walker's crossed ones were merely dull.

"Safer that way, ain't it?" Walker continued. "For you? Dead men don't cause no fuss."

Ash turned his back to Walker and offered Steele his hand. "I'm sorry about your brother, Henry. I'll do my best for you."

"Watch yourself," Steele warned.

"I will," Ash agreed. "I've gotten kind of fond of living."

Four days later, in the mountains northwest of Sweetwater, Tamsin murmured and threw an arm over her face. She was only half-awake, still savoring the warm happiness of being a child on her grandfather's farm again. Both parents had died of cholera when she was too young to remember them, but her grandparents had given her all the love and caring anyone could ask for.

In her dream, Tamsin had been sitting beside her grandfather on the porch swing, drinking lemonade and listening to Gram sing and play the piano in the front parlor. It was summer. The floor-to-ceiling windows were open, and the sweet words and tune of the old ballad "Lord Bateman" drifted out to blend with the chirping of crickets and the soft, rushing sounds of the river.

> *They made a bargain, and they made it true,*
> *For seven long years to stand;*
> *If you wed no other lady,*
> *I vow to wed no other man. . . .*

Something fuzzy rubbed across Tamsin's face, and she brushed at it, then opened her eyes with a start. Fancy was standing over her, nuzzling Tamsin's cheek with her warm nose. The mare pricked up her ears and blew gently through her lips.

Tamsin chuckled. "What are doing? Trying to wake me?" She rubbed her eyes and looked around. The canyon seemed as peaceful as Eden. The sun was up, a golden disk in an azure sky. Overhead, a jay chattered noisily, and chipmunks scampered up and down the trees.

Tamsin stretched and looked around for her stallion. "Where's Dancer?" As soon as she spoke his name, she heard an answering whinny and caught sight of him grazing just beyond a clump of bushes. She always left the horses loose at night.

The mare nudged Tamsin with her velvety nose.

"All right, all right." Tamsin stood up and rubbed the aching muscles in her back. "I must have slept away half of the morning," she murmured. Tonight, she would have to remember to make a bed of leaves to spread her blanket on.

The first twenty-four hours after she'd fled Sweet-water, she'd done little more than ride. On the second day, she'd had to slow down and allow the horses to graze. Without grain or hay, she had to give them time to forage.

She'd expected to be chased by a posse, but she'd seen no one. She'd ridden across flatlands and through foothills, forest and rocky slopes. She had a compass and a map, but even with those, it was easy to become con-fused and go in a circle. For the last two days, she'd been following a rocky creek upstream toward what she sup-posed must be the Great Divide, the high place where water ran either east or west toward the Pacific Ocean.

Her plan was simple. She intended to travel through the mountain passes to Fort Bridger and then join a group going on to California. She didn't have enough money to pay her way, but she could work. Few men knew as much about horses as she did. She could treat their illnesses and injuries and even trim their hooves and shoe them if she had the right farrier tools and a proper forge.

Tamsin's stomach protested. She was hungry, and she'd been hungry when she'd gone to sleep the night be-fore. Unfortunately, there was little left in her saddlebags to eat.

She hadn't planned on heading into the wilderness without restocking her supplies. She'd had enough food for the first days, and when that was nearly gone, she'd traded a packet of needles to an Indian woman for a hot meal, a container of dried berries and meat, and a birch-bark box of honeycomb. The old lady spoke no English, and Tamsin didn't understand a word she said in her own language. But they hadn't needed a translator to ex-change goods.

Before she'd left Tennessee, Tamsin had purchased a

goodly supply of needles, good silk thread, and four pairs of German embroidery scissors. She'd expected to trade with people on her western journey, and the sewing things were light and indispensable.

Tamsin had eaten the last of the honeycomb at noon yesterday. Since she'd run from Steele's ranch, she'd been afraid to make a fire. The weather had cooperated by being unseasonably warm for April, but she would need a fire this morning. She intended to have grilled trout for breakfast.

Breaking off a willow branch, she stripped away the twigs and leaves and tied her fishing line to the pole as she walked through the trees to the stream. Her grandfather had taught her to fish in the Cumberland, and that river made these Colorado rivers looks like puny creeks.

Tamsin quickly found a few grubs under a rock and cast her line into an eddy. An instant later, she had her first bite, and within half an hour, she had three speckled trout. On the way back to her camp, she gathered a few ferns that looked like some that had grown near the Cumberland. Her grandmother had served those with oil and vinegar. Tamsin didn't have either, but the ferns weren't bad, if a bit chewy.

Both horses watched curiously as she lit a small fire, cooked her fish, and ate them. Then she threw dirt over the coals and stamped on them. Tamsin was just about to mount Fancy when she noticed a column of white smoke in the sky to the west.

She doubted that the smoke could be from the men she supposed were chasing her. A more likely answer would be other travelers or Indians. Since her food supply—other than a pound of tea leaves—was nonexistent, she decided to investigate.

The smoke was farther away than Tamsin had thought. She rode through the morning and into the heat of the afternoon sun. She traversed woods and meadows, gullies and ridges, crossing and recrossing the same creek where she'd caught the fish.

Tamsin was tired, sore, and thirsty by the time she dismounted and tied Fancy to a tree. Late afternoon shadows cast dark smudges across the landscape, and the air had an odd, almost sulfuric, odor. Leaving the animals behind, she crept cautiously closer. Curiously, there was no longer one spiral of smoke, but many, some thicker than others.

If she was sneaking up on an Indian camp, it had to be an entire tribe.

Tamsin grimaced. Doubtless, her curiosity would be her undoing. It had often gotten her into trouble, as her departed husband—God rest his withered soul—had repeatedly scolded.

She was just like her granddad, she thought. Once she started to question something, she just had to follow through until she'd solved the puzzle.

Ahead, through the foliage, she could see a clearing, but still no sign of people. Birds were flitting overhead and singing, giving no sign of alarm. Tamsin moved from tree to tree. She stepped carefully, waiting and listening over and over again before advancing.

Finally, she parted a clump of bushes and stared in amazement. What she had seen wasn't smoke at all. It was steam, bubbling up from mineral springs. Across the small green valley, pools and streams shimmered and splashed. Laughing, Tamsin stood up, intending to go closer when suddenly, not ten yards ahead of her, a naked man rose from the water. His back was to Tamsin, allowing her a clear view of hard, bare thighs, tight buttocks, and broad, powerful shoulders.

As she watched, he wiped the water from his face, shook his head—sending a mane of black hair flying, and dove under again. Her heart thudded against her chest. Had she seen what she'd thought she'd seen? Or had the sun gotten to her and made her imagine a native swimming in the altogether?

Tamsin held her breath as he surfaced again, splashing and sputtering. This time, he looked in her direction, but she didn't move, and the curtain of leaves hid her presence completely.

Lord save us. It was the bounty hunter she'd seen on the street back in Sweetwater. What was his name? Morgan? And what was he doing here? Had they put him on her trail?

She shivered.

He'd looked tall on horseback, but he was bigger on foot. She guessed he topped her by half a foot, and she was as tall as most men.

Morgan was big, but he didn't carry an ounce of extra weight. His arms were corded with sinew; his scarred chest bulged with muscle. She put his age as near to thirty, perhaps a little younger, perhaps older. And he was ruggedly attractive. She wouldn't call him handsome. His chiseled features were too fierce and masculine for that, and his mouth was all too . . . She shook her head, unable to describe those sensual lips in her mind. The only word she could think of was *dangerous*.

Her cheeks grew warm, but she could not tear her eyes away. Curiosity, she told herself, simple scientific scrutiny. Any reasonable woman would look. If he hadn't wished to be stared at by any passersby, surely he would have kept himself decently dressed.

Tamsin moistened her dry lips. The only naked man she'd ever seen had been Atwood, and Morgan put him to shame. Compared to this thoroughbred, her husband had been a knock-kneed, swaybacked plow horse.

When he dove under the water again, she backed quietly away. Morgan's presence here meant nothing good for her, but she was still hungry. She couldn't help wondering if he had food in his saddlebags. Her fish had been delicious, but she'd gone without dinner and soon it would be suppertime.

She backtracked several hundred yards, then worked her way up to the clearing again, this time far to the right of where she'd seen Morgan. Her hunch was rewarded when she saw a strawberry roan gelding hobbled and grazing beside a saddle, a bedroll, and a pile of neatly folded clothing. To reach them, she had to cross an open, grassy spot, but the steam from the hot springs would hide her progress.

She hoped that the bounty hunter would continue his bath. If he decided to return to camp suddenly, she'd be at his mercy.

With a sigh, she decided that the risk was worth taking. She dashed out of hiding and ran to where he'd left his garments. Boots, a broad-brimmed slouch hat, and a coat lay on the grass beyond the saddle.

Quickly she knelt beside the saddlebags and untied the strings. Out tumbled a cloth bag containing biscuits and cheese. She snatched up the food, left a packet of needles in trade, and fled back into the woods. Then, using her compass, she hurried back to where she'd left the horses.

Swinging up into the saddle, she kicked Fancy into a hard trot. She hadn't cheated the stranger, but it wouldn't do to let him come upon her unawares. The best thing to do was to put distance between them.

She ate half of the bread and cheese and rode for the better part of an hour before stopping to drink from a stream. This time, she mounted Dancer. Riding the stallion was always a risky endeavor. No one had ever been able to stay on him except her. Atwood had been thrown so many times that he'd threatened to shoot the animal. If Dancer hadn't been so valuable as a stud, her grandfather would never have kept him on the farm.

Sometimes, when he was feeling particularly ornery, Dancer bucked her off as well. This time he rolled his eyes and tossed his head, but after a little side prancing and theatrics, he allowed her to guide him farther into the heavily wooded foothills.

One minute it was dusk, and the next, it seemed full dark. Tamsin reined in the stallion and slid down. She could barely see to unsaddle her animals and take her blanket and coat from the bags.

Far off, she could hear the cry of coyotes or wolves, and she supposed that a campfire would keep them at a distance. But Morgan might have tried to follow her, and she didn't want to take the chance of showing him where she was camped. Instead, she said a prayer, wrapped herself in her blanket, and stretched out on a mossy bank beside the creek.

Frogs croaked and small things rustled in the bushes. An owl hooted and another answered. Stars blinked on, so close that Tamsin thought she could reach up and grab one. Tennessee had been beautiful, but Colorado was glorious. She swallowed, touched by the magnificence of velvet sky and primeval forest.

Hours passed. She lay awake, tired but unable to sleep. So much had happened in the past year that it seemed unreal. Lying here alone, she could sort out the good and the bad and make plans for the future.

Marrying Atwood MacGreggor had been the worst decision of her life. She'd been uneasy about him from the first, but her grandfather had been so sure that the man was the answer to all their prayers.

Granddad's health had been failing steadily, and she'd watched him grow weaker season by season.

"A woman can't manage this farm alone," he'd reasoned. "I worry about you, Tamsin. I've had a good life. I wouldn't mind dying if I knew you were safe."

She couldn't put all the blame on Granddad. She'd wanted a man to pay attention to her, to escort her to dances and parties, to tell her the things suitors told other girls. But she was too tall and too set in her ways for any of the neighborhood boys. Willie Maxwell had asked her to ride home from church one Sunday in his buggy, but Willie was nearly fifty with thirteen motherless children at home.

Tamsin liked children well enough, but thirteen scabby-kneed, Maxwell boys—ranging from two to eighteen years of age—was unreasonable. Considering Willie as husband material was worse. She wasn't that desperate, not if she'd had to live out her life as a spinster.

So she'd let Atwood sweet-talk her. She'd bought his lies and his excuses, and trusted him. And he'd ruined everything her grandfather had spent a lifetime building . . . not to mention her dreams. Atwood hadn't wanted babies. She had, but now . . . Now she was glad he'd spilled his seed over her good lace coverlet instead of planting it where it would do the most good.

She'd lost all respect for her husband and gradually come to dislike him intensely. When he'd died, she'd felt nothing but relief.

"Good-bye and good riddance," she murmured sleepily.

Maybe she wasn't a woman who made good choices when it came to men. She'd nearly fallen prey to another predator back in Nebraska when she'd allowed good-looking Jack Cannon to take her to dinner a few times.

Jack had seemed a gentleman at first, nicely dressed and well spoken. But he'd presumed on her friendship and become frighteningly possessive. All too soon, she'd discovered aspects of his personality that she couldn't tolerate. After the last incident, she'd had enough of his attentions and left town.

I must be an awful judge of character, she thought. I'm better counting on myself, than looking for a man to—

Dancer nickered loudly.

"What is it, boy? What's wrong?"

Fancy snorted and moved close to where Tamsin curled against the cold. The stallion squealed and pawed the ground. Stones rolled under his iron-shod hooves.

Tamsin scrambled to her feet, mouth dry. Her fingers clutched the grip of her heavy Navy Colt. Then the hair rose on her neck as the sound of a woman's unearthly scream split the darkness.

The mare panicked and bolted away, but Dancer held his ground and trumpeted a fiery challenge.

With trembling hands, Tamsin raised her weapon, trying to locate the source of the danger. Then she caught an overpowering scent of cat, and a snarling shadow hurled out of the treetops, coming to earth between her and the rearing stallion.

Chapter 4

Ash shoved the MacGreggor woman out of the way and fired three quick shots into the big cat. The woman went down on her hands and knees, and the cougar roared in pain. Ash took aim at the source of the animal's cry and fired again. This time there was only the thud of a heavy weight toppling onto the rocky ground and the echo of hoofbeats above the sound of his own harsh breathing.

"You all right?" he demanded as he fumbled for a match.

She didn't answer.

"Are you hurt?" He hoped she hadn't fainted. Females did that all the time, and he never knew if it was for real or an act.

He kept his pistol ready in his left hand and struck a light against a rock with the other. Murderer or not, it went against his grain to stand by while a woman was ripped apart by a mountain lion. But being soft-hearted didn't make him fool enough to let her shoot him while he was saving her life.

The match flared, casting a circle of yellow illumination in the pitch-blackness of the moonless night. The suspect didn't seem injured. Her eyes were wide open, staring at the cougar sprawled inches from her feet. She didn't look like a hardened killer. She seemed young and vulnerable.

"Stay where you are," he warned, motioning toward the dead cat. "I didn't use all my shots on him."

He lit another match and kicked some leaves and sticks into a heap on a flat section of bare rock. In no time, he had a small fire. The MacGreggor woman still hadn't made a sound or moved a muscle.

"You're not deaf, are you?" he asked. He rolled the dead animal over, proved to himself that it was a male, and noted the crippled hind leg. The cougar was young, maybe a two-year-old. Ash reckoned the animal's weight at nearly two hundred pounds, but he was thin and in poor shape. His ribs stood out like fence slats, and his tail was matted and balding in spots.

He knew that most mountain lions feared the scent of man and stayed clear of them. Doubtless this one's weak leg had hurt his ability to hunt game. If the animal had been stronger, he decided, it would have attacked the horses instead of a human.

He felt a pang of sympathy for the cougar as he ran his fingers over the tawny hide. You're better off, he thought. A bullet's easier than a slow death by starvation.

The wounds were easy to find. Two of his shots were killing ones, one had shattered the cat's bad hip, and another had missed altogether.

Ash shrugged. The middle of the night wasn't the best time for hunting predators. A few seconds later with the last shot and either he or Tamsin MacGreggor would have had a lifetime reminder of the incident, provided they'd survived to remember. A cat this size, even a crippled one, had razor teeth and claws that could disembowel a human in seconds.

The woman sat up and brushed gravel off her hands.

"You could have killed my horse." Her voice was throaty and southern, but she was clearly educated.

Ash's eyes narrowed. She was scared, but obviously trying not to show it. "I saved your life."

"My stallion would have killed the beast."

He scoffed. "The horse that's still running down the canyon?" She was beyond the circle of firelight, too far away for him to make out the color of her eyes or the expression in them. He wondered if her answer was false bravado, or if she was that naive. "You believe that stud would have stood and fought that cougar, and I could convince you to hand Texas back to Mexico."

"He would have killed him! Dancer didn't run until you started taking shots at him."

"You're under arrest," he said quietly. "I've a warrant on you for murder and horse thieving."

"I didn't kill that man."

"An eyewitness says you were covered with blood."

"I rolled him over to see if he was alive. I didn't shoot him."

"I'm authorized to bring back runaway felons," he said, ignoring her protests. "Keep your hands where I can see them, and move over into the light."

She rose to her feet. "Are you a lawman?"

"Not exactly."

She stiffened. "You're taking me back to Sweetwater for money, aren't you?"

"Partly. Partly because I don't approve of murder."

"You've made a mistake, Mr. Morgan. I'm no criminal. The horses were stolen from me in the first place."

She was tall and big-boned for a woman, but she moved with the fluid grace of a yearling doe. "That's far enough," he warned gruffly. "Don't try anything foolish." He tapped his holstered pistol. "I'd hate to have to shoot you."

"Sam Steele was dead when I found him." She smoothed her skirts as if she were standing in church instead of a steep hillside in the middle of nowhere.

"It's not my job to decide who killed him. It's my job to bring you back, dead or alive."

"You're trying to frighten me. If you'd wanted me dead, you would have let that thing"—she motioned toward the cougar— "devour me."

"Maybe I should have. You made this personal when you stole my supplies. I'd rather see you stand trial."

She didn't back down. "I didn't take your bread and cheese. I traded fairly for them."

"Needles?"

"Good ones, imported from Germany. Actually, I'm not certain I got the best of the deal. The biscuits were rather tasteless and the cheese—"

"Never mind the cheese," he snapped. "Are you armed?"

"What?"

Ash felt his patience draining away. "Are you carrying a gun?" He liked to think he could remain a gentleman with any woman, regardless of the circumstances, but this Tamsin MacGreggor was exasperating. "I have to search you. I've got no interest in your body, so long as you're not hiding a pistol or a knife."

Her face blanched. "You mean to put your hands on me?"

He moved toward her. "So long as you don't try any tricks, I won't hurt you."

She trembled as he patted her down. She wasn't wearing a corset, and her breasts were soft. He tried to remember that she was part of Cannon's gang. But when he stepped back and looked down into her face, he felt an odd unease, akin to shame.

"What? A bounty hunter with scruples?" she asked.

He ignored her sarcasm. "I've got to go back and get my horse. I'll have to make sure you don't run away on me while I'm gone."

"Please . . ." Her voice cracked. "I won't go anywhere. Don't tie me. What if there's another mountain lion?"

"Not likely," he replied. "Pumas are solitary animals."

"Pumas?"

"Pumas, cougars. They're the same thing. I've heard old mountain men call them painters, as well." He pulled a pair of handcuffs from his belt. "Turn around." She didn't protest as he fastened her hands behind her back. "Sit here by the fire," he ordered. "I won't be long."

Tamsin watched until he vanished into the darkness of the surrounding forest, then got awkwardly to her feet. Between the strong feral scent of the mountain lion and the blood, her stomach was doing flip-flops.

The terror of the cat's attack and Ash Morgan's sudden appearance had left her shaken. She was grateful that he'd come when he did. That didn't mean she intended to meekly return with him to Sweetwater and face certain conviction for a crime she hadn't committed.

Her fears for her own safety weren't so great that she was able to forget the immediate danger to her horses. Her granddad had always taught her to do what was needed and save her tears for later.

Fancy and Dancer were somewhere out there on the mountainside, unprotected, perhaps even injured. She had to get to them, and she had to think of a way of getting free from this Ash Morgan.

She couldn't act rashly out of panic. She'd made a bad mistake when she'd attracted the bounty hunter's attention by taking his food.

She'd underestimated the man. And if there was one thing she prided herself on, it was in never making the same mistake twice.

Morgan was too powerful to fight with her wits and bare hands. She would need an equalizer.

Quickly, Tamsin began to search the area near where she'd fallen when the mountain lion attacked. It didn't take long to find her revolver, half-buried in a pile of leaves. She knelt and fumbled for the handgun, praying that it wouldn't accidentally go off.

It was difficult to pick up the Navy Colt with her hands cuffed. Twice she dropped the weapon, but finally, on the third try, she was able to tuck the weapon into the pocket under her skirt.

Her cheeks still burned from the indignity of having the stranger touch her where no man but her husband ever had before. He'd tried to pretend that he was unaffected, but she'd heard the change in his breathing when he ran his hand between her breasts.

"Snake," she muttered. If he searched her again, he'd discover her hidden pistol. She'd have to make certain that she gave him no reason to be suspicious.

She couldn't hear anything but the normal night noises, the rustle of branches, the moan of the wind through the rocks. She strained to see into the darkness. Dancer and Fancy must have run a long way, but she hoped the mare would find her way back.

In February, Tamsin had bred the two. Since Fancy hadn't come into heat again, it was likely that she carried Dancer's foal. It would be some time before the mare would swell with her pregnancy, but Tamsin hoped to be settled in California for the birth. That was another reason not to allow this Ash Morgan to drag her back to Sweetwater.

Her grandfather had often said that he was an honest man in a dishonest world. Well, she was an honest woman, and she was prepared to do whatever she must to survive. If it meant deceit, so be it.

A twig snapped and Tamsin turned to stare in that direction. "Fancy?" she called. She listened, certain that she heard the click of a horse's hooves on stone.

Disappointment washed through her as the bounty hunter materialized out of the forest. He rode his mount into the firelight, then swung down out of the saddle.

"We'll spend the night here, then look for the horses in the morning," he said.

She stood and looked him over, beginning at the toes of his high, black leather boots and moving up over the tight-fitting trousers of pin-striped wool. Beneath the calf-length black leather coat, she caught a glimpse of a gun belt and a red shirt.

Morgan's face was rough-hewn and clean-shaven. His skin was tanned to the shade of peach honey, and his cheekbones were high and sharp. A proud nose bore the faint marks of being broken more than once, and his lips were thin and sensual. The wide brim of a felt plainsman's hat kept her from seeing the color of his eyes, but instinctively, she felt that they were as dark as his hair.

"Seen enough?" he asked, breaking into her intense scrutiny.

"Mr. . . . Mr. Morgan . . ." she began.

"Ash will do."

She forced herself to think clearly. Morgan's hands were clean. In the time he'd been gone, he'd obviously found water and washed away the mountain lion's blood. It was strange behavior for a man of his following. Cleanliness, in her mind, was more an attribute of a gentleman. "My horses . . ." she stammered. "If they smell the cat, they may not come back."

"My warrant's not for the animals. It's for you."

"But . . . the creature stinks." She wrinkled her nose. "Surely, you don't mean to sleep in the midst of . . ."

"Normally I'd skin out the hide, but this one's in bad

shape." He stared at the dead creature for a few seconds, then shrugged. "I'll drag it off into the woods if it bothers you."

She nodded. "I'd appreciate that."

He took a rope from his saddle and looped it around the dead cat's neck. Then he mounted and snugged the rope tightly around the saddle horn. His strawberry roan gelding flicked his ears nervously and rolled back his lip, but Morgan spoke to him in soft tones and urged him backward, step by step.

The cat's carcass slid over the loose rock and gravel. Morgan guided his horse between the trees. Soon they were out of sight, but Tamsin could hear the crunch of undergrowth and the snapping of twigs.

She shivered, moved closer to the fire, and wondered if she had more to fear from this man than from the mountain lion. He didn't seem a bully or a rapist, despite his rough exterior. She hoped that he wouldn't assume that she was a woman of loose character because a warrant had been issued for her arrest.

Her grandfather's old Colt revolver hung heavy on her hip, giving her comfort. She wasn't helpless. If Morgan tried to lay hands on her, he'd suffer the consequences. She'd come this far—surely halfway to California. And no one was going to stop her.

"This used to be the border between the Southern Shoshone and Arapaho territory," Morgan said as he returned, leading his horse. "In '65, after the Sand Creek Massacre and the trouble that started, most of the Cheyenne and Arapaho were pushed onto reservations in Indian Territory. The Southern Shoshone moved north to join their kin, and I've heard reports of scattered bands of hostiles. These mountains are still wild, no place for a woman alone. Whatever red men or white that roam here, they're to be steered clear of."

He tied his gelding to a tree and proceeded to un-saddle the animal and drop a bedroll on the ground. "As I said, you're safe enough from me, so long as you don't try anything. You'd best curl up beside me here by the fire."

"I'd sooner sleep in a snake den," she answered fervently. "What kind of a fool do you take me for?"

"Suit yourself, but don't be surprised if a diamondback crawls into the blankets with you." He slid a .44-caliber Winchester rifle out of a saddle holster and stood it against a pine tree. "They slither out of the rocks this time of year, and they favor a warm place to sleep, the same as you."

"I'll take my chances." She sucked in a deep breath. "How do you expect me to sleep with my wrists shackled?"

He tilted the brim of his hat and gazed at her across the fire. "On your stomach?"

"I think not."

He studied her for a long minute; then the hint of a smile played over his thin lips. "All right." He unlocked one cuff and snapped it around the loop of his lariat. "About six feet of rope should do you," he said as he tied the other end to his forearm. "I warn you. Move sudden in the night, and I might take you for another puma and shoot you."

Tamsin clenched her teeth to keep from saying the same thing to him. She curled up in her own blanket facing him.

A deep cough sounded from the woods higher up the ridge. Morgan reached for his rifle as brush crackled below them.

Tamsin rose on her knees and looked around anxiously. "What is it? What's that—"

"Hush!" The bounty hunter was on his feet, rifle in hand, muscles tensed.

A branch snapped and a steel-shod hoof struck rock. Morgan's roan raised his head and nickered. Morgan raised his rifle.

"Don't shoot!" Tamsin struggled up and circled the fire until she stood beside him. "It's my horses."

An answering snort came from the forest, and two dark shapes loomed out of the night. Tamsin ran toward the mare and was brought up sharply when she reached the end of the rope.

"I told you. I said they'd come back. Good Fancy, good girl!" Her mane and tail were tangled and pine needles clung to her side, but she seemed sound.

Tamsin glanced back at Morgan. "You can put your rifle down. You're hardly in any danger from these two." Fancy stepped daintily forward until she was close enough for Tamsin to rub the horse's velvet nose.

Dancer squealed and tossed his head.

"Yes, I see you back there," Tamsin said. The stallion pawed the loose stones and grumbled in short, deep huffs.

Suddenly, the lariat binding Tamsin to the bounty hunter went slack. She turned to see him staring uphill, away from her and her horses. "Now what—" she began, but her question was cut short by a bloodcurdling scream.

The eerie howl echoed down the ravine and sent the three horses into a plunging, snorting frenzy. Gooseflesh rose on Tamsin's arms.

"What is it?" she whispered.

Morgan's terse reply made her knees go weak. "Another cougar."

Sweat trickled down her spine. "But you told me they only travel alone. You said—"

He shook his head and peered into the trees. "Hell with what I said. There's another cat out there, and unless I miss my guess, he's stalking us."

Chapter 5

"Can't we saddle the horses and ride out of here?" Tamsin asked breathlessly. She'd managed to get the rope around Fancy's neck and tie her to a tree beside the fire. Morgan's roan gelding stood trembling, legs spread, eyes rolled back in his head. Dancer had torn away into the darkness. She could hear him crashing through the undergrowth, but she didn't know if he was trying to escape the mountain lion or attack it.

Tamsin was acutely aware of the scent of the frightened horses and the pungent smell of crushed spruce boughs under their hooves. She could hear Morgan's breathing and the metallic click of his revolver as he spun the cylinder. If he was afraid, she could see no sign of it by his relaxed, precise movements.

Tamsin had known only three men well in her life. One was her grandfather, and the second a former slave and expert horseman. The third was the sorry excuse for a man she'd married. This Ash Morgan was unlike any of them and he puzzled her. Truth be told, he frightened her as much as the cougar circling their camp.

A sharp crack tore her from her reverie.

Morgan snapped a branch with his boot heel and tossed it on the blazing fire. "No, we can't leave camp."

"What?"

"You asked me if we could outrun the cat," he said

gruffly. "It would be suicide to try. None of us can see in the dark like that puma can, and the horses could break a leg if we tried to move fast. We wouldn't get a hundred yards. He'd leap out of a tree and—"

"I understand." She didn't care to hear more. Images of the dead puma's ivory fangs were all too clear in her memory. She could imagine the ferocious roar, the screams of the horses, and the feel of the slashing claws tearing her apart.

Morgan nodded. "I saw what was left of a man killed by a big cat once...."

She shuddered.

"I should build a second fire, but there's not enough dry wood nearby." He dug extra rifle bullets out of his saddlebag and dropped them into his shirt pocket. "And it would take a bolder man than me to go out there"— he motioned to the circle of darkness around them— "hunting for more."

"Not bolder," she replied. "Stupid." She leaned against the mare and whispered soothing endearments as she ran her hands over the silken hide. Each time the cougar snarled, Fancy shuddered and tried to rear. The rope stretched taut, cutting cruelly into her neck. Tamsin wanted to ease the knot, but she was afraid that Fancy would slip out if the tie was looser.

"You said there couldn't be two mountain lions." Tamsin shivered despite the crackling fire.

Suddenly, Morgan raised his rifle and fired. Tamsin's ears rang from the explosion, but she caught a brief glimpse of two green-glowing coals high up in a tree. Then she saw only blackness. "Did you hit it?"

"Shhh!" he ordered. "Listen." He placed a big hand on her arm, and she jerked back from him as if she'd been burned.

"Quiet." His deep voice was whisper soft, but his tone brooked no argument.

Her breath caught in her throat.

A dry cough sounded to their left, near the place where he had abandoned the carcass of the first puma. Heart pounding, Tamsin moved closer to Morgan and slipped her hand inside the slit in her skirt to grip her pistol.

Minutes dragged by. The horses pawed restlessly and sniffed the air. Then the quiet was broken by a long, drawn-out scream from the gully below.

Hair rose on the back of Tamsin's neck. Her mouth felt dust dry, and her feet seemed rooted to the ground.

Morgan lowered his weapon and swore softly under his breath. "Missed it."

"Maybe you wounded it." Her voice echoed oddly in her head.

"No such luck." He kicked a rock into the fire. "This is all wrong. I've never seen a cougar act this way." He glanced at her. "You might as well get some sleep. I'll keep watch."

Tamsin shrugged. The way her heart was racing, she'd have as much chance of sprouting wings and flying. "Do you think my stallion Dancer . . . Do you think he's in danger?"

"Sure. Who the hell knows? By rights, that cat should have been after him, not us. Humans stink to high heavens. Lions are afraid of them, but horseflesh is fair game."

"But it didn't go after Dancer."

"Nope." He uttered a sound of derision. "The Shoshone say these mountains are haunted. They'd tell you that wasn't a live puma at all. They claim a spirit cat hunts red men and white alike." Morgan looked at her with fierce eyes. "You believe in ghosts, lady?"

She swallowed, trying to ease the constriction in her throat. "I have a name. It's Tamsin."

His features remained hard. "Well, Tamsin, do you believe in ghosts?"

"No. And I doubt if you do either."

"I don't believe in much I can't see, hear, or touch."

"Except the law."

"You're sharp, I'll give you that."

"I'm innocent."

"Then you should welcome the opportunity to clear your name." He hunkered down with his back to a big spruce tree and laid the rifle across his knees. "You ought to thank me for catching you. You wouldn't have lasted long out here by yourself."

"That, Mr. Morgan, is a matter of opinion."

"No need to *mister* me. Ash will do. Get yourself some shut-eye. Dawn comes early on the trail."

She tugged her bedroll as close to the fire as she could get without scorching herself. "I'd appreciate it if you could take this handcuff off me."

"Cuffs on both wrists or the rope. Your choice."

"You're no gentleman."

"And you're obviously no lady or we wouldn't be here, would we?" He tied the end of the rope to a tree.

"What if I have to run from another cougar?"

He shook his head. "No need. Not with me standing guard."

She wanted to remind him that he hadn't been quite so vigilant when she'd spied on him and taken his supplies. Morgan stood between her and freedom, and she couldn't afford to antagonize him.

Instead, she lay down, her back to the fire. There would be little sleep for her that night. As weary and sore as she was, she couldn't forget the mountain lion's scream or those terrifying green eyes.

Sometime in the night, Dancer returned to camp. He sniffed Ash's gelding, snorted a warning, and trotted over to lean his head against Fancy's.

Overhead, glittering stars appeared one by one until the sky seemed strewn with diamonds. The temperature dropped and Tamsin curled tighter in her blanket. Every forest sound became ominous, and it took all of her willpower not to show how frightened she was.

Each time Tamsin opened her eyes, she saw Ash keeping watch. Occasionally, he stood and walked around the perimeter of the camp, then returned to his resting spot without making a sound.

The twittering of birds announced the day long before the darkness gave way to light. One after another, small creatures began to stir. First a squirrel scampered down the tree Ash was leaning on; then a mouse peered out of a heap of pine needles not three feet from where Tamsin lay.

She sat up and stretched. The insides of her eyelids were scratchy and her head ached. She had never done well without sleep, and the night that had just passed was no exception.

"Morning," Ash said. She hadn't heard him leave the camp, but the coffeepot he was propping on the coals was full of water. "I'd offer you bread and cheese," he said, "but someone stole my provisions." He reached down and unlocked her handcuff.

Rubbing her wrist, she got to her feet and tried to comb the twigs out of her hair with her fingers. "Is the cougar gone?"

He nodded. "Horses been quiet since about two o'clock."

"How can you tell the time? Do you have a watch?"

"Not on me. I broke the crystal in a little tussle. I left it in Sweetwater to be repaired."

"Then how do you know the time?"

"I swear, woman. You're the talkingest prisoner I've ever had." He grinned at her, and his smile was as bright as the sun breaking through a storm cloud. His teeth were white and even. Smiling made him look younger and not nearly so forbidding. "You can tell time by the stars if you spend enough time sleeping under them."

"I don't need constellations to tell me that I'm ready for breakfast," she replied. "I've fishing line in my pack. If you let me go to the creek for an hour, I'll catch us the main course."

He studied her for a minute, then smiled. "Don't suppose it will do any harm to let you try. I'll just walk along with you, so you don't get lost."

"So I don't run away, you mean." She shrugged. "That's fine, so long as you're gentleman enough to allow me . . ." She felt a flush rise up her throat. "I have personal needs."

"By rights I shouldn't give you any privacy after you got an eyeful of my assets."

"Oh, I . . ." Embarrassment made her speechless. How could he have known that she'd seen him in the altogether?

His obsidian eyes glittered with mischief. "Your tracks told the story, Tamsin. I was careless and let you sneak up on me. Had you been a rogue Cheyenne, my scalp would be waving from a tepee pole." He dusted his hands on his coat. "Hope you enjoyed the sight."

"It wasn't what you think," she protested.

"Hard to think anything but the worst," he drawled. "A lady hiding in the bushes, watching a man Adam-naked in his bath."

Tamsin was mortified. "I thought you were an Indian," she explained. "I was only trying to see—"

"Ladies in Tennessee make a habit of such?"

"No, they do not."

He cradled his rifle in the crook of his arm and stood. "Glad you did. If you'd have ridden past, I might have missed your tracks and not caught up with you for a week. As it was, a six-year-old Arapaho could have followed your trail here. You're a hell of a horsewoman, but not much of a scout."

"I'll keep your observations in mind," she said as she fumbled through her belongings for her fishing line.

Ash chuckled as he followed her downhill to the steep-banked stream. The watercourse wasn't more than three yards wide, but it was fast-moving and waist deep. Likely there were fish there. If she had the gear to catch a few, so much the better.

Had he been alone, he would have found himself a likely spot, lain on his belly, and tickled a fat trout or two. Catching fish with his bare hands was a trick his daddy had taught him when he was a child. It worked, but it took time. And he didn't trust Texas Jack Cannon's woman enough to allow her to stand behind him with all these rocks strewn around.

Maybe he should think about another line of work after he brought Cannon to justice. Ash had never intended bounty hunting to be a permanent occupation. Those who made their living with a gun usually ended up in boot hill before their hair turned gray.

For a few brief seconds he let his mind flash back to the spread he and Becky had carved out of empty prairie near Colorado City. She'd begged him to give up the job, but he hadn't listened. He worried about having enough money to see them through the winter, and he'd decided to go after one more road agent. The reward on Red Bucky's head would be enough to pay their bill at the feed store and buy a good bull.

It had been the worst argument they'd ever had, and

he'd rode out and left her crying on the front porch. He hadn't even kissed her good-bye.

He'd been so sure that he knew what was right, but he hadn't counted on Cannon's committing a robbery in Colorado City or on his Becky being a witness to the crime.

He'd gotten his outlaw. He'd brought Red Bucky back, collected the bounty, and bought Becky a music box for her birthday. But when he got home and called her name, nobody answered.

In that one night, Ashton Jefferson Morgan had lost his wife, an unborn child, and everything he'd worked for. Something had died inside him. He'd given up caring about anything but the law and settling his score with Cannon, his brothers, and the rest of the gang.

Ahead of him, Tamsin was breaking off a tree branch to use as a fishing pole. She was a hand taller than his Becky, fox-haired instead of wheat-blond, and striking rather than pretty. Tamsin's sensual mouth was too bold and her chin too sharp for conventional beauty. But this Tennessee enigma had a glow about her that drew a man's eye.

He half suspected that Tamsin might be telling the truth about the horses belonging to her. But all the evidence pointed to her being the back shooter who'd killed Sam Steele. As he'd told her, deciding who was guilty and who was innocent wasn't up to him. All he had to do was serve the warrants and bring the suspects to justice.

Sunlight filtering through the evergreen canopy lit sparks in Tamsin's tangled locks and stirred something deep in Ash that had best remain sleeping. Losing Becky had hurt him worse than being orphaned at ten, but it hadn't turned him off women.

Someday, when he'd finished what he'd started, when he'd rid himself of the itch to keep moving, he'd find a good woman and settle down. He wanted kids, and he wanted a piece of land he could call his own. He didn't fool himself that he could ever feel about a second wife the way he had for Becky. But plenty of solid marriages were built on respect and friendship. He'd known real love, the kind you'd rush into fire for, and he didn't look to see it again this side of the hereafter.

He damn sure wasn't looking for it in a female like Tamsin MacGreggor. If she stirred his nether parts, it was pure lust and nothing more. He was a man with as strong a hunger as any other, but he prided himself on being able to control his physical needs. She was his prisoner. He'd shoot her if he had to, but he'd not take advantage of her.

He settled onto a flat boulder and waited for Tamsin to beg him to find her a worm and thread it on the hook. To his surprise, she turned over a few stones, found what she was looking for, and baited the hook herself.

Mosquitoes buzzed around Ash's head, and he was glad for his coat despite the heat. He stretched out his long legs and massaged an old scar he'd received during the war.

The tip of Tamsin's pole bobbed, then dived toward the surface of the water. She set the hook and pulled in a two-pound trout. "See," she called to him. "My breakfast. I'll see what you're having next."

She got another nibble and then nothing. Ash cleaned the first fish. Minutes passed.

"Do you want to try this while I . . ." She left the rest unfinished.

He nodded. "Long as you go downstream away from the camp. Not too far, around that bend. I doubt you'll try to escape without those horses."

"Right now I'm more interested in food than getting

away," she replied coolly. "I do have a change of clothing in my saddlebags. These are—"

"Quit while you're ahead." He took the fishing pole from her.

She looked unconvinced. "I have your word you won't . . . won't spy on me?"

"Lady, we just spent the night together. If I meant you harm, there wouldn't have been a damn thing you could do about it. Go wash your unmentionables."

Tamsin muttered under her breath as she picked her way through the bushes along the creekbank. Ash turned his attention to fishing. Immediately, something nibbled at the bait. He missed that one but soon caught another trout. He stayed where he was, but he couldn't stop his thoughts from wandering down the creek. He wondered what Tamsin MacGreggor looked like without her clothes. She was slim, not nearly as well endowed as most of the ladies at Maudine's, but he would have bet his saddle she was prime.

Thinking that way was enough to make a man overly warm. He ran a forefinger under his collar and called to her. "You still there?"

"Yes!"

He brought in two more fish before Tamsin rejoined him. Her cheeks were scrubbed rosy, and she'd braided her wet hair into a single plait that hung down her back. She smelled good, woman-clean without a hint of heavy perfume.

"About time," he grumbled. "I've got two fish apiece. With the coffee, that should do us. Of course, we could use biscuits."

"The bread you had in your pack could never be considered biscuits," she replied. "Heavy, stale, nasty lumps of flour and grease."

"You ate them, didn't you?"

Ignoring him, she undid her fishing line from the pole and coiled it up and put it in her pocket. "I'm the prisoner," she said. "You can cook the fish."

"Intended to. That way I'll know it's cooked."

They walked in silence back to the camp, and Ash forced himself to tear his gaze off the sway of Tamsin's shapely hips in that riding skirt.

It was easy to see why Jack Cannon would be attracted to her, even if she was a cut above his usual choice in women. Ash wanted to ask her why the outlaw had let her ride off alone into these mountains and where she intended to meet up with him, but he didn't. It had been Ash's experience that a lady would lie to protect her man faster than a horse could trot. Just listening usually paid off in the end.

Back at the fire, Tamsin found more kindling and saddled her mare while he grilled the four trout. They drank the black, acrid coffee and devoured the hot fish with a minimum of chatter.

It was when he turned away to saddle his gelding, Shiloh, that she hit him in the back of the head. He saw stars and sagged to one knee, half turning to face her just as she brought the chunk of firewood down across his skull again.

Chapter 6

Ash knew he'd been hit a second time. He tried to react, but his muscles wouldn't obey. "Son of a—"The remainder of his oath was muffled in the spruce needles as he slid face first onto the ground. Bright lights were exploding in his brain, and his vision was fading.

"I'm sorry," Tamsin said. "But you wouldn't listen to reason."

Rage boiled in Ash's chest as he tried to get up. His head seemed made of lead; his arms, quicksand. "Don't . . ." he managed. Even his tongue felt odd, too thick for his mouth. The stars were fading, and in their place sprouted two distinct centers of pulsing pain. He tried to speak, but his words slurred. "Can't . . . take horse . . . my horse."

"I have to," Tamsin replied.

Through the slits where his eyes had been he saw two blurry, red-haired women lift two rifles.

"Not my gun . . ." he rasped, and spat sand from his mouth. "No . . . not take . . ."

"I'm not stealing your weapons."

He thought that's what the witch was saying, but he also felt a tugging at his holster. Then his pistol passed before his eyes.

"I'll leave them on the far side of the campfire," she

said. "That way, you won't be tempted to shoot me while I'm riding away."

"Shoot you . . . in the back . . ." Ash forced himself up on his hands and knees and reached for her. She stepped aside and the effort sent him plunging to earth again. "You're the bushwhacker." He gasped, trying to clear the confusion from his mind.

Shot in the back. Someone was murdered. Who? Ash knew that he should remember, but it seemed so long ago. There was a man lying on the ground beside him . . . a big man.

Moisture clouded Ash's vision.

"I'm sorry," Tamsin repeated. "You'll be all right. I didn't hit you hard enough to kill you."

Ash heard the creak of saddle leather. His horse nickered. Hooves scraped on rock, then faded in the distance. "Tamsin!"

The only answer was the loud chatter of a hairy woodpecker from a bough overhead.

Ash's fiery oath startled the bird, and he caught a glimpse of black-and-white feathers as it took flight through the aspen grove.

Ash closed his eyes and sank against the earth. Something warm trickled down the back of his neck, and he smelled the sweet scent of blood. The scent of blood had filled his head that day his father was murdered.

This blood wasn't his daddy's. It was his.

The MacGreggor woman's killed me, he thought. *I hope she's killed me. If she hasn't, she'll soon wish she had.*

There was nothing worse than a common back shooter. A renegade Comanchero had killed his daddy from ambush. If Ash closed his eyes, he could see his father sprawled in the red dirt.

"Daddy, get up. Get up, Daddy."

Ash didn't know if he was hearing an echo from the distant past or if the words were coming out of his mouth now. His father had taken him fishing. It was his tenth birthday and his daddy had given him a man-sized pocketknife.

Ash couldn't recollect too much . . . didn't want to. But it was impossible to forget the sickly sweet smell of blood or the puzzled look on his father's face when he fell.

All night, he'd sat there beside the body, holding Daddy's tin star. He hadn't wept. His loss was too deep for tears. One minute he'd been Big Jim Morgan's boy, and the next . . .

He was alone.

Until the Comancheros returned in the first gray light of dawn to steal the horses and weapons and scalp his father.

And the bad times started.

Ash cradled his head in his hands as dusty images of pain and fear washed over him. Vaguely, he knew what he was seeing in his mind was long past.

Reason told him that he had to get on his feet . . . had to go after his escaped prisoner. But his skull was splitting. It was easier to lie on the warm ground and think about nothing at all.

A branch whipped across Tamsin's face, but she paid no heed to the sting and spurred Ash Morgan's strawberry roan into a hard trot.

She hadn't planned on bashing him over the head, but she'd found herself standing there with the stick in her hand. She'd realized that she would probably never have a better chance of getting away. If she hadn't taken his horse, he'd soon be on her trail again.

Ash would survive. He'd have a long walk back to Sweetwater, but she'd left him his rifle and handgun. What more could he ask?

She wondered if she was going to spend the rest of her life running. Horse stealing was a hanging offense. She'd been innocent of that charge when they'd written up a warrant for her arrest. Now she was as guilty as sin.

"Horse thief." She tried out the phrase. It sounded ugly ... despicable. She'd never stolen so much as a penny's worth of candy in her life.

No wonder there were so many desperadoes in the West, she mused. One mistake, and an honest person could find themselves on a wanted poster.

For what it was worth, she intended to leave Ash's roan gelding at the next town, but that probably wouldn't count for much if she was captured and faced a jury.

A rabbit dashed out of the bushes, and the gelding leaped sideways. Tamsin kept her seat easily. Her two horses were following close behind. She'd thought it wiser to ride Ash's mount. Leading an unwilling horse would have been a problem in these trees, especially since Dancer kept sneaking up to take nips out of his rump.

Tamsin hoped the mountain lion was far away. It had fled uphill, leaving her an escape route back down the way she had come the day before. She knew from her map that she needed to find a pass through these foothills, and she remembered the entrance to a promising valley she'd seen on the way in.

Ash would think the worst of her. She hated to leave him with the impression that she was a killer and a horse thief.

"Damn you, Atwood MacGreggor," she swore. "I hope your coffin leaks." It was all his fault. If he hadn't been such a jackass's behind, she'd be back in Tennessee sipping lemonade on her own front porch. . . . And maybe Granddad's heart wouldn't have given out so soon.

She'd realized that she'd made a mistake on her wedding night. Atwood had embarrassed her with crude remarks and selfishly taken his pleasure on her rigid body. Worse, he'd blamed her when his red-faced thrusting met no resistance.

He'd called her a whore, accusing her of not being a virgin. That was a lie, but she'd had no way to prove her innocence . . . any more than she could prove her innocence to Ash Morgan.

Her honeymoon with Atwood had been a great disappointment. Afterward, she'd wondered what all the fuss was about mating and why some women were willing to risk everything for illicit affairs with men not their lawful husbands.

Tamsin removed her hat and wiped the sweat off her forehead. If Atwood MacGreggor had looked anything like Ash Morgan in the altogether, perhaps she could have mustered a little more enthusiasm for his husbandly attentions.

Just thinking about Ash's naked body made her mouth go dry and butterflies flutter in the pit of her stomach. There must be something sinful in her if she could take such pleasure in remembering the dark sprinkling of hair that ran down his flat belly to the tightly curled mat above his sex. . . . Or the way drops of water glistened on his muscular arms.

Even if things were different between them, if Ash hadn't been a bounty hunter paid to bring her back to Sweetwater, it would make no difference. A good-looking man like Ash Morgan would never be interested in her.

Growing up, she'd had no woman to teach her feminine ways. Her mother had died giving birth to her, and her grandmother had never gotten over the shock of losing her only child. Gran had lived in a wispy world of ghosts and voices only she could hear. She was always happy, always ready to give her granddaughter a hug or a sweet. The trouble was, she couldn't remember Tamsin's name or who she was.

Tamsin didn't blame anyone for her inability to fit into Three Forks society. Her grandfather's wealth couldn't make up for her unconventional ways. Her hair was too red and too unruly to be smoothed into a proper coiffure, and her dresses were always torn from climbing fences and trees. All her life she'd heard remarks, some whispered, some rudely spoken aloud.

"Too broad-shouldered for my taste," a neighbor's son had remarked. "They say all heiresses are beautiful, but I'd rather court one of her grandfather's racehorses."

Atwood hadn't said any of those things, not until after she became his wife and he had control of her inheritance. Then he'd taunted her with far worse. He'd said she was too mannish and stupid to boot.

She knew he was wrong. The only truly stupid thing she'd done in her life was to accept Atwood's proposal of marriage.

She'd known about her husband's gambling and foolish business ventures, but she hadn't guessed the extent of the damage. And in the end, the mare and stallion were all she had to start a new life.

She was well rid of him. She would build again in California, bigger and better. She didn't need a husband to take care of her. She was quite capable of managing her own—

Tamsin reined up the gelding. She'd been so busy dredging up old memories that she'd nearly ridden past the entrance to the valley. She dismounted to drink and let the horses drink their fill from the stream.

Once in the saddle again, she pushed hard up the valley. Ahead mountains rose in folds, some still snowcapped. She had a compass and a map showing two passes through the Rockies. Now she was cutting too far north to find either one. She couldn't go back to Sweet-water, nor could she go south without taking a chance on meeting up with Ash again.

"I'll simply have to find another way."

She rode on through the heat of the noonday sun, seeing nothing more threatening than a golden eagle winging overhead and a coyote with two pups trotting after her. The air was so clean and sweet that she inhaled it in great gulps, savoring the bite of evergreen on her tongue.

In midafternoon, Tamsin rode past a herd of elk grazing peacefully in a meadow of yellow flowers not un-like the buttercups that had grown so profusely at home. A massive bull with spreading horns raised his head and gazed at her, but the cows and long-legged calves seemed unconcerned.

Tamsin was amazed by the vastness of the country. Other than Ash, she'd not seen a single human being since she'd left Sweetwater behind. Moved by the panorama of endless sky and mountains, she rode in si-lence, filling her eyes and memory with the tranquil beauty. The creak of saddle leather and the comforting cadence of the horses' hooves were almost hypnotic, lulling her into a sense of deep peace.

Abruptly, the valley narrowed, and trees lined the passageway. Already shadows lengthened, telling Tam-sin that it was time to look for a place to camp for the night. But she had found no other stream, and she was reluctant to make a dry camp.

A rock fall from the ridge above made her look up in alarm. Small stones tumbled down, unnerving the horses. Laying his black ears flat against his head, Dancer rolled his eyes and snorted. Fancy mouthed the bit and pressed up behind her mate.

Prickles of apprehension played up and down Tamsin's

spine and the leathers felt suddenly damp against her palm. She urged her mare on, but Dancer blocked their way. Skin rippled over his powerful chest, and he pawed the stony ground.

"Go on!" she shouted, bringing her reins down across his rump. He sprang forward, leaping fallen logs and rocks. The mare sped after him with the gelding hot on her heels.

Then a ferocious snarl echoed down the canyon. Twisting in the saddle, Tamsin caught a flash of tawny movement high above her. Heart thudding, she flung the lead line free, letting the roan find his own pace.

It was all she could do to stay in the saddle as the chestnut sailed over a waist-high boulder, slid in the loose gravel, and nearly went down on her knees. Ash's horse scrambled partially up the steep bank to gallop past them, as Fancy regained her balance and raced on with Tamsin clinging to her mane.

The ravine widened to embrace a muddy creek. Dancer splashed through the water and continued on up the gulch. The sides of the gorge grew higher, and trees lined the divide, sometimes closing overhead to block out the fading light.

Tamsin didn't know how far they'd come since she'd seen the mountain lion, but Fancy was visibly tiring and the other two animals were streaked with sweat.

Gradually, Tamsin checked the mare's pace to a trot and then a walk. The other horses matched their gait to hers. "It's all right," Tamsin soothed.

Ahead of her, Shiloh stopped, looked back, and whinnied. Tamsin rose in her stirrups and glanced about nervously.

Then something struck her, tumbling her forcefully out of the saddle. She hit the ground hard. Terror stricken, she opened her mouth to scream, but the fall had knocked the wind out of her. She curled into a ball, clenched her eyes shut. Her last conscious act was to attempt to protect her head from the cougar's attack.

Chapter 7

"Get up!" Ash ordered as he climbed to his feet. "No, don't! Stay where you are." He stifled a groan. He'd landed with his left shoulder taking the shock of his weight, the one he'd dislocated in a fall off a broomtail last autumn.

Tamsin rolled onto her back. She opened her eyes and stared at him in stunned disbelief. "I thought you were a mountain lion."

"Shut up. Don't say a word. And don't you dare move from that spot." He rubbed his aching shoulder and muttered a string of foul curses under his breath. He was thirty-six, too old to be leaping off cliff faces onto a horse and rider. He gritted his teeth and shook the kinks out of his back.

Tamsin's green eyes looked stunned, and her oval face was chalk-white beneath the smears of dirt. From the corner of her mouth, a thin trickle of blood marred her bottom lip.

For long seconds she didn't even breathe; then she drew in a deep, shuddering gasp and her eyes filled with tears. "I . . . I saw . . . the cougar," she said. "I thought you were the . . ."

He gave her a look that would have soured milk. "You would have been better off if a lion did jump you."

"I thought—"

"I told you to be quiet, you conniving witch!" Damn if his knee didn't feel like it was screwed on backward. He forced himself to put all his weight on it.

"I'm sorry, I—

"Not one swiving word!" He limped away and picked up the end of the rope trailing behind his horse. Shiloh's chest and belly were lathered, and foam dripped from his mouth.

The roan nickered a greeting and flicked his ears as Ash approached and ran a hand appraisingly down the gelding's left front leg. Murmuring to the animal, he fingered a bloody scrape on the horse's shank. A patch of skin was torn away, but the wound wasn't deep.

Ash glanced back at Tamsin and saw she was sitting up. "Get down!" She obeyed and he continued his inspection of Shiloh's injuries. Ash lingered over the task, using the time to master his anger.

He'd never hit a woman, but he wanted to hit Tamsin. Just thinking about slapping the hell out of her took some of the venom out of his seething anger.

Seven hours! He'd spent seven backbreaking hours climbing a rugged mountain in this heat to get here ahead of her. And he'd done it with a splitting headache, carrying all his gear.

He'd guessed she'd double back and take this canyon. If she hadn't, he would have had trouble catching her on foot. But he would have found her eventually, even if he'd had to trail her into the mouth of hell.

The other two horses stood head to head a few yards away. Ash walked over and gave them a quick look. The stallion's flanks were wet, but he wasn't even breathing hard. And the bay had enough spit left in him to snake out his neck and bare his teeth.

Tamsin's chestnut mare appeared as weary as his roan

but sound. As far as Ash could see, she didn't have a scratch on her.

"You could have killed me," Tamsin accused.

Ash turned to face her. She was wide-eyed and shaken, but on her feet. Her tears had turned the grime on her cheeks to mud.

"I told you to shut up and stay put!"

"All right. You don't need to shout."

Some of the sass was coming back into her tone, but he wasn't amused. Any sympathy he'd felt toward Tamsin MacGreggor had vanished when she'd nearly cracked his skull with that chunk of wood.

"You'd be wise to pay heed to what I told you," he said. "I get the same reward if I hang you from the nearest tree and take you back head down across a saddle."

She shook her head. "I left you your guns. If you wanted to kill me, you had the chance. You won't shoot me, and I refuse to allow you to bully me."

He took a deep breath and exhaled slowly, mentally counting to ten. "Shooting you would be too easy. If I kill you, I want it to be slow and painful. Do you have any idea how far I've walked today?"

She glanced toward the foothills he'd crossed to reach this divide. "I think so."

"Don't think. Don't even speak."

Tamsin sniffed. "You would have done the same thing if I was the bounty hunter and you were the suspect." She took off her hat and tried to mold it back into shape. "I am sorry I hurt you."

She was wrong, he thought, ignoring her apology. If he was on the run, he'd never have left her armed. And maybe not alive. If Tamsin was a murderer, she was damn poor at her job.

"You could have crippled these horses," he accused.

"Are you stupid? Running them in this canyon? With this uneven ground and all these rocks?"

A single tear crept down her muddy cheek. "They bolted on me. The cougar . . . It must have followed us."

"You're a greenhorn," he scoffed. "You saw a deer or a bighorn sheep and mistook that for a puma. Then you panicked, and rode these horses hell-for-leather."

Tamsin took a limping step toward him. "I know the difference between a mountain lion and a deer."

"Sit down." He pointed to a rotten log. "There. And keep your hands where I can see them."

"I said I was sorry."

"Save it." Ire seethed in his gut. Men—hardened outlaws—didn't give him this much trouble. Any male prisoner who'd knocked him senseless would be spitting teeth out of his arse.

Tamsin could have split his skull like a rotten pumpkin. Maybe that's what she'd intended, and all these pretty words were more lies. Because she was an attractive woman, he'd taken chances he never would have with a man. It had nearly cost him his life.

Tamsin MacGreggor was as dangerous as a cornered rattlesnake.

"You're my prisoner," he said. "From now on, I treat you like one."

"I didn't kill Sam Steele," she argued. "I'm sure the judge did it himself. If you take me back to face his court, I'm guilty before I say a word in my own defense."

"Put your hands behind you." She did as he ordered, and he clamped the cuffs around her wrists. Both palms were filthy and stained with blood. He hardened himself against feeling compassion for the pain she must be in. "There's water about a mile ahead. We'll camp there."

He whistled and Shiloh came to him. Strapping his

bedroll and plunder to the saddle, he mounted the gelding.

"You can do the walking for a change," he said to Tamsin. "See how you like it."

She didn't protest as they wound through the narrow cleft in the rocks. The mare and the stallion kept just ahead. Ash didn't think there was much chance of her climbing up on one of them with her hands secured behind her back, and it did his heart good to see her stumbling over the rough ground.

Ash smelled smoke before he reached the creek. He thought of leaving Tamsin there and scouting ahead to see what was causing the fire. But if he fastened her to a tree and something happened to him, she'd be helpless. And if he didn't, he doubted she'd be here when he came back.

Reluctantly, he stopped and uncuffed Tamsin, then offered her his hand. "Swing up behind the saddle," he ordered. "Hold on tight. If there's trouble, we may need to ride like there's no tomorrow."

"You don't mean you'd run the horses over this rocky ground?"

"Put your arms around my waist and shut your mouth. If there is someone up ahead, let me do the talking." He cradled his rifle in the crook of one arm and hoped Tamsin's silence meant she'd follow his orders.

As they drew closer to the water, the horses pricked up their ears and broke into a trot. Shiloh picked up his pace in spite of the double load.

A dog began to bark somewhere ahead of them. As Ash and Tamsin rounded a bend, two Indians barred their way.

Ash felt Tamsin stiffen and heard her sharp intake of breath. "Steady," he whispered. "They're Ute, usually friendly to whites."

He raised his right hand, palm open. "Greetings," he called in the Ute tongue. "We come in peace."

The older man, round-faced and unsmiling, answered in stilted English, "How-dy." His graying hair hung in two long braids, and he wore a woolen vest over a plaid shirt, and buckskin leggings. Around his neck gleamed a silver Peace Medal, and his left hand clutched a flintlock musket.

Four horses were tied beneath the trees, two pintos, a black, and a buckskin. A thin black dog with bristly hair and a curly tail dashed out from between their legs. Barking furiously, he rushed at Shiloh.

The younger brave smiled and lowered his rifle. "You and your woman alone?" he asked in the Ute language. He wore traditional leggings and a fringed hunting shirt decorated with geometric embroidery.

Ash nodded. He knew more Cheyenne than Ute. Although he was certain he'd understood what the second man had asked, he was quickly using up his vocabulary. "Just us two."

"Come. Eat." The gray-haired man wearing the Peace Medal motioned to Ash. "You are welcome." He struck his chest lightly. "I am Mountain Calf. This is my sister's son, Wrestler."

"We will accept your hospitality, Mountain Calf," Ash replied. "I am called Ash Morgan, and this is my wife, Tamsin."

"Wife?" Tamsin whispered.

Ash felt Tamsin flinch as he grasped her arm. "Let me help you down. These kind gentlemen have offered us supper."

Alarm showed in Tamsin's eyes as she slid to the ground, but she didn't protest. Ash dismounted and walked toward the Utes. Solemnly, he shook hands with

Mountain Calf and then his nephew. The dog continued to bark.

Wrestler pumped Ash's hand up and down vigorously. "A white man who brings his wife comes as a friend." He grinned at Tamsin. "This man has heard that some white women have hair like winter-dried grass, but he has never seen one with fire hair and eyes like spring grass. It will make a good tale when Wrestler returns to his own village. This man hopes that his friends will believe him." He shook his head and laughed. "You must tell them, Uncle."

Mountain Calf put two fingers to his lips and uttered a shrill whistle.

From the trees beyond the stream came an Indian woman carrying an infant strapped to a cradleboard. "My wife," Mountain Calf explained to Ash in the Ute language. "She is called Shadow. She is a good cook. You must taste her broiled venison."

"An Ute who brings his wife comes as a friend," Ash said.

Mountain Calf nodded. "It is so." He spoke sharply to the dog, and the animal crouched on its belly and grew still.

"Do you go west over the mountains into Ute land?" Wrestler asked.

Ash shook his head. "No." He pointed east. "We turn back tomorrow toward the place of the rising sun."

"Good," Mountain Calf observed. "All of my people are not so hospitable to strangers."

"My mother's brother likes white men," Wrestler said. "You need have no fear at his fire."

"An Ute's word is good," Ash replied. "And honest men of any color have much to talk about." He glanced at Tamsin. "The Utes treat their guests with honor."

"But will they steal the horses?"

"Our belongings are safe in a brother's camp," he said,

loud enough for both Utes to hear. "As safe as in the Creator's hand."

"Whatever you say, *husband*," Tamsin murmured sarcastically.

Wrestler grinned. "Good wife. Ute women not so obedient. Have strong will." He studied Tamsin more intently. "She has power, this woman, and she sits a horse well. A shame she is not Ute."

"A pity," Ash replied.

"Yes," Tamsin agreed. "A pity."

Hours later, she rolled up in her blanket a short distance from the campfire. Ash and the two Ute men were still talking, and the woman, Shadow, was nursing her baby.

Tamsin had found the Indian woman fascinating. She and Shadow shared no common language, but they had managed to communicate. Tamsin had admired Shadow's fringed leather dress and her beautifully fashioned moccasins decorated with dyed porcupine quills. She even played with Shadow's baby, an adorable three-month-old boy with huge, sparkling, ebony-colored eyes.

For the second night, Tamsin found herself tired beyond belief but unable to sleep. She kept thinking of the cougar. If it had crossed the hills, would it follow them to this campsite? Ash had told the Indians about the cat's strange behavior, and they'd assured him that their dog would keep close watch during the night.

"He is a bear dog, that War-et," Wrestler had said. "He is small, but he has the heart of a grizzly."

Shadow had showed Tamsin how to make a soft bed of pine boughs. Using only pantomime, she had explained that the pine needles would keep away insects and snakes. Tamsin was all for that.

But even though her bed was comfortable, Tamsin could not stop her thoughts from racing. Everything that had happened since she'd hit Ash and escaped this morning kept spinning in her head: the mountain lion, the furious dash down the canyon, the beauty of the wilderness, and Ash's fury when he caught up with her.

She ached all over from her fall. Somehow, she hadn't lost her pistol when Ash had landed on top of her. She'd managed to conceal the heavy weapon until she'd unsaddled her horses. Then she'd slipped under Dancer's neck and hid the weapon in one of her bags.

Ash had told the Indians that they were heading east in the morning. He intended to take her back to Sweetwater. She couldn't let that happen, but short of shooting him, she wasn't sure how she could get away.

"Slide over, Mrs. Morgan."

Tamsin's eyes snapped open and her heart skipped a beat. Ash was standing right over her. She had been lost in her own thoughts and hadn't heard his footsteps.

"I said move over, woman."

She pushed herself up on her elbows. By the fire, she could see Wrestler standing, looking in their direction. "What?" she asked. "What do you—" Fear raised gooseflesh on her arms.

Ash pulled off one boot. "I'm coming to bed."

A heavy weight seemed to crush her chest. "With me?"

He removed his other boot and stood them beside his rifle, then tugged at his shirt. "You heard me," he said. "Where else would a man sleep but beside his loving wife?"

Chapter 8

"You can't do this!" Tamsin whispered thickly.

"Shut up, woman. It's for your own good." Ash's trousers and socks followed the shirt, leaving him wearing only his hat.

She clutched the blanket against her as Ash neatly folded his clothing and laid it next to his boots. "You cannot sleep here," she insisted.

"You want me to tell Wrestler that you're not my wife? That I lied to him?" Ash balanced his hat on top of his boots. Then he seized the edge of the blanket, jerking it tighter over her breasts to give him room to ease under. "That's better." He lay down beside her and slipped his left arm under her head.

Tamsin tried to get up, but she was tangled in the blanket. Fear and a curious excitement made her tremble. "I don't want to do this."

Ash pulled her close. "Wrestler likes your hair," he whispered. "He's offered to trade me two horses and a stack of beaver hides for you."

She pushed against his naked chest with both hands, trying to put distance between them, but Ash was as unmovable as a granite wall.

"Stop squirming," he said.

"Get out of my bed!"

83

"Wrestler said he'd make you first wife. You might want to consider it."

The suggestion shocked her nearly as much as having this naked bounty hunter wrapped around her. "Marry him? I'd sooner wed you."

"I haven't proposed," he reminded her.

"I should have said I'd sooner wed the devil."

He chuckled. "I make it a practice never to marry a woman who's likely to shoot me."

"I don't think this is funny."

"Taking Wrestler for a husband would beat hanging, wouldn't it?"

"I doubt it." She was fully dressed, but the heat of his skin burned through the layers of her garments. Scents of tobacco and leather, gunpowder, and horses enveloped her as Ash's long legs tangled with hers, and his bare hip and firm thigh pressed intimately into her flesh.

Ash frightened her tonight, but her own emotions terrified her even more. It had been a long time since a man had held her like this. Atwood's shoulders were never so wide, nor his body so hard and muscular.

A distinctly male odor emanated from Ash's hair and skin. It wasn't unpleasant, Tamsin thought, trying to calm her inner trembling. To the contrary . . . she found his aroma enticing, almost exciting.

Ash was exceptionally clean. She had watched him scrub himself in the stream before supper, rubbing his limbs with sand and washing his hair with a foamy substance that Shadow had given him.

Then she stiffened as she smelled something else, a hint of alcohol. Was it possible that he'd been drinking? She was sure of it when his mouth brushed hers and she tasted the bite of whiskey. "You're drunk!" she accused, no longer bothering to keep her voice down. "You're despicable."

"I'm not a drinking man," he answered. "Hardly ever touch the stuff."

"Don't lie to me. I smell it on—"

He cut her off with a kiss, a caress so hot and demanding that it seared her lips and took her breath away.

"Tamsin," he rasped.

She gasped as he threaded lean fingers gently through her hair and slowly drew her lower lip between his. She felt the tip of his warm tongue trace her sensitive skin and heard his nearly inaudible groan.

She tried to turn her face away, but his mouth found hers, and this time his kiss was so sweet and tender that her resistance crumbled.

Against her will, her lips parted and the tantalizing kiss deepened. He cupped her chin in one broad hand, sending giddy sensations spinning through her.

When he drew back, her lips tingled and an odd heat glowed in her stomach. She wanted to run, but her limbs were oddly weak.

He touched her face, tracing the line of her cheek with one rough finger.

"Don't," she protested. His breath was warm on her face, his mouth only inches from her own.

Another kiss sent her reason spinning.

"No!" She pushed him away, fighting sensations of heat that spread up from her core.

"What's wrong? You want me as much as I want you."

"I'm not one of your whores."

He pushed himself up on one elbow. "Sorry I'm not Jack Cannon."

"What?" She gave him a hard shove with the palm of her hand. "What does Jack Cannon have to do with this?" A numbing fear seeped through her. How did he know about Jack?

"Everything." Ash's voice deepened. "I know about the two of you. I've trailed you since Wheaton, Nebraska."

"You followed me? Why?" She balled her fist and struck him again. This time he caught her wrist and pinned it to the ground.

"Stop," she protested. "You're hurting me."

"I'll let go when you stop punching me."

"All right," she muttered.

He released her, and she turned her back to him, trembling with anger. "What happened between Mr. Cannon and me is my own business. None of yours."

"He was with you when you shot Sam Steele, wasn't he?"

"Jack?" She squirmed around to face him. "I told you, I didn't kill anyone. The judge shot—"

"Right."

She made a sound of disbelief. "You're drunk and a liar. I don't know why I'm even having this conversation with you."

"Lady, you could teach me a thing or two about lying. Jack Cannon's a thief and a killer."

"You must have the wrong man. Jack's a rancher. He—"

"Admit it, MacGreggor. You're his fancy woman, and that cakes you with the same horsesh—"

"Don't be vulgar. I am not his woman. He took me to dinner a few times. Period."

"Nice company you keep. Cannon's face is plastered on wanted posters from Texas to Arizona. He robbed the bank days after you left town."

She felt suddenly sick to her stomach. "I don't believe you," she insisted. It couldn't be true. Jack Cannon had a bad temper, and he didn't take no for an answer, but surely he wasn't a murdering criminal. She couldn't have misjudged his character that badly. "Why should I believe you? You lied to me when you said you hadn't been drinking."

"It wasn't anything that could be avoided, more of a medicinal swallow than anything else."

"Medicinal?"

"Wrestler passed a jug, and it would be bad manners to refuse. Could be dangerous to a man's health to insult an Ute. They're proud people."

"What makes you such an Indian expert?"

"I lived with outlaw Comanches for two years."

"Comanche Indians?"

"These were renegades, thieving murderers of the worst kind, shunned by their own tribe."

"And you were one of them?"

He groaned. "I didn't have a choice. I was ten years old when they killed my father and carried me off."

She buried her face in her hands, unwilling to listen to him. How could she tell truth from lies when her own mind and body so quickly betrayed her. "You're not ten now," she managed. "And you gulped down enough rotgut to give you courage, then crawled under my blanket thinking that I would—"

"I was wrong," he said brusquely. "I thought you'd be willin'. I'm not a man to force any woman."

"Now that that's settled, get your own bedroll."

"Can't. How would it look to Wrestler and Mountain Calf, a man sleeping alone on the cold ground when he has a wife to keep him warm?"

"I'm not your wife. You can shoot me, but I'll not be taken advantage of by you or any other man."

He swore softly. "Don't carry on so. I'm not going to rape you."

"No, you're not."

"Does it sound as though Shadow's being abused by old Mountain Calf?"

Tamsin listened; then her face grew hot as she realized what activity was causing the groans and whimpers coming from the far side of the camp. "Lecher," she hissed. She'd not heard the couple until Ash mentioned them. Now it was impossible to ignore their lovemaking.

"If I was a lecher, you'd be making more noise than she is."

"Blackguard!" She tried to slap his face, but he blocked her blow with a muscular arm. "Try anything again, and . . . and . . ."

"Maybe I should let Wrestler have you," he grumbled. "Those are some nice-looking ponies he's got."

"You can't frighten me," she lied. "You're a bounty hunter. Your duty is to arrest me. You said that yourself. You won't let him have me, not even at the cost of your own life."

"I didn't say that."

"I'm a good judge of horses and men," she said. "I know you wouldn't turn me over to the Indians. You couldn't sleep nights if you did."

"Damn if I'm getting much sleep tonight."

"Or anything else."

He grunted and settled down alongside of her, molding his body to hers.

"Please," she murmured. "Sleep somewhere else. I won't go anywhere. I promise."

"The trouble with you, MacGreggor, is that you don't have sense enough to know when you're ahead. Now, shut up and go to sleep, before I forget I'm not a snake like Cannon."

She bit back an oath.

"That's better," he said sleepily. "You're softer than the rock under my spine." He dropped his arm around her waist. "But I warn you, trying to get away could get you killed. I come up out of a sound sleep shootin'."

* * *

Sometime before dawn, the dog began to bark frantically. Ash leaped up and reached for his rifle. The horses,
banded together in a small roped-in pen, snorted and
whinnied, stamping restlessly.

Tamsin stirred.

"Stay where you are until I find out what's wrong," he
ordered. See if Jack Cannon and his boys are payin' us a
visit, he thought.

Damn if his head didn't feel like he'd been caught in a
prairie twister. His mouth was as dry as gunpowder, and
his gut was none too steady as he yanked on his clothes
and boots.

He wondered if he was coming down with fever until
he remembered the firewater Wrestler and Mountain
Calf had shared with him around the campfire. "Nothing
like bad whiskey to make a man a fool," he muttered
under his breath.

The Utes were all on their feet. Shadow was throwing
more wood on the fire. Wrestler held the yapping dog by
the scruff of his neck. War-et's hair was roached up and
his teeth were bared.

"What is it?" Ash called to the Indians.

Mountain Calf gestured toward the far side of the
stream. *"Gato!"*

It was the cougar out there, not Cannon. Ash glanced
back at Tamsin, wondering if she'd be disappointed.
She'd denied a relationship with the outlaw, but that was
to be expected. If the liquor hadn't been talking, he'd
never have mentioned Jack to her.

As he watched, Tamsin snatched up the blankets and
her boots and hurried over to join Shadow.

Wrestler's inscrutable bronze face glowed in the firelight. The Ute was on his knees, holding the struggling
dog with both arms. "War-et is brave, is he not?" Wrestler

asked. "Alone, this dog would throw himself into the teeth of the puma."

"I saw the cat," Shadow said in her own language. "He came out of the night without fear of the fire." She handed her sleeping baby to Tamsin and continued adding fuel to the flames.

Her husband nodded. "This man, too, saw the mountain lion. When War-et began to bark, I thought it might be a raiding party."

"There are hostiles in the area?" Ash asked. "What tribe?"

Wrestler shrugged. "Arapaho and Cheyenne. Together. Angry young men, a few women, mostly warriors. Dog soldiers among them. Those fierce ones who hate the white men for the killings at the place you call Sand Creek. They will not lay down their arms and go to Indian Territory as the white president says."

Ash frowned. He knew there were scattered bands hiding in the mountains, but he'd not heard of any fighting men in numbers. "How many?"

"Thirty, maybe more. Some men could have been hunting when we saw them pass."

"We hid," Shadow said. "The Arapaho and the Cheyenne are not always friends of the Ute."

"These are not friends to any man," Mountain Calf pronounced. "Many scalps hang from their lodge poles. All are not white scalps."

"What is this Sand Creek?" Tamsin asked.

"A disgrace," Ash said, as he scanned the trees for movement. "In early winter of '64, John Chivington led an attack on a peaceful camp of Southern Cheyenne and Arapaho and massacred men, women, and children. No one knows exactly how many were murdered, maybe hundreds. But it was pure butchery. I've fought Indians when I had to, but it sickened me when I heard of the brutality and senseless killing."

"You would do well to walk wide of those my nephew speaks of," Mountain Calf said. "Men who have lost everything have nothing to lose. They would shoot you down like a rabid wolf."

Ash nodded. "I value my scalp as much as you do, my friend."

They stood watch until morning light turned the forest from black to a shimmering gray-green. Once they heard the puma cough, but it came no closer to the camp.

Later, he and Wrestler searched the far side of the stream. They found cat tracks, larger than Ash had ever seen, and they located a tree with shredded bark.

"The cougar wait there," Wrestler said, pointing to a limb about ten feet from the ground. "She watched us."

"She?" Ash questioned.

The Ute nodded. Crouching a few feet from the tree, he brushed aside the bushes to reveal fresh scat and stains of urine. "A female. In her prime. This man believes she craves the taste of horseflesh."

Ash wondered. The puma had stalked Tamsin's fire on the far side of the mountain, as it had here. It was unnatural behavior for a mountain lion and growing stranger all the time.

"Mountain Calf does not like this place," Wrestler confided. "We had planned to go on north to trade with others of our own kind, but now . . ." He stroked his chin thoughtfully. "Now I think we will take our trade goods and return to our village."

Ash waited, certain that the Ute brave meant to say more.

"I think I am fortunate that you did not accept my offer for the woman."

"My wife, you mean?"

Wrestler smiled with his mouth, but his hooded eyes remained cool. "The red-haired woman. I think she brings danger with her. You must not trust her too much, whoever she is. She has power, this female who talks to horses. And this man, for one, would not sleep easy with her at his side."

"I slept easy enough last night. What did you put in that whiskey?"

A smile spread over Wrestler's face. "Trouble is, white man, you no can hold liquor."

Tamsin accused him of the same vice once the three Utes rode off through the trees. "We've venison and some sort of roots for breakfast, if you're not too hungover to eat. I traded Shadow a pack of sewing needles for enough food to last us through the day."

Ash rubbed his forehead. "I'll admit I had more spirits than I should have. I apologize for offending you last night."

"In more ways than one."

"I said I was sorry."

"But you don't believe I'm innocent. And now you're accusing me of having an immoral attachment with someone that you say is an outlaw."

He pulled his hat low on his brow. "Don't talk to me about Cannon unless you can tell the truth. And hear it."

"I didn't know him that well. He came into the store where I worked and seemed pleasant. Mr. Cannon escorted me to a church social and to eat in a public hotel. I've nothing to be ashamed of."

"You've got my sympathy, lady. People keep makin' up lies about you."

"I've heard what kind of women you're accustomed to associating with. Doubtless you're used to their fabrications, but I can assure you that I'm not—"

"Peace, MacGreggor. Your yammering is hard on my aching head. We'd best talk about something else, if you insist on talkin'."

"How can I convince you—"

"I'll put the coffee on if you'll tend to the cooking," he said, ignoring her argument. "But stay close to the fire. That cat's probably a long way from here this morning, but we can't be certain."

She rested both hands on her hips and stared at him through narrowed eyes. "The cougar? The cougar that you told me I couldn't possibly have seen yesterday afternoon? Maybe it wasn't a mountain lion at all. Maybe those prints you and the Indian found were deer tracks."

"Maybe so," he agreed. "But if it was a doe instead of a puma, it was one that could climb trees."

"It wouldn't surprise me in the least," she replied sarcastically.

Unwilling to continue a conversation that he was obviously losing, Ash went to check Shiloh's injured leg. As he'd suspected, the shank was swollen. He untied the gelding and led him down to the stream to drink. To his disappointment, Ash saw that the horse was definitely limping.

"We won't be breaking camp today," he said to Tamsin as he fished his coffeepot out of his saddlebag. "Shiloh's leg needs rest. The torn flesh is a little puffy. There may be infection, thanks to you and your riding."

"We can lead him into the stream," she said. "Running water's good for swelling. And I've a little salve in my pack. He should be right as rain in a day or two." She used a green branch to pull hot coals over the spot where she'd buried the roots to bake. Dusting ashes off her hands, she said, "I've never cooked roots. I hope they're fit to eat."

"If you're hungry enough, you'll eat dog and fight to get it."

"I doubt that."

He shrugged, not bothering to answer her. He wished he hadn't spoken of the bad times to Tamsin. He didn't know why he had. It wasn't something he liked to think of, let alone tell a woman.

The old memories chafed at his mind as he went to the creek to fill the coffeepot with water.

He'd used his daddy's birthday knife to try to kill the half-Mexican Comanchero that gray Texas morning. But he'd not been a man yet, and he had a lot to learn about fighting a bigger opponent. First, the trader had beaten him half to death, and then he'd tied him across his daddy's horse and led him a hundred miles back to camp.

These renegade Comanche made a living stealing from the Texans and selling horses, loot, and captives south to Mexico. But Juan Fat Knee, the man who'd shot Ash's father, didn't trade him away. He'd kept him, as a cross between a slave and a pet, taking perverse pleasure in seeing how much he could mistreat a boy without killing him.

Ash had eaten dog all right. He'd gnawed the blackened bones and chewed the skin. It had made him so sick, he'd prayed to die, but he hadn't. He'd survived to relish a lot worse, including raw horse meat and lizard so rank that the camp curs wouldn't touch it.

He'd survived two years with the Comanche marauders, and come away wondering if the Lord wouldn't have done him a favor by letting him take that bullet instead of his father.

When Ash returned to the fire, he silently added coffee, noting that there was only enough left for one more pot.

"Were you in the war?" Tamsin asked.

He nodded, glad for the excuse to stop thinking about the past.

"I thought you must have, giving your horse that name." She looked at him through thick dark lashes. This morning she'd pulled her hair into a single knot on the back of her head, but curling strands had come loose around her freckled face. She looked fine, he thought, fine enough to kiss.

He'd been drunk the night before, but not so drunk he couldn't remember the taste of her mouth or the feel of her womanly body cuddled up against his. He was glad she'd stopped him. Getting involved with Cannon's lady friend and a woman who would likely hang for murder wasn't a smart move.

"What side were you on?" Tamsin asked. "In the war."

"You feel a need to talk all the time?"

"I asked you a simple question. Are you ashamed of the answer? Did you fight for the North or South?"

"North. I don't hold with slavery." Couldn't, he thought, not after knowing what it was like to be a slave . . . to be owned body and soul by Fat Knee.

"I never could stomach slavery either," Tamsin said. "But my home was in Tennessee, and all my friends and relatives were for the Confederacy."

She sat on a rock and offered him a faint smile. Her teeth were even and white, pretty teeth in a pretty mouth.

"My dead husband, Atwood, should have joined the army, but he kept finding excuses," she continued. "Once, he even broke his own foot with a hammer to keep from going. He was a coward, of course."

"Don't sound like a man I could have much respect for," Ash said.

"Me either. Not then, not now."

When the food was ready, they ate. The deer meat was

good, the roots gritty and tough. His coffee, as usual, was strong enough to melt nails.

Afterward, Tamsin and he walked to the stream to wash. Then he pulled the handcuffs from his belt. "Arms behind you," he said. "It's lockup time."

"What?" Her face paled. "Where am I going to go?"

"Don't even bother. All the sweet talk in the world won't help me if you decide to murder me when my back's turned."

"No!" She stepped away, then turned to run toward the horses.

He caught her in a dozen strides and wrestled her to the ground. "Lay still!" he shouted. Holding her without hurting her was like trying to pin a bee-stung badger with one hand tied behind his back. Tamsin kicked and twisted, pulling out of his grasp and crawling away.

He grabbed her ankle, and she kicked him in the chin with her other foot. Ash swore as he seized the hem of her skirt.

"Damn you," she cried, rising up on her knees and planting a solid fist square in the center of his forehead. "You . . . you Yankee bully! Stop that!"

"You made the rules between us," he answered grimly as he straddled her. "Now you pay the price."

Chapter 9

"No! Not again!" Tamsin cried.

"Don't make this harder than it has to be." The blow to Ash's chin and her last well-aimed punch had set his head to throbbing. Shame at having to manhandle a woman, any woman, this way fueled his anger toward her and sickened him.

"Please," she begged. "Don't put those things on me. What if the cougar comes?" Tears filled her eyes, but she was still fighting him with every ounce of her being.

"Be still, damn it!" He didn't want to hurt her. But neither was he fool enough to let her murder him. "You'll try something the minute my back is turned."

"I won't."

She twisted and bit his arm, and when he let go of his hold on her to pull away, she balled her fist and punched him again. The blow glanced off his bad shoulder, sending a jolt of excruciating pain up his neck.

Anger dulled his chivalry, and he captured her flailing fist and pinned it roughly against the earth. "Don't lie to me!" he flung back. "You'll jump on one of those damned horses and ride out of here to find Cannon. And . . . And . . . I'll have to hunt the both of you down."

Tamsin's breath came in hard, deep gasps, but she wouldn't stop struggling. Face flushed, bosom heaving, she strained against him, transforming his honest anger to something darker.

His knees clamped tighter around her hips.

Having her helpless beneath him shattered the barriers he prided himself on possessing. He shuddered, caught in a sudden rush of primitive lust that any decent man should keep in check. In vain he tried to smother a devilish urge to lift Tamsin's skirts and drive himself between her warm, soft thighs.

The woman scent of her filled his head. He knew he was stronger than she was. He could have her here and now. Maybe she even wanted him to do it. Ash groaned and swallowed the sour gorge that rose in his throat.

Maybe he was no better than the scum he'd vowed to destroy—the outlaws who'd raped and murdered his wife.

The thought washed over him with icy dread. "I'll let go if you keep your hands to yourself," he managed.

She gritted her teeth and glared at him with green hellfire in her eyes. Suddenly, as if she realized what she was doing to him, she stopped squirming. A flash of terror crossed her face.

He felt like dirt. "Truce?"

"For how long?"

Frightened or not, she wasn't cowed. "Today. Tonight," he rasped. His loins ached with need. He had to take his hands away from her, had to put distance between them before he lost control.

"Until daybreak tomorrow?"

He nodded and slowly got to his feet, turning away to keep her from seeing his obvious arousal. He removed his gun belt and flung it across the creek. "Go for my rifle and you'll regret it," he said thickly as he dropped belly down on the rocky streambank. Melting snow from the mountain peaks fed the tumbling course, making the flow slightly warmer than freezing. Bracing himself for the shock, Ash scooped up handfuls of running water and splashed his face and arms.

The frigid water couldn't wash away his desire, but it did keep him from making a total bastard of himself. He glanced back at her to make certain she wasn't stalking him with a rock. "You pack a mean right," he said.

Tamsin's freckles stood out starkly against milky white skin. "I'm sorry," she stammered. Fear was still evident in her expression. She looked at him as if she expected him to tear off her skirts.

The hell of it was, he wanted to.

Ash dunked his entire head under the water and came up sputtering. Need churned in his loins. He wanted to see the shape of her breasts and bury his face between them. He wanted to taste her skin and feel her nipples harden against his tongue.

He stripped off his boots and socks and plunged into the stream. The water was only waist deep but swift, splashing over and around the mossy time-washed boulders that littered the ancient streambed. He submerged completely, letting the sting of the cold liquid wash away the evil from his mind.

He came up gasping for air.

"What in God's name are you doing?" Tamsin demanded. She stood on the bank staring at him. Her clothes were dirty and disheveled, and her glorious red hair hung over her shoulders in wild abandon.

Ash took one look at her and dived under again. He might not be able to quell his growing attraction toward her, but he could cool his ardor. This time when he surfaced, he brought his sense of humor with him. "Come on in," he dared. "The water's fine."

"Are you out of your mind?"

He laughed. "Probably."

"You expect me to undress?"

He shook his head. "Hell, no. Come in like you are. What better way to wash your clothes?"

Tamsin glanced toward the horses.

"Don't even think it," he warned. "We've a truce, remember? You gave me your word."

"Under duress."

Goose bumps rose on his skin, and his teeth began to chatter. "Where's your nerve, woman?"

A mischievous gleam danced in her eyes. "How do I know you won't hit me with a rock?"

He laughed again. "If I didn't finish you off after you punched me, you're probably safe until dark. Then I mean to throw you to that mountain lion."

She tugged off her left boot, raised her skirt, and rolled down one black stocking.

Damned if she didn't have a fine-looking ankle. Her bare foot was narrow, high-arched, and very clean. He'd always liked his women clean. "Hurry up," he said brusquely, "before I come out and throw you in."

She removed her second boot, quickly shedding the other stocking and then her vest. She undid the top two buttons on her bodice, but before his imagination got too randy, she held her nose and jumped in.

She shrieked as the cold water closed over her. The current knocked her off balance, and she fell on her bottom. But before the force of the water could wash her onto the rocks, he caught her around the waist.

Tamsin clasped his neck, and before he realized what was happening, her mouth was on his. Instantly, incandescent desire leaped between them, drawing him deeper into a fevered kiss of searing heat.

His heart thundered as her lips parted to receive the thrust of his tongue. He felt her tremble in his arms, and his craving for her came flooding back.

She urged him on with tiny whimpers of pleasure as he

molded his body to hers, crushing her against him. Then he tore his lips from hers and began to kiss her neck and the soft rise of her bosom.

"We can't," she murmured. "Not like this."

He groaned in disappointment but made no effort to stop her as she broke from his arms and sank into the water. Seconds later, she scrambled up. The dazed expression was gone, replaced with laughter.

"Let's get out of here before we drown each other."

Swearing under his breath, he climbed the bank and helped her up, trying not to think how perfectly Tamsin's hand fit his. Her fingers were long and graceful. He wondered how it would feel to have them stroking him . . . touching him.

Awkward silence hung between them for a heartbeat; then she laughed again. "I hope you've got dry clothes," she said matter-of-factly. "If not, you're going to catch your death."

"I do." His mouth still tingled from the touch of her lips. His arms remembered how she felt.

This is Cannon's woman, he reminded himself. You're playing with fire.

"What have we started?" she asked, almost as if she could read what was going on in his head. Then she shook her head. "I've never kissed a man like that. Never knew . . ."

She's lying, he thought. She has to be lying. But the words slipped out. "Me, either."

"I hope not," she teased. "You don't seem the type to kiss a man at all."

"Hardly." He drew in a deep breath. "What are we going to do about it?" To hell with Jack Cannon. Maybe she was telling the truth. Maybe the outlaw was nothing to her, but that didn't matter now. What was real was the ache in his gut and the need to hold her again.

"Under the circumstances? Nothing." Her eyes held him. "Unless . . ." She sighed. "I'm a respectable woman, Ash. I've never been with a man, other than my husband. . . . not in the biblical sense. And I'm too old to learn new tricks."

"I'm not." He stripped off his wet shirt and fumbled with his belt. "And I don't think *tricks* was the word you were looking for."

"Where are your manners?" She turned her back. "I've dry clothing in my bags. Do I have your permission to fetch them?"

He peeled off his soaking pants and stood bare in the sunshine. The radiating warmth felt like a taste of heaven. "Why didn't you go for my rifle and shoot me while I was in the creek?"

She kept facing away from him, but he saw her muscles tense. "I'm not a murderer."

"So you keep telling me." So they all said. He'd never known a killer to admit his crime.

Tamsin didn't fit his image of a back shooter. Maybe she was innocent, but it wasn't his place to make that decision. Once a man started figuring the guilt of another, he'd lose all respect for the law. "Put your dry things on," he ordered. "I'll not look at you."

"All right." Then she laughed.

"What's funny?"

"Your gun belt is on the far side of the creek. You've got to go back in that freezing water to fetch it."

"Auugh." He shuddered at the thought. Damned if he wouldn't throw a bridle on Shiloh and ride across. One bath like that was enough for a day.

By the time Tamsin had retrieved her change of clothing, dressed, and tamed her hair, Ash had sliced venison into small strips to bake on a rock beside the fire. She approached him hesitantly, unsure of what to say.

Things had gotten out of control. His kiss had left her both excited and confused. She'd behaved shamelessly, and now all she could think of was having his arms around her again.

She stopped a few feet away and waited for him to speak first. When the silence grew between them, she searched frantically for something to ease the growing tension.

"Are you a marrying man, Mr. Morgan?"

His eyes registered amusement. "Is that another proposal?"

She uttered a sound of derision. "Hardly. I was but making polite conversation."

"I think we're beyond that, Tamsin MacGreggor."

"Do you?" She sat on a rock, rested her elbows on her knees and her chin in her hands. "You didn't answer my question. Are you a devout bachelor?"

He squatted and pushed hot coals around the base of the coffeepot. "I don't discuss my personal life with my prisoners."

"Is that what I am? Simply another prisoner?"

"You think a kiss changes things?"

"You know that was more than a kiss."

"You're damned outspoken for a woman." He tugged his hat brim lower over his eyes.

She noticed that his blue shirt and doeskin trousers were clean and less wrinkled than her own clothing. Ash had taken the trouble to shave and comb his hair. Damp and shining black, he'd tied it neatly back with a beaded strip of leather.

A bead of blood showed along the left jawline. Tamsin thought he must have nicked himself while shaving, and it was all she could do to keep from touching the graze.

"We've a truce for today, remember," she murmured,

wondering why a man of such obvious character had become a bounty hunter.

Ash moistened his lips. "So we have."

"Then I believe you should show courtesy by answering my—"

"I'm a widower," he answered abruptly. The coffeepot tilted to one side, and Ash grabbed the metal handle to keep it from spilling. "Damn!" Snatching his burned finger back, he popped it into his mouth. "See what you made me do?"

Tamsin chuckled. "Look, Lord, see what the woman *you gave me* has done. She made me eat that forbidden apple." A smile lit her eyes. "I've heard that one enough. Why are men never willing to take the blame for their own mistakes?"

"You're one of those, are you? A man hater."

"Me?" She chuckled again. "Not at all. I grew up around men. My grandparents raised me, and my grandmother lived in a world of her own. Actually, I've always preferred men to other women. Women never say what they think."

"And you do?"

"Usually." She pointed to the venison. "Mind that. It's cut thin. It will overcook if you don't—"

"You're bossy, too."

"That's true. Although people rarely accept my good suggestions. Do you have children?"

"None that I've ever heard of."

"How did you lose your wife?"

"Didn't lose her. She was murdered."

"How terrible for you," Tamsin said. "I'm sorry I—"

"No reason for you to be sorry. You didn't cause her death." His eyes clouded. "Like as not, you've seen your own share of trouble."

"Atwood?" She shook her head. "I never shed a tear over his grave."

Ash stood and rubbed his hands on his pant legs. "You must have cared for him once. Why did you marry him?"

She glanced away. That was a question she'd asked herself a thousand times. She guessed she'd done it because her granddad wanted her to. . . . Because she was a poor judge of men's character.

"Stupid, I guess," she said to Ash. "Very young and very stupid."

"If that was a crime, I'd have more work than I could handle."

She tilted her head. "Did you love her . . . your wife?"

He didn't answer with words, but she needed none. Ash's craggy features grew taut, and his eyes narrowed. "You ask too many questions."

"I'm sorry. I shouldn't have pried."

He drew in a deep breath. "It was a long time ago."

"No," she countered. "Not long enough."

His Adam's apple flexed. His shirt lay open at the throat. His skin was sun-bronzed and tinted with gold.

Tamsin knew it must be a sin to envy a dead woman. "She must have been special."

"She was." The affirmation came so softly that she nearly missed it. "She was to me."

"Did she die while you were away at war?"

"You worry a man like a dog with a bone. Let it lie."

She nodded. "I've a tear in my skirt. Is it all right if I fetch thread and needle and stitch it after breakfast?"

He poured her a steaming cup of coffee. "Do as you like so long as you stay away from the horses and my guns."

She set the tin mug on the rock to cool and accepted a portion of the deer meat. It was tough and chewy, but she was hungry. "You've a loose button on your shirt," she said when she'd eaten two pieces of the venison. "I could mend that, too, if you like," she offered.

"I can sew it myself. No need in you doing me favors." His voice hardened. "We're heading back tomorrow, Tamsin. You can't sweet-talk me out of that."

"I don't trust that Sheriff Walker. For all I know, he and Sam Steele were part of the plot to steal my horses. They're worth a great deal of money, you know. Fancy's bloodline goes back directly to the Godolphin Arabian, and Dancer is descended from both the Byerley Turk and Bulle Rock."

"They're fast enough on flat ground, I imagine," Ash replied, ignoring her comments about the sheriff and the dead rancher. "But with those long legs, your horses aren't bred for these mountains. I'd rather have a tougher mount, smaller, stockier, deep chested, something with mustang blood. You take your average mustang. They'd look like coyote sh—"

Ash flushed slightly and continued. "I mean to say they look like coyote dung next to your high-priced animals, but they can live on scrub and weeds, and they've got staying power. They're tireless. Give them a little decent feed and the proper training, and I'd put a western pony up against any fancy horse in the country for covering ground or working cattle. Hell's fire, woman. Your thoroughbreds have style, but they'll get those long legs tangled around a steer and end up under him."

"I'm taking them to San Francisco. With all the gold men have found in California, there'll be a market for racehorses," she said.

"Maybe you're right," he said. "Maybe you will get clear of this trouble and find your way over the Rockies and across the desert, through Indian country, past the desperadoes and the desperate would-be miners with gold fever. I hope you do. But I doubt it. Even if you're found innocent and released, I wouldn't give you the chance of a rabbit in a bunkhouse of ever seeing the Pacific."

"You're not the first one to tell me that," she answered softly, "and you won't be the last to be proved wrong."

ivory button, or bit of bright ribbon. Her life has meant no
more to them than a rabbit's does to a fox. In spite of her
faults, I couldn't leave her to the barbarities of such
human predators."

"You're saying that you could lead them to the spot where
Reynard and his woman died—back to the place where you—"

Chapter 10

The day passed quickly for Tamsin. Under Ash's stern
supervision, she examined the horses' hooves and led
Shiloh into the creek so that the running water would
ease the swelling.

"He's a fine animal," she said after she'd anointed the
scrape on the gelding's leg with a healing salve. Ash's fingers brushed hers as she passed the animal's lead line to
him, and she felt a tingling sensation up and down her arm.

She pulled away quickly, but Ash seemed not to notice. He hobbled Shiloh and turned him out to graze
with the other two horses. Ash's hands were gentle as he
handled the animal, and again, Tamsin observed how
gracefully he moved for a big man.

"You're good with horses," she said. It had been her
experience that a man showed his character when he
dealt with animals.

Ash's eyes narrowed as he studied her. It seemed to
her as though he'd been staring at her since they'd kissed
in the creek. She didn't know whether the uneasiness she
felt was fear or attraction.

Forcing a smile, she tried to ease the tension by
making ordinary conversation. "How did you pick that
name for your horse? Were you at the Battle of Shiloh?"

"Nope. I've never been east of the Mississippi." Ash

plucked a few leaves from a clump of wildflowers and ate them. "Try it," he said. "It's yellow monkeyflower."

Tamsin tasted the leaves and grimaced. "Sour."

"Just takes getting used to, like a lot of things in this country. Eating just meat or fish will sicken you if you stay in the mountains long enough. Think of this as lettuce."

"Maybe it would be better with oil and vinegar," she suggested, but forced herself to chew and swallow a little more of the odd vegetation.

Ash folded his arms over his chest and rested his back against a tree. "I bought the horse from a Pennsylvanian heading to Arizona. He told me the gelding's name was Shiloh."

"But you did fight in the War between the States?"

He nodded. "It's easy to see you're from back east. Folks out here in the west prefer to forget what's happened in the past. They look on too much curiosity as prying into what's private."

Tamsin settled onto a mossy outcrop and curled her legs under her skirt. "You fought with the Union," she persisted, ignoring his broad hint.

His eyes were as dark and glittering as an Indian's. Looking into them, she could read a will as strong as her own . . . and something more . . . bone-deep sorrow.

"Colorado volunteers," he answered. "I wasn't in too long, but what I saw was hot enough. We went head to head with Sibley's Texans at a place called Glorieta Pass."

"In Colorado?"

"New Mexico."

She stroked the soft green moss with her fingertips and waited. For minutes there was no sound but grazing horses, the gurgle of rushing water, and the melodious whistle of a wren echoing down the canyon.

"I was wounded at Glorieta," Ash said huskily. He slid

a lean hand down his upper leg and massaged a spot midway between knee and hip. "The ball missed bone, but it bled like hell. It got infected, and I spent nearly a year recovering."

A picture formed in her mind of Ash lying near to death, leg swollen, and skin burning with fever. She shuddered. "After that?"

He gestured with his hands. "Hostile Indians and cutthroats were raiding outlying ranches—stealing, burning, murdering innocent folks. When my leg mended good enough to ride, I gathered a few friends and we organized a home defense force." Ash shrugged. "Never did get back into the war proper."

"At least you volunteered," she replied. "Even if it was for Lincoln." She sighed. "More than I can say for Atwood."

"How did he die?"

She didn't miss the suspicion in his voice. "Don't look at me. I was at a church meeting the night he drowned in a mud puddle behind Lacy Satin's River House. Nine gentlemen swore that Atwood left the establishment stone broke and too drunk to ride." She shook her head. "Not that it mattered. He didn't have a horse left to ride home on. He'd just lost my gray Tennessee walker, Alabaster, to a Yankee lieutenant in a hand of poker."

Ash frowned. "Sounds fortunate for you, to be rid of such a husband."

"Yes and no. I'd not wish Atwood dead, although I did wish him in China many a night. I'm glad to be rid of him, but he cost me dear. A woman may as well be a slave under the law. Her husband has complete control of her funds."

"Slavery's done with."

"Not for wives. If we had the vote—"

"Why stop at the vote? Why not a woman governor of the territory?"

"You're making fun of me," she said. "Do you truly believe that women are born inferior to men?"

He pushed his hat brim up with a long forefinger. "I've known women who would put most men to shame when it came to thinking. My Becky was one. But I never heard her clamoring to vote. I expect she was content to leave such matters to me."

"But why?" Tamsin demanded. "Why should only men have the vote?"

Ash scoffed. "Damned if I know, Tamsin. It's always been that way. It's not a thing that's ever kept me awake nights wondering about."

"Maybe you should." She remained silent for a few minutes, then leaned toward him slightly and asked, "Were you really a prisoner of the Comanche when you were a child?"

He shook his head. "Outlaw Comanche. No self-respecting Indian would have them in his village. They were outlaws, torturing, bloodthirsty killers. They robbed the Texans, other tribes, and the Mexicans."

"How did you survive?"

He made a tight, bitter sound in his throat. "Who says I did?" He stared off into the trees. "I wanted to die, God knows. I prayed to die."

"How did you get away from them?"

"I put a bullet through the man who murdered my father, took his horse, and rode south to Texas."

"At ten? Eleven?"

Ash shook his head. "Twelve. I told you. I was with them for two years, give or take a month. It's not too clear in my head."

"They didn't come after you?"

"Maybe. They sure as hell didn't catch me."

"Texas was your home? That's where you grew up?"

He nodded. "Daddy was a Texas Ranger. I was born in the back of a wagon, somewhere north of Austin. I can't tell you much about my mama, only that he claimed I got her black hair and that she came from a highfalutin family in New Orleans. He said her folks were French, that they'd lost all their money and come west to make a new start. I wouldn't know about that. She ran off with a man named Jules Valjean when I was two weeks old, left Daddy a note telling him that she couldn't abide Texas or raising a child on the frontier."

"Your mother just left you?"

"Left us both. Daddy never married again. He brought me up himself. He was a federal marshal when he was killed."

"Did you have family to go to when you got back to Texas?" she asked.

"Uncle Matt and Aunt Jane took me in. They weren't real kin. Uncle Matt was a ranger, same as my daddy. The two of them were close as brothers. I was loco as a bee-stung mustang and half-starved, but Aunt Jane filled me full of hot soup and biscuits, scrubbed off two years' worth of dirt, and tucked me into her feather bed. I must have slept for three days straight. When I woke up, Uncle Matt was sitting there beside me with tears rollin' down his cheeks."

Ash's voice grew husky with emotion. "I needed somebody, and I guess they did, too. They never had any kids of their own that lived. I stayed with them until I was seventeen. Then they died of spotted fever, and I quit school and hired on to drive a herd of cattle out here to Colorado."

"It must have been very difficult, losing your father and then your . . . your aunt and uncle."

"Aunt Jane didn't have more than eight years of

schooling, but she was the finest lady I've ever known. As for Uncle Matt, just ask any decent folks in Texas about Matt Bell. They'll tell you that they don't make men like him anymore."

"I never knew my own mother," Tamsin began. "She—"

Suddenly Dancer threw up his head and whinnied. Fancy sidled close to him and stared down the valley, the way that they had come the day before.

Tamsin tensed and her heartbeat quickened. "The cougar?" she whispered urgently. "Do you think—"

"Quiet!" Ash went to the campfire and retrieved his rifle. His pistol hung around his waist. He'd recovered the handgun earlier. "Bring the horses into camp," he said.

"All right." She tried to whistle, but her mouth was so dry that it came out a squeak. But Fancy's keen ears caught the sound. Instantly, the mare turned to look at her. Tamsin whistled again, and Fancy trotted toward her with the nervous stallion close behind.

Ash scanned the woods line as she put a rope on Fancy and tied her to a tree. A jay screamed a warning overhead. On the ground, a few yards away, a squirrel raced by, then scampered up a trunk and vanished in the green leaves.

"Shall I fetch Shiloh as well?" Tamsin asked. She pressed her hands against her sides so that Ash wouldn't see her trembling. She could imagine the mountain lion leaping on her as it had before. Her legs felt as though they were made of wood.

"Might as well." Ash's dark gaze continued to rake the surrounding forest. "Something spooked the horses. It may be nothing, but you don't make many errors in judgment in these mountains and survive."

Then, as Tamsin forced herself to step out of the shade and into the sunlight of the clearing, she caught a flicker of movement on the far side of the creek. "There!" She pointed. Something black appeared, then vanished again in the thick foliage.

Ash took careful aim at the bushes with his rifle. Dancer snorted and muscles rippled beneath his glossy hide. Tamsin didn't move.

She waited, expecting to hear a bear growl or the cougar snarl. But to her surprise, the sound that rose from the brush was a whine.

"It's all right," Ash called.

"I don't—" Tamsin broke off as the Utes' black dog emerged from hiding. The wretched animal's tail curled between his legs and his belly hung close to the ground.

Ash crouched and slapped his knee. "Come here, War-et."

Instantly the little dog plunged into the stream and paddled across. Wet and shivering, still whining pitifully, the dog slunk to Ash's side.

"Where's your master?" Ash murmured. "Where's Mountain Calf?"

Tamsin grabbed the strawberry roan's bridle and hurried back to the fire. "Why did the dog come back here?" she asked.

"That's what I'd like to know." He patted the animal's head. "Poor pup. He looks as though he's had a rough time."

Tamsin saw that one of War-et's ears was bloody and that he was covered with scratches.

"Nothing deep enough to be a puma attack," Ash said, answering her unspoken question. "But it's odd he'd leave on his own."

"He looks hungry. Do you want something to eat?" she asked the animal. Sad eyes stared back at her. She glanced at Ash. "Can I—"

"Yes, cut him off some of that venison. We've more than we can eat before it starts to turn anyway."

Tamsin sliced off bits of raw meat and fed them slowly to the dog. When she decided he'd had enough, she shook her head. "That's it. You'll be sick if I give you more."

War-et's tail flicked hopefully.

"No more," she said.

With a final whine, he curled at her feet.

"Maybe it chased the mountain lion and got separated from the Utes," Tamsin suggested.

Ash remained alert, rifle cradled in the corner of his arm. "Maybe," he replied. He didn't think so. And suddenly, this hollow didn't seem like a perfect campsite anymore. An uneasy feeling gnawed at his innards. "Saddle the horses," he said to Tamsin.

"What?" She rested one hand on her hip and stared at him in puzzlement. "But you said—"

"Forget what I said. We're backtracking. Now!" He began to kick dirt over the fire.

"You said that Shiloh's leg should rest today. You—"

"Damn it, woman. Can you never accept a simple order?" He didn't owe her any explanations. He had none to offer. And he'd already said too much to Tamsin. He'd told her about Glorieta Pass and Aunt Jane and Uncle Matt, private things he hadn't spoken of to another living soul in years.

Something about Tamsin made him want to trust her with his innermost secrets, but common sense told him that was foolhardy. If he wasn't careful, he'd let his personal life interfere with his job, and that was one rule he never broke.

He had an itch for Tamsin. Hell, it was more than that. He wanted her. He couldn't keep his eyes off her. She made his hands sweat, and his blood race, and his imagination run wild. The way she moved, the tilt of her head when she laughed, the sparkle in her green eyes, all drew him like a thirsty mustang to water.

He'd been too long without a woman when he'd let his ballocks rule his head. It would have been far better for him if he'd accepted Shelly's offer. He could have pulled her into Maudine's tub and scrubbed her from head to toe first. Shelly was none too bright, but she gave a man honest reward for his money.

And he didn't have to worry about Shelly shooting him in the back.

He tried to think of Shelly. She barely came up to his shoulder, and her hands and face were lily-white and soft. Her cupid mouth was painted scarlet, her eyes outlined in kohl as black as her hair. What clothes Shelly wore were feminine, tight-fitting, lacy, intended to entice a man.

How was it that he'd rejected a willing little baggage like Shelly to be tempted by a tall, freckle-faced outlaw's woman with callused hands and a will of iron?

Hellfire and damnation. Another night rolled in a blanket with Tamsin and that southern-sweet whiskey voice of hers would convince him that Henry Steele had murdered his own brother, and she was the next thing to a cross-wearing nun.

He stirred himself from thoughts of Tamsin and glanced around. Birds and squirrels still rustled in the trees; the horses seemed to have lost their fear once they saw the dog. Yet, he could not shake the feeling that something was wrong.

Maybe Jack Cannon and his boys were near, or maybe it was just his nerves stretched too tight.

Tamsin tightened the cinch on Shiloh's saddle. "Which way are we going?"

"You have to ask?" He motioned to the narrow passageway that led east.

"This canyon ends here?" Tamsin eased a snaffle bit into the mare's mouth and slipped the headstall behind the animal's ears. Fancy stood unmoving, ignoring the stallion who pranced behind her, showing his teeth, and laying back his ears.

"It narrows again, then opens into a valley. But it runs west. We're going back toward Sweetwater."

"Oh, I just wondered." She pursed her lips thoughtfully. "Then I was going in the right direction. West, through the mountains."

"I just said so, didn't I?"

She nodded and turned away from him, toward the big bay.

"Will you tell me one thing?" Ash asked as Tamsin swung the plain Texas stock saddle over the mare's back. "Why is it you put a western saddle on that sweet-tempered chestnut, and an English rig on that devil stud? Why not the other way around? I'd think you'd need more saddle under you to ride him."

"I don't ride him much," she said. "Dancer's full of surprises."

"If you'd had him properly broken, he wouldn't be so damn flighty."

"The Texas saddle seemed more practical for such a long journey," Tamsin continued. She approached the stallion carefully, crooning softly to him.

The animal squealed and shied away, but she kept talking and moving closer. Finally, she was able to grab his halter and snub him to a tree. Ash kept watch as Tamsin secured her packs and tied them to Dancer's saddle. "All done except for your bags and bedroll," she said. She undid a strap on a leather pouch and adjusted the contents.

"It will just take me a minute," Ash answered. He switched his rifle to his left hand and reached for his blanket with his right.

"Stop there!" Tamsin said. "Drop your gun."

"What—" He spun toward her, then froze in his tracks when he saw the big Navy Colt in her hands.

"I said drop the rifle."

"You won't shoot me."

She squeezed the trigger, and a bullet whizzed past his left ear and thudded into a tree behind him. "I mean it," she warned. "I don't want to hurt you, Ash, but I'm not going back to face that judge."

Ash was certain he could get at least one shot off, but the bullet would tear a hole in Tamsin a man could throw a steer through. His muscles coiled, but he couldn't do it. He didn't want to kill her. He dropped the rifle onto the stony ground.

"Shall I turn around?" he demanded. "Would you rather take aim at my back than look me in the eye and shoot?"

"I'm a good shot, Ash. I could have put that lead between your eyes if I'd wanted to. Step back."

He swore an oath that would melt leather, but he did as she ordered.

"Now draw your gun with two fingers. Don't make me kill you, Ash."

He watched her eyes, saw the moisture pool in them, read the determination there.

"You won't get away. Murder me, and more men will come after you. California isn't far enough to run, Tamsin."

She kicked his rifle away. "Do as I say." Her voice cracked, but her hands held the Colt steady. "Throw your revolver into the creek."

"There are hostiles on the move. That strawberry hair

of yours will end up on some young buck's scalp belt. And if the Indians or the cougar don't get you, you'll lose your way in the mountains and starve."

"The pistol. Toss it."

White hot fury boiled in his gut. "Damn you—"

She fired a second time, sending gravel flying from a spot beside his left boot. "No more warnings, Ash. Next time, I shoot you. I'll start with your knee."

Still cursing, he flung the pistol into the water.

"Good. You follow it. Take off your boots and wade into the water."

"You'd better kill me. I'll hunt you down for this," he swore.

"Move." She picked up his rifle.

War-et growled and moved to Tamsin's feet.

Ash's chest felt constricted; his breathing came in deep shuddering gasps. His skin stretched taut across his temple, and his head pounded. It took every ounce of his will to keep from rushing her, ripping that Colt out of her hands, and strangling her. How could he have been so damned stupid?

The cold water rose to his waist, shocking him, making his thinking clear and precise.

"I'm sorry," she called as she swung up into Shiloh's saddle. "I really like you, Ash Morgan. I just don't like you enough to die for."

Chapter 11

Tamsin struggled all day, often having to dismount and lead the horses through rockfalls and tangles of thick-growth pine. Again and again, she found the way impassable and had to retreat to try another pass through the mountains. By dusk, she was utterly lost, not certain that she'd traveled more than a few miles from where she'd left Ash and the mountain lion.

She hadn't been able to lose the black dog. At first, she'd tried to chase the animal away. But War-et hadn't obeyed; he'd just kept following. Now that the light was fading, however, she was glad of his company.

Hungry, muscles aching, Tamsin crouched in the shelter of an overhanging rock face. Her two horses she unsaddled and turned loose to graze, but she didn't let Shiloh off his rope for fear that he would wander away.

She'd quenched her thirst and filled her canteen from a spring in the canyon wall two hours earlier. Now she wished that she'd made camp there. She had nothing left to eat but dry venison and nothing with which to wash it down.

"A fine fix," she muttered to War-et as she fed him pieces of her supper. He whined and crept closer to her.

Even her campfire was a pitiful effort. She'd dragged a rotting log into the front of the shallow cave and started a small fire beside it. The wood was too damp to burn without smoking, and she'd waited too long to gather additional fuel.

"It's going to be a long night," she said wearily.

Guilt over what she'd done to Ash had ridden beside her all day, pricking her conscience and making her wonder if she shouldn't have done what he wanted and gone back to be tried by a court of law.

California and a new life far from a Tennessee torn by war and bad memories seemed an impossible goal. A single tear trickled down her left cheek.

Then something damp and scratchy brushed Tamsin's hand. She looked down to see War-et's homely face. "You stupid dog," she whispered. "You're as lost as I am." But she stroked his ragged head and made no protest when he wiggled into her lap.

"You've probably got fleas." The dog licked her chin and wagged his curly tail enthusiastically. "One vermin bite and you're out on your ear," she warned as she hugged him close.

Tamsin's eyelids grew heavy. The flickering flame was hypnotizing, and she felt herself nodding off.

Her dreams were a shadowy turmoil of nightmare and memories as she relived Ash Morgan's kisses and the surreal terror of the stalking cougar. Sweat poured from her body. War-et's warning bark became a puma's snarl. Tamsin broke free of Ash and tried to run, but her feet seemed frozen to the ground. When she looked back, Ash's features had hardened to a grotesque mask.

"No!" Tamsin's eyes widened. Suddenly the figure looming just beyond the fire wasn't Ash's but the form of a painted Indian.

The brave shrieked a war cry and leaped over the burning log brandishing a spiked club. Still dazed, Tamsin raised her pistol and fired point-blank. The warrior fell back into the flames as Tamsin scrambled to her feet.

The stench of burning cloth and hair filled her nostrils as she fled toward the spot where she'd left Shiloh tied.

The horse was gone.

Heart in her throat, she dashed headlong into the woods, heedless of the branches striking her head and the vines tangling her legs. She'd not gone twenty feet when another howling Indian crashed through the undergrowth and blocked her way.

Tamsin stopped in her tracks as a dark shadow raced past her and lunged at the brave nearly hidden in the trees. She couldn't see well enough to tell man from dog, but she could hear the thud that changed War-et's snarls to agonized whimpers.

Sickened, Tamsin ran back toward the fire, nearly colliding with Dancer's charging fury. The stallion's shoulder struck her a glancing blow as he pounded past with teeth bared and ears laid flat against his head. She spun through the air and landed in a tangle of brush as the squealing stallion reared and lashed out with his front legs.

The Indian's war hoop shattered as iron-shod hooves crushed flesh and bone. For the space of a dozen heartbeats the only sound Tamsin heard was Dancer's enraged snorting.

Shaking, still clutching her pistol, she tried to rise. But before she could disentangle herself from the clinging vines, a sinewy arm clamped around her throat and an overpowering stench of bear grease filled her head.

Choking, half-mad with fear, Tamsin swung the Colt, striking her assailant. She heard him grunt with pain and felt the pressure on her throat ease. Gasping for air, she twisted away. A heavy blow knocked her to her knees, and she twisted onto her back.

The Indian flung himself on top of her, and she dragged the gun up and pulled the trigger. Pushing free of his thrashing body, Tamsin crawled away.

Without warning, another warrior seized her by the hair and yanked her head back. He spat a jumble of angry words that she couldn't understand, but she needed no translation. The cold steel of a knife blade pressing against her throat spoke volumes.

She tried to raise her pistol to shoot him, but powerful fingers clamped around her wrists, twisting until the weapon dropped from her hand. In shock, she closed her eyes and tried to pray as she prepared herself for the death thrust.

Seconds passed like hours. She could feel wet, sticky drops oozing down her neck and his hot breath on her face. The sound of the brave's harsh breathing rasped in her ears.

Inhaling deeply, she looked into the ocher-streaked face above hers. Fierce eyes, ringed with circles of paint, stared back at her. She caught a glimpse of a naked chest and bands of copper around the arm that held the knife to her throat.

"You die!" Venom radiated in the soft, almost lyrical English.

Shards of terror pierced Tamsin's breast. "White. You're white," she whispered hoarsely.

"No speak!" The blade wavered. She felt a sharp sting but not the piercing agony that she expected.

Another man shouted to her captor. He answered, then slowly released his grip on her hair and removed the knife.

Teeth chattering, Tamsin rolled to a sitting position and drew searching fingers over her lacerated throat. When she glanced down at her hand, it was smeared with blood. Her breath came in strangled gasps, and she trembled as intense cold seeped through her bones.

The white Indian with the ringed eyes kicked her. "Get up!"

She staggered to her feet.

Four braves, one with torch in hand, moved from the shadows. Two carried a broken body and laid it beside the dead man at the campfire. A huge warrior with a shaved head and human finger bones thrust through his earlobes crouched over a third fallen figure. The injured man, obviously badly hurt, moaned softly.

Tamsin drew a ragged breath and looked back at the white savage who'd threatened her with the knife. His grotesquely painted face twisted with hate as he laughed and raised the knife again.

"No." Tears sprang to her eyes, and she threw up an arm to protect her face. "Please! Don't kill me!"

The giant with the bones through his ears shouted something to Ringed Eyes. Then he pointed to the injured warrior, raised the butt of his musket, and made a smashing gesture.

Tamsin didn't need words to understand the warrior's meaning. He was urging the white Indian to kill her.

"You attacked me," she said hoarsely. "I was only defending myself."

"Prisoner no talk!" her captor ordered as he slid his knife back into his belt sheath. "You talk, you die."

Her stomach lurched as she smelled the mingled stench of blood, rancid fat, and sweat on his near-naked body. He wore nothing but a strip of beaded leather around his loins and moccasins on his feet. Every inch of his pale skin was smeared with red and yellow dots of paint.

"You can't blame me for what happened," she argued.

He grasped her throat and forced her head back, then brought his face so close to hers that she could feel the heat of his flesh. "No talk!" he repeated.

Tamsin swallowed her protests and stared him full in the eyes.

He released her and laughed. "White-skin woman brave." His sweating face shone in the flickering firelight. "Die good." He seized her wrists and bound them tightly with a leather cord.

Another man led Shiloh forward, and her assailant grabbed her by the waist and heaved her up into the saddle. The brave who held the horse's reins, a short, stocky man with bowed legs, tied her ankles beneath Shiloh's belly.

"Where are you taking me?" Tamsin dared. Hope was beginning to blossom within her. If they hadn't killed her yet, maybe they didn't intend to.

Ringed Eyes glared at her. "You know place white men call Sand Creek?"

Tamsin nodded.

"Many Cheyenne die there. Children, old woman, old man. Many die."

"I know," she said. "That was wrong. Evil. But I didn't—"

"You white!" he accused.

"You're white yourself!"

His face flushed purple beneath the paint. "Not white! Father white. Buffalo Horn great dog soldier!"

"Dog soldier? I don't understand," she said. "Are you Cheyenne? Are these men Cheyenne?"

"Cheyenne?" He struck his chest with his fist as he had done before. "White man call us that name. We are the People."

"Please. What is your name?" Tamsin moistened her dry lips. "I am Tamsin MacGreggor. I've never done anything to hurt you."

"You are the enemy." He hawked up a gob of phlegm and spat on the ground. "You think Buffalo Horn let you live when his mother die in Black Kettle's camp? When his sister, big with child, used like whore and butchered by white soldiers? You not live, white woman. You die slow. Die as Buffalo Horn's sister die. But you with hair like fire—you die in fire."

A mile to the east, Ash lay on his back and watched the stars reel across the sky. He'd chosen not to build a fire, despite the faint roars of the cougar he'd heard since dusk. At noon, he'd traded his worn-out boots for the Arapaho moccasins of a scalped miner he'd discovered in a gully.

There'd been nothing he could do for the man or his two companions. All lay dead, two slain with bullets, one clubbed with a heavy object. As far as he could tell, Tamsin had ridden within two hundred yards of the massacre and never seen the bodies.

The war party was Cheyenne. They were mounted and moving fast. Smoke from a trapper's cabin had drawn them off to the south. Otherwise, Tamsin would have ridden right into the hostiles.

He'd noticed the smoke at once, more than a chimney would release and less than a forest fire. Ash didn't need to cover the four miles through rough country to know that the cabin had been burned. There was no way of telling whether or not the owner had escaped alive. Hell, he couldn't even spare the time to bury the three miners. If he was going to find Tamsin, he had to get to her soon.

The dead men had owned several mules and at least one shod horse. One mule had been shot and butchered by the war party, one led off with the horse. It had been a stroke of luck to find the remaining animal wandering in a draw. Ash had ridden that animal hard until it was too dark to see.

Chasing Tamsin MacGreggor down in the teeth of a Cheyenne raiding party wasn't in his job specifications. The reward he'd get for bringing her in wasn't worth getting staked out on an anthill or being skinned alive. But Tamsin's second escape had changed everything between them. Catching her was no longer simply his duty. Bringing her back to trial in Sweetwater had become personal.

"You've not seen the last of me," he swore as he wiggled farther back into the dirt hollow he'd dug for himself in the ridge. He hadn't had a decent night's sleep since he'd first laid eyes on her.

And now he was about to risk everything to save her from a worse end than hanging. That is, he'd try to save her . . . if she wasn't already dead.

If there was one thing that attracted Cheyenne warriors more than whites trespassing on their lands, it was fine horseflesh. Ash figured most dog soldiers would give fingers off their right hand to own animals like Tamsin was riding.

"A man with the least bit of common sense would turn back, tell the sheriff and the judge the MacGreggor woman was dead, and collect his pay," he muttered.

He'd have been in far better shape to tackle a war party of hostiles with his rifle in hand and a good mount under him. Naturally, Tamsin had taken both with her, leaving him with nothing but a dead man's pistol, his belt knife, and an aging mule.

"I'll kill her myself."

He pulled his hat low over his eyes to shut out the moonlight, but sleep wouldn't come. Sweat trickled down the back of his neck every time he heard a branch creak or a mouse rustle in the leaves. Expecting two hundred pounds of puma in his face at any moment didn't help a man relax.

"When I get back to Sweetwater, the first thing I'll do is rent the whole damn fancy house, have a hot bath, and sleep for two days."

He'd had to halt when it got too dark to read Tamsin's trail, although God knows a child could follow it in daylight. He hadn't stopped to eat. He'd chewed dry venison on the move. Tomorrow, he might be down to eating roots. Shooting anything or lighting a fire to cook would be suicide. A gunshot or a campfire would bring every hostile for miles.

Something with a lot of legs crawled up his back, and he twisted around and smashed it.

"I'll strangle Tamsin with my own two hands."

What was it about her, besides the obvious sexual attraction, that had gotten to him? Why had he forgotten who and what she was? She'd made a fool of him, not once, but twice. If he got himself killed in this mess, he deserved to die.

"Stupid," he whispered. "I'm plain stupid." Done in by a shapely backside and a sweet southern accent.

He almost hoped the Cheyenne had finished her off.

Almost, but not quite. He had better plans for her.

A nagging thought rose to trouble him like an old war wound. She'd been his prisoner. And as much as he hated to admit it, the conniving, thieving, probable murderer was his responsibility.

Unbidden, an image of his dead wife flashed across his mind. Becky hadn't been pretty and laughing that morning after Jack Cannon had left her. Things had been done . . . things it sickened him to think of even now.

"I couldn't save her," he muttered. "I should never have left her alone when she begged me not to."

There was nothing he could do for Becky now, but he might keep Tamsin from coming to the same end at the hands of the Cheyenne. He'd seen his share of dead women, but it never got any easier to stomach. And not even a back-shooting female deserved to die that way.

He'd promised his Becky that her killer wouldn't escape justice in this world, and he meant to keep that vow. He'd caught sight of Texas Jack during the battle of Glorieta Pass, but he hadn't been able to get close enough to him to get a decent shot.

This time would be different. If he could get Tamsin MacGreggor back from the Cheyenne in one piece, he could use her for bait to trap Cannon and send him to hell.

Ash wasn't much of a religious man, and he had little hope that he'd ever find his way to heaven in the hereafter to join Becky. But just maybe . . . with a little luck . . . he could find Tamsin MacGreggor before it was too late.

Chapter 12

Rain had been falling all night in Sweetwater, filling the mossy bottoms of the rain barrels and making the main street a muddy morass. Few citizens were about this morning, but outside the sheriff's office, Roy Walker tacked a new wanted poster for Tamsin MacGreggor beside the sketch of Texas Jack Cannon's face.

Henry Steele, always at his desk by 7:00 A.M., stopped to see the notice. "Morning, Roy," he said as he balanced a steaming cup of coffee in one hand and a stack of files in the other. "Not much of a likeness of her, is it?"

The sheriff shrugged, rolled two additional posters, and tucked them into his pocket. "Peddler over at the boardinghouse drew the picture. Guess it ain't too good. But I'm not likely to pencil a better one." He frowned and scratched at the back of his starched collar. "Not too many tall, red-haired women riding around on fancy, stolen horseflesh. I imagine anybody who sees her will remember her."

"I want her caught and hanged. The sooner the better." Henry scraped some of the muck off his good shoes. The wooden sidewalks the town had put in on this side of the street were a help, but they didn't extend to the livery stable where he'd left his horse a few minutes ago.

Walker nodded. "No more than the rest of us do. Your

brother was a hard man, but I liked him. A lot of honest folks don't hanker to see a bushwhacker go free."

A hard man? It was all Henry could do not to tell Walker just how he felt about his brother. Sam had been the spitting image of their father, and he'd driven their mother to an early grave.

But prudence held his tongue. Walker wouldn't understand. Blood was blood, and people expected one brother to mourn the other, regardless of what might have passed between them in a lifetime.

"I put the two-hundred-dollar bounty on her head," Henry said, motioning to Tamsin's picture. "The county put up the other hundred. I imagine that when Morgan finds her, he'll find Jack Cannon, as well."

The judge stepped back, put his reading spectacles on, and studied the other wanted poster. "A thousand dollars for Cannon, dead or alive. You'd think that would bring the varmints out of their holes. His own mother would turn him in for that much gold."

Walker folded his arms. "Shame Morgan filled them two road agents that helped Cannon rob the bank in Wheaton full of lead."

"Sánchez and Johnson? I agree. We might have gotten something useful out of them."

The sheriff gave a snort of amusement. "Heard Morgan's got a way with a knife. Heard tell he can get a man to say everything he knows and then some."

Henry pursed his lips. "I've been told that that Morgan has some unorthodox methods of interrogation."

"Wouldn't be surprised none if that stage robbery outside of Pueblo two weeks ago was Cannon's work. The driver and one of the passengers were shot through the head."

"I agree. Company records show two men unaccounted for on that stage. They vanished without a trace." Henry removed his glasses and tucked them into his coat pocket.

"You think Cannon or some of his gang were on the stage?"

"He's done it before. Inside jobs are the easiest, and Cannon hates to leave witnesses. It's why he killed Morgan's wife, back before the war. She saw him hold up a mining office. Cannon didn't get her that day, but he went to Morgan's ranch and murdered her a week later."

"Bad business, killing a bounty hunter's wife," Walker said.

"So far, he's gotten away with it. I hope his luck doesn't last."

The sheriff tucked a fresh plug of tobacco inside his lower lip. "They say a rabbit's foot is lucky, but every dead rabbit I ever saw had four of them."

Henry took a sip of his coffee. It was stronger than usual, and he decided that the boardinghouse cook must have added gunpowder to the coffee grounds. "Cannon killed Morgan's wife back before the war. Texas Jack's kept one jump ahead of him ever since. They claim that the three Cannon brothers and Parson Bill Marsh lost their taste for playing soldier after Glorieta Pass. They deserted and hid out in Mexico. But the parson played loose with one too many married women, and a jealous husband put a bullet through his head."

"Saved us the trouble of stringing him up. The parson was a dangerous man. He killed a friend of mine during a bank robbery in Missouri." Walker leaned his hammer against the wall. "I was just fixin' to go and get me some breakfast, Judge. You had yours yet?"

"Yes, before I left home," he lied. He'd barely eaten since Sam's shooting. His stomach felt as though he'd swallowed a keg of ten-penny nails and they were working their way out, one by one. "You go on. I need to finish up some paperwork for Sarah. My brother handled all the financial matters for the ranch, and I'm afraid my sister-in-law's at a loss."

"She gonna keep the place or sell out?"

Henry frowned. "We haven't discussed that. I think she's still in shock at Sam's death. We all are."

"Never figured him to go like that, shot in the back by a—" He broke off as a horse and buggy stopped in the street. "There's Mrs. Steele now."

A woman peered out of the front of the carriage. "Henry?"

Walker touched the brim of his hat. "Morning, ma'am."

"Good morning, Sheriff." Sarah's head and face were hidden in a cloud of black mourning veil. "Henry . . . I'm going out to the cemetery, and I wondered if you—"

"Want to go with you?" Henry finished. "Certainly." He handed Walker his cup. "Take this back to the saloon for me, will you?"

Henry descended the slippery steps to the street. Sarah slid over on the buggy seat as he climbed in and took the reins. "What are you doing out on such a nasty morning?"

She rubbed small, black-gloved hands together nervously. "The rain," she said. "I thought about Sam's grave, all bare. I wanted to take some wildflowers to lay on it."

Her voice sounded as though she'd been crying. Henry's throat constricted. His brother was a son of a bitch with a rotten temper, but he'd never wanted to be rid of him that way.

"It was a bad end," he murmured. "Murdered in his own stable by a ruthless woman."

Sarah brought a lace handkerchief to her face. "I can't sleep. I can't stop thinking about it . . . the way he looked, lying in his casket, so white and still." She broke down and began to weep.

"Don't cry, Sarah. I can't stand it when you cry."

The buggy rolled past the last house and onto the rutted lane that led to the church and burying ground. "Sam was a difficult man to live with, but I never wanted him dead."

"Neither of us did," Henry agreed.

It was damned hard to keep his conscience from nagging him. He and Sarah had loved each other for more years than he could remember. Everyone had assumed they would marry until a stupid argument over another girl had broken them up. Hell, he couldn't even remember the other woman's name now. Sam had stepped in and started squiring Sarah to dances and church dinners, and before either of them realized it, it was too late to patch up their falling out.

Sarah had married Sam, and he'd tried to make the best of it. He'd thought he could love Sarah from a distance, and he had until things between her and his brother deteriorated.

"I'm a terrible sinner," Sarah whispered. "I made a mockery of my marriage vows and—"

"Not alone you didn't." He slipped an arm around her. Sobbing, she leaned against him. He let the lines fall, and the horse stopped. "No more tears," he begged her. "Sam's dead. He's dead, and we're alive."

"I wanted you to take me away," she answered in anguish. "But now he'd dead and he'll always be between us."

"It won't be like that, I promise." His heart ached to see her like this, clad in black widow's weeds from head to toe. Sarah liked fine clothing, bright colors. He'd give them to her again.

"Never." She wept softly. "You don't understand. There's something I have to ask you. . . ."

"Ask me? Ask me what?"

"Did it happen the way you said, Henry? Did that MacGreggor woman shoot Sam?"

He stiffened. "Why would you ask me that, Sarah? Haven't we been over this a dozen times?"

"It's just . . ." She pushed the veil away to look into his face. "He knew about us."

"Hell, yes, he knew. What's wrong with you, Sarah? What did you think that argument was about, the last time I saw him alive? When he threw me off the Lazy S." He lifted her chin and met her questioning gaze. "Do you think I killed him? My own brother?"

More tears spilled from her swollen eyes. "No . . . I don't. . . . I wanted to hear you say it, say you had nothing to do with . . . with what happened."

"Don't even think such a thing. Sam caught Tamsin MacGreggor stealing his horses, and she shot him. I'm as innocent of his death as you are. And I'm as anxious to see justice done."

"I prayed to be rid of him . . . but not that way. Never that way," Sarah said.

"My brother's death won't go unpunished. I'll see the MacGreggor woman hang if it's the last thing I do. The Bible says, 'An eye for an eye.' I would have shot her that night if I could, but I'll settle to see her dangle from a rope in front of the courthouse."

"Her death won't change anything. It won't bring Sam back, and it won't change what we . . . what I did."

"I love you, Sarah. I've always loved you. We'll wait a decent time, and then we'll be married. Just as we should have been a long time ago."

"I was miserable with him, and now that he's dead, I'll always be unhappy."

"Don't say that. You're all upset, and rightly so. You were a good wife to him, Sarah."

"A good wife?" She made a small sound of despair. "When I slept with his brother like a common harlot?"

"Never say that again," he admonished. "What happened is in the past. The future belongs to us. We'll get through this, see justice done, and then we'll be wed."

"You don't understand."

"I do. And I have to live with the fact that I betrayed him with—"

"But I'm with child."

"What?" Stunned, he stiffened. "You're what?"

"I'm going to have a baby."

His chest felt as though it were squeezed in a vise. All these years he'd secretly envied his brother, and he'd been glad that his marriage was barren. But now that Sam was gone, was it possible that he'd have to live with Sam's son?

"Say something?" she begged. "Tell me you're glad."

"Sam's child? You're having—"

"No, you great ninny! Not Sam's. We haven't been together in years . . . not like that. It's yours, Henry, your child."

"But . . . but . . ." Dumbly, he began to grin. "Mine? Ours?" Joy bubbled up inside him. "My son?"

"Or daughter."

"You're not pleased?" She didn't sound pleased. Sarah had always said she wanted children, but . . .

"Of course I'm pleased, Henry. Why wouldn't I be? It's just that now . . . now, we can't marry. Not for months, maybe years. People will talk. They might guess that—"

"Hell with what people say," he said. "What difference does it make what gossips blab about? What could be more natural than I'd marry my brother's widow and care for—"

"His child, Henry. Unless we want our child branded a bastard, it must always be Sam's child."

Suddenly, a thought struck him and he sobered. "Did he know? Did my brother—"

"He knew," Sarah said brokenly.

"A son." Henry leaned close and kissed her lightly on the mouth. "Nothing could make me happier," he said. "And I'll make you happy. I swear it. I'll protect you and care for you, Sarah. And I'll make you forget all this unhappiness."

"Will you, Henry? Can you?" She touched his cheek with a gloved hand.

"I swear to you, we'll make a new life. Here or somewhere else, the three of us."

"Yes," she agreed. "I want to go away, back to St. Louis, back to civilization. I want to forget what happened here."

Around the bend, toward them, came the minister's chaise. Quickly, Henry released Sarah and picked up the reins. "We'd best take those flowers of yours to the grave."

"Yes," she answered. "We should show proper respect. Flowers make a grave less . . . less . . ."

"Good morning, Reverend," Henry called to the minister.

"A blessed day to you, Judge, and to you Mrs. Steele," the cleric replied.

"Reverend," Sarah said.

Smiling, Henry clicked to the mare and drove on through the pouring rain.

The first light of morning found Tamsin and the war party riding up mountainsides and plunging into ravines that she wouldn't have believed a goat could traverse. Low-hanging branches scraped at her skin and hair and tore her clothing. Thirst plagued her, and it was impossible to forget Buffalo Horn's threats of burning.

If she let her mind dwell on torture, she would lose all reason. She kept remembering the Indian she'd shot at the campfire and the stench of burning hair when he fell.

Since she was a child, Tamsin had heard horror stories of Indian captives burned at the stake. She didn't want to die, but if there was no hope of survival, she would rather be shot in an escape attempt than to meet such a horrible fate.

Tamsin feared as much for her horses as she did for her own safety. Fancy and Dancer were thoroughbreds, unused to such rugged country. One misstep and either of them could snap a leg.

One of the Cheyenne braves rode Fancy, but none could stay on Dancer's back long enough to make it worth his while. They'd dropped rawhide ropes over his head and wrestled him to the ground, but the big bay had fought them hoof and tooth. And after an hour's struggle, the braves had given up and simply fastened a lead line to a loop around his neck.

As the hours passed and her thirst grew worse, she tried to fill her head with other thoughts. She tried to imagine what her new farm in California would look like. She built imaginary barns and paddocks and filled them with sleek mares and beautiful foals.

She could almost see Ash Morgan leaning on a split-rail fence and—Ash? How had he slipped into her innermost thoughts?

It was better not to remember how safe she'd felt with his arms around her . . . and better not to hope that he would come for her.

But he will, she thought. He'll follow me to where I stopped for the night, and then . . .

Sweet God in heaven, why would Ash want to risk his

life for her after what she'd done to him? Not once, but twice.

She glanced around cautiously. Last night she'd counted four uninjured Cheyenne. In daylight, she'd seen that she'd missed three more, making a total of seven. The wounded man was barely conscious, his shirt stained with blood. She supposed he was the one she'd wrestled with and shot, apparently in the side. But he was too weak to lift a weapon, so that made the odds against Ash seven to one. Not even Ash could fight off so many Indians. Could he?

When the sun was high overhead, the Cheyenne stopped to rest beside a cascade of tumbling water. Men slid down from their mounts to bury their faces in the foamy stream, and the horses eagerly drank deeply.

"Please, I'm thirsty," she called to Buffalo Horn. "Loose my hands for just a minute so that I—"

In the bright sunshine, the paint on his face had smeared and faded, but his eyes were just as hard. Ignoring her plea, he turned to a companion and said something in Cheyenne that made the other men laugh. He seized her by the shoulder and dragged her from the horse.

Tamsin fell on one knee, then screamed as he shoved her back on the ground. "No!" Her head struck a rock, and for an instant the pain nearly overshadowed the realization that Buffalo Horn was tearing at her skirts.

Hysterically, she kicked at him and struck out with her bound hands. "No! No!"

Jeering, the others closed in around her as his weight pressed her down. Buffalo Horn's hand clamped over her mouth. She twisted and sunk her teeth into his flesh, biting down until she tasted the salt of his blood.

Suddenly, Fancy shrieked a high-pitched whinny of fear, and the animals went wild. Shiloh plunged past, nearly crushing Tamsin and her assailant under his hooves.

A man shouted.

Buffalo Horn raised up on his knees as an enraged roar slashed through the pandemonium of kicking, rearing horses. Before Tamsin could draw another breath, the mountain lion leaped from an overhanging tree branch onto a brave's back.

It seemed to Tamsin that time stood still. For an instant, Buffalo Horn, the other Cheyenne warriors, and the terrified horses were imprinted on her mind. Tamsin was certain she could smell and taste the sour scent of the big cat, the animal's sweat, and the odor of wet leaves trampled underfoot. Even the colors seemed clear and distinct, the tawny yellow of the cougar, the white of the young brave's eyes, and the intense blue of the cloudless sky.

Then the scene began to unravel as the cat's claws and teeth rained blood on the scattering warriors. The dying man's screams mingled with those of the fleeing horses and the puma's snarls.

A rifle cracked, and Tamsin caught a final glimpse of ivory-yellow teeth and gushing red before the cat vanished into the underbrush. More guns went off, and the Cheyenne's cries had turned to war whoops as they raced after the cougar.

Heaving dry sobs of terror, Tamsin got to her feet and backed away from the dead warrior. Stumbling, shaking with fear, she edged closer to the nearest horse, an Indian mustang.

He snorted, laid back his ears, and trotted away, still trailing a single rein. Tamsin strained at her wrist bindings. If her hands hadn't been tied, she would have run after the horse, flung herself onto his back, and attempted an escape.

A brave's grip on her arm dashed her hope. He spun

her around to face him and glared into her face. "Demon Claw," Buffalo Horn muttered. "Spirit cougar. You bring bad medicine. We go from this place quickly."

Maybe he's right, Tamsin thought as he put her on the trembling pinto. There was something eerie about the mountain lion. Maybe it hadn't come for the Cheyenne. Maybe the big cat had come for her, seeking revenge for Ash's killing the smaller cougar.

And for the space of a heartbeat she wondered if she wouldn't have been better off if the beast had killed her. Even that death would be better than the rape and torture Buffalo Horn had planned for her.

Chapter 13

The Cheyenne rode until it was too dark for Tamsin to see her horse's head. Then, when she thought they would go on forever in blackness, Buffalo Horn called a halt and ordered her to slide down off the pinto.

She winced as his knife slashed the leather bonds at her wrists. He pushed her roughly to a sitting position on the damp leaves, and she waited, rubbing her hands to bring back the circulation.

She heard the crack of flint and steel, and a spark came to life in the darkness. The flash of light extinguished but was quickly followed by another and another. In a matter of minutes, a tiny fire illuminated the faces of men crouched close around it.

Apparently one of the braves had slain a mountain sheep during the day. Tamsin watched as two of the youngest men built a fire and butchered the ram. They sliced the bloody meat into small pieces and suspended them over the coals on green branches. Soon the air was filled with the tantalizing smell of broiling mutton.

Tonight there was none of the laughter and camaraderie she'd seen between the men in the morning. They all seemed tense, keeping their weapons close at hand and nervously glancing over their shoulders at every night sound. Buffalo Horn's face was taut as he chewed every last morsel of flesh from a leg bone and tossed it into the bushes.

No one offered Tamsin a bite as the war party devoured the meat. She tried to keep her gaze averted, but she couldn't keep from salivating. She was so hungry that her stomach growled and ached.

The Cheyenne had taken her higher into the mountains than she'd been before. A cold wind whistled down from the peaks, the temperature was dropping fast, and she was getting cold.

Tamsin edged closer to the fire. One chunk of fatty roast remained, clinging to a skewer. A brave on the far side of the hearth glanced at the meat and reached out to take it. Boldly, Tamsin snatched it first. Without worrying who had touched the mutton or whether it was done, she began to gobble it with as little propriety as the warriors had shown.

Juice dribbled down her chin, but she didn't care. The ram was old and tough, but it was food. She'd gone too long without nourishment to be particular. She was nearly finished when she heard a loud cough from the trees behind the camp.

Instantly, a Cheyenne jerked up his rifle and fired in the direction of the sound. Tamsin jumped. Her heart pounded, and her chest felt tight.

Two men rose and rushed toward the aspen grove, but they stopped at the edges. Horses whinnied and stamped their feet. Tamsin heard Dancer snort nervously.

She stared into the darkness. Wind whistled through the branches, rattling leaves, and raising gooseflesh on her arms.

Tamsin looked around her at the startled men. She didn't need to understand Cheyenne to know that they thought the cougar had come back, that it was crouched out there, watching, waiting.

Then, from another direction came the drawn-out hooting of an owl. A stout man with graying braids laughed nervously. The huge Cheyenne with the bones in his ears stood and paced, rifle ready.

Minutes passed without any unusual sounds. The moon rose, a pale crescent of ivory. Single stars winked on, one by one, and talk began to flow around the fire.

Tamsin shivered. Her face and front were warm, but fear of what might happen made her start at every stamp of a horse's hoof or snap of a twig.

Then the owl hooted again.

The giant with the shaved head shouted angrily and leaped to his feet. Buffalo Horn put a restraining hand on the dissenter's arm, attempting to argue, but the huge warrior jerked away and stalked into the woods followed by a second malcontent.

Minutes or an hour later—Tamsin couldn't be certain—the bald man returned alone. Buffalo Horn questioned him. He shrugged and looked worried.

Buffalo Horn glared malevolently at Tamsin. "You are a witch." He rose to his feet and came toward her.

Shuddering, she leaped up and backed away.

"Did you bring Demon Claw?" he demanded, snaking his knife from the sheath at his side.

"No," she protested. "I—"

Something huge, dark, and braying broke from the trees. Men and horses scattered as a mule burst into the center of the clearing, trailing a ball of fire. Shots exploded wildly. Coals and sparks sprayed in all directions.

Buffalo Horn whirled and dived for his rifle. Tamsin didn't wait to see what he would do. She ran for cover amid a volley of frenzied shots, shouting men, and stampeding horses.

An Indian mustang galloped toward Tamsin, trailing a

rope. She seized a handful of mane and tried to pull herself up, but the animal shied sideways and lashed out at her with his teeth.

She caught a glimpse of Buffalo Horn taking aim at her with his rifle, and she dived for the earth. A squealing bay horse leapt over her and careened into the darkness.

Tamsin tasted dirt and rolled, shielding her face with her arms. A rifle cracked, and a limb shattered over her head. She started to crawl away, then heard another horse bearing down on her.

"Tamsin!"

Ash's voice cut through her terror. She looked up to see him pounding across the clearing on Shiloh. Behind Ash, Buffalo Horn whooped a war cry and threw himself onto the nearest Indian pony.

One chance, she thought. I've got only one chance. She waited, frozen, as Ash galloped closer and closer.

Then he leaned from the saddle and snatched her up. His arm clamped around her as she shut her eyes and scrambled to find something solid to grab on to as they plunged into the trees.

Before she could get a grip on Ash or the saddle, Shiloh reared and skidded on the loose stones. Ash dropped her on her feet.

"Take cover!" he yelled.

"Don't leave me!"

He reined the gelding around and spurred back the way they came. Tamsin heard the crash of underbrush and saw Buffalo Horn galloping toward him.

Two rifles barked as one.

Ash stiffened and wheeled his horse in a tight circle. An Indian pony trotted past. Buffalo Horn clung to the animal's mane for a few yards, then fell forward to sprawl on the ground.

Tamsin started toward the riderless horse.

"No," Ash said. "Get up behind me." He offered her his hand again and kicked loose his stirrup. She thrust a foot into it and accepted his help to mount behind him.

Ash urged Shiloh on, pausing only to slap the barrel of his rifle against the Indian horse's rump. The animal squealed and charged off in another direction.

"What about the cougar?" Tamsin whispered as Ash slowed his gelding to traverse a steep stretch of gravel.

"Me," he replied. "I wanted to make them nervous."

"It worked."

A branch tangled in her hair and scraped her back. "What about my horses?"

"I cut them loose," he grated. "Right now, I'd like to worry about my scalp."

She could hear the Indians behind them, and the cry of anger when they discovered Buffalo Horn. She buried her face in the back of Ash's shirt and held on with all of her strength as they reached a break in the undergrowth and galloped pell-mell down the wooded incline.

All night they played cat and mouse, following rocky streambeds and rugged coulees. Often they heard shots, and once they dismounted so Ash could hold Shiloh's nose to keep him from whinnying as two Cheyenne rode by.

At dawn they discovered a small clearing with a mule and three horses grazing there. "Dancer! Fancy!" Tamsin cried hoarsely.

"Shhh, keep your voice down. Wait to—"

The stallion raised his head and nickered. Shiloh returned the greeting. Tamsin dismounted and found she was almost too stiff to walk.

"Fancy! Here, girl," she called softly.

The chestnut snorted and trotted over, followed by an

Appaloosa mare. Murmuring endearments, Tamsin stroked Fancy's soft nose and neck.

"She's safe," she said to Ash. The Cheyenne hadn't even bothered to unsaddle her. Her bridle was missing one rein, but Ash used several pigging strings from his saddlebag to make up for it.

"Mount up," he said tersely when Tamsin had tied the rawhide together to make another rein. "We need to put distance between us and them."

Too weary to question his orders, she pulled herself up onto Fancy's back and fell in behind Shiloh. Dancer, the Appaloosa mare, and the mule followed. The mule had scratches along his sides and singed spots on his rump.

"Poor thing," Tamsin murmured. "What did you do to him?"

"Tied a Texas tornado to his tail. Lit brush and a few cartridge shells."

"That's cruel," she replied.

"I figured the rope would burn through before the fire got to the mule. It must have, because he looks a hell of a sight better than you do."

She nodded. She wanted to thank him for saving her life, but she knew if she said one word, she'd choke up and lose her nerve. She'd given Ash every reason to abandon her, but he hadn't. He'd risked his life for hers. He was still risking it.

"How long will they follow us?"

He shrugged. "I wounded one at the campfire and killed that brave that came after us. That's bound to make them mad."

"One Cheyenne went off into the woods, after the owl hooted, but before—"

"Where do you think I got the rifle?"

"You killed him?"

Ash didn't answer, and she felt foolish. Of course he'd killed him. Tears welled up in her eyes and wet her cheeks. She wiped them away, but more trickled down.

He glanced back at her. "Why are you crying now?"

"I don't want to die."

"Reckon them Cheyenne didn't either. It was just a game to them, until things went the wrong way."

"You shouldn't have come for me," she said, urging her mare up beside Ash's weary horse. "After what I did to you . . . Why did you—"

"Don't ask. You might not like the answer."

She bit her lower lip and tried to control her emotions. "Thank you," she whispered.

He didn't say anything for a long time, not until the sun was high overhead. Then he looked back at her, and she noticed how gray and gaunt his features looked.

"You know I can't let them capture you," Ash said.

She roused herself out of a stupor. "What?"

"I can't let the Cheyenne take you prisoner."

Her lips were cracked. Her mouth was almost too dry to speak. "What are you saying?"

"I'll keep you safe, Tamsin."

His words were meant to be comforting . . . but somehow, they only made her more afraid.

No longer making any effort to hide their tracks, Ash kept the pace at breakneck speed. They crossed rocky gullies, scrambled down bare slopes, and galloped across alpine meadows knee-deep in blue-green grass and wildflowers.

They raced down canyons and led the horses along goat paths too narrow to ride where the threat of rock slides made Tamsin breathless. And then when the boiling sun was directly overhead, they stopped on a high ridge to spell the horses. Ash shaded his eyes, looked back the way they had come, and swore softly.

"Look there." He pointed to a string of horsemen that spilled across an open hollow.

"Cheyenne?" Tamsin shivered despite the midday heat.

"Too far off to say for certain."

"It's them, isn't it?"

"Switch your saddle to the Appaloosa."

Tamsin shook her head. "I've never ridden her. I'd feel safer on Fancy."

"Save her for an open stretch. That's a Nez Percé pony. They don't breed tougher horseflesh anywhere. I don't know where Buffalo Horn's bunch got hold of her, but I'd trade both thoroughbreds for her any day. She's fast and surefooted, and she's got a heart as big as these mountains."

"Why don't you ride her? Your Shiloh's worn out."

"I'll ride the devil's whelp," he said.

"Dancer?" She was too exhausted to do more than shake her head. "You can't ride him. You're not used to an English saddle, and he's not trained to a western."

"You put a rope on him and tie him to a tree. I'll ride the bastard or know why."

"He'll kill you," she warned. "I can barely ride him."

"If I don't kill him first."

It took the best part of ten minutes for her to coax the stallion near enough to slip a bridle over his head and switch the supplies to Shiloh's back. Then she mounted the Indian horse. She didn't bother to put a lead line on Fancy. She'd follow, and if Shiloh didn't, having him on a rope would only endanger them all.

Ash took Dancer's reins in one hand and put his foot in the stirrup. The stallion squealed with fury and reared, nearly throwing them both off the edge of the mountain.

Tamsin stifled a scream as loose rock crumbled and Ash flung his weight forward and lashed the horse's rump with the ends of the leathers. Dancer's white-rimmed eyes rolled as he fought to regain his balance.

"Please, God," Tamsin groaned.

The big bay's front feet found solid ground, and he lunged forward onto the narrow trail. "Yaaah!" Ash yelled, driving his heels into the animal's sides.

Dancer reared again, scraping the sky with flashing hooves, slammed into the earth, twisted sideways, and jackknifed. Ash rode him up and down, sticking to the English saddle with the tenacity of a greenbrier.

Unable to stand the tension any longer, Tamsin slapped the Appaloosa's neck. "Get up!" she cried. The mare leapt forward, rounding the bend, scrambling up the last rise, and plunging down the far side with Ash's gelding and Fancy hot on her heels.

Dust rose in swirls as the Indian pony's hooves churned up the twisting trail. It was all Tamsin could do to hold on and pray that her mare's bone-jarring flight wouldn't hurl them off the path and into the abyss. She couldn't think about Ash, couldn't take time to wonder if he and Dancer had survived.

Tears streaked Tamsin's dirty face, blinding her to everything but the mare's head and neck and the sheer rock wall flashing past. One misstep, one gap in the weather-carved track, and her life would be over in a split second.

Then, behind her, Tamsin heard a roaring rumble as the mountain groaned and shifted. Boulders crashed, and a wave of loose gravel and pumpkin-sized rocks bounced around them. Unable to see, Tamsin clenched her eyes shut and clung to the horse's mane as she felt the horse leap over an obstacle, stumble, and slide.

Before she could catch her breath, the mare's hind legs buckled, and Tamsin lost her footing in her right stirrup and felt the saddle pull away from under her. Desperately, she tried to hold on to the Appaloosa's mane, then screamed as she lost her grip and fell.

Chapter 14

Ash clenched his teeth against the pain as he whipped
the bay stallion harder while the mountainside slid away
beneath the horse's feet. The roar of falling rocks drowned
the thunder of Dancer's hooves as they pounded down
the ever-narrowing trail that wound around the edge of the
cliff.

In the first minutes after he'd swung up into the
saddle, Ash had been certain that Tamsin was right. Not
only wasn't he strong enough to control the stud, but
Dancer was going to kill both of them to prove it. When
they'd nearly toppled off the edge, Ash had felt his hair
turn gray. But once Tamsin started down the mountain,
the stallion seemed to forget the man on his back. He
was bound and determined to follow the other horses.

The stud hadn't made that decision a moment too
soon. Either Dancer's craziness or Tamsin's stampede
had started a rock slide. The mountain sheep path they'd
followed over the peak had vanished in the blink of an
eye, wiped clean as though it had never existed, leaving
them all running for their lives.

Between the falling debris and the animals ahead of
him kicking up dust, Ash found it impossible to see anything farther than the stallion's head. There was nothing
to do but trust Dancer's instincts and urge him forward
even faster.

The big horse didn't fail him. Leaping rocks with the agility of a wild mustang, Dancer came down off the peak as though the hounds of hell were hot on his tail.

Ash spat dirt and breathed a sigh of relief as the shelf wound around a corner and widened. Sheltered by an overhanging ledge, the air was clear enough to give him a hazy view of the downhill trail. He tried to rein in Dancer, but the horse had the bit in his teeth and his temper up.

Then, without warning, a yawning crevice opened in front of them. Ash tried to gauge the width of the gap, but it was too late to stop. Instead, he leaned forward and dug his heels into the stallion. Dancer tensed his muscles and leapt, flying over the missing section of rock and landing securely on the far side.

The bay gained on Tamsin and the other horses with each stride. Spraying dirt and gravel, he tore past the sweat-streaked chestnut on the left, forcing the mule close to the inner wall. Ahead, Ash saw Tamsin's Appaloosa mare stumble and nearly go down, and his heart skipped a beat. He knew that if she fell, the other four animals would be unable to stop. All five would go down in a tangle of hooves and thrashing bodies, crushing her beneath them.

Then, as he watched, Tamsin lost her balance and fought to stay in the saddle. The Nez Percé horse struggled up, her stride broken, but still moving fast. Shiloh skidded behind her. With only one foot in the stirrup, Tamsin held on for long agonizing seconds while Ash cursed the stud and whipped him faster.

At the last possible instant Dancer drew neck and neck with the Appaloosa mare. Ash leaned out of the saddle and plucked Tamsin from midair. He winced and crushed her against him as the big bay took the lead and continued his wild downhill gallop.

A hundred yards ahead, the steep track spilled into a tiny alpine meadow. Ash reined in the stallion to a canter and pulled hard on his left rein. Circling tighter and tighter, the horse slowed to a trot and finally halted.

Tamsin, her face milk-white beneath the dust, trembled from head to foot and clung to Ash as though she would never let him go. "Shhh, shhh," he soothed. "I've got you."

Pain gnawed at his side and made him light-headed as he dropped Tamsin onto her feet. He drew in a jagged breath and sat perfectly still for the space of a dozen heartbeats.

"What is it?" she demanded. "What's wrong?"

"This savin' your butt has become a habit," he managed. Bracing himself, he swung down out of the saddle.

His legs felt like wet clay, and his head was pounding. He clamped a hand against his side and walked toward a fallen tree. It was only a few yards away, but the distance seemed daunting.

Dancer raised his head and emitted a shrill trumpet as the other horses trotted into the high grass. The stallion was breathing hard, and his sides were streaked with sweat. Yellow foam dripped from his mouth and nose, but his obvious exhaustion didn't keep him from herding the mule and the mares and nipping at Shiloh's hindquarters.

Tamsin was suddenly at Ash's side, slipping an arm around his shoulder. "You're hurt! Oh, my God, you're bleeding!"

Ash exhaled slowly and sank onto the log. "It's nothing, a graze."

She pulled his hand away and her eyes widened with alarm. She snatched back his vest and saw the widening circle of red around the hole in his shirt. "What is it? Did a rock . . . Oh, Lord, that's a bullet hole. You've been shot."

"What are you worried about?" he said. "Your horses are fine. Not a broken leg among any of them." Or you, he thought.

She ignored him, tugging at his clothing. "You're losing blood."

"Ow." He groaned, pulling away from her. "Damn, woman, you'll kill me trying to see—"

"Back there," she interrupted. "When you shot that Indian . . . I didn't know you were hit." She slipped his vest off his right shoulder. "The bullet came out the back."

"Damn good thing it did," he muttered. "If it was still in there, I wouldn't have made it off that mountain, not riding him." He nodded toward Dancer.

"But you've been bleeding all night." She laid a hand on his temple. "Your face is hot. You're running a fever."

Ash shook his head. "No. I told you, it's not deep. The bullet plowed a furrow along my rib, maybe cracked one from the way it feels. But it only bled an hour or two." He uttered a exclamation of black humor. "Until a few minutes ago."

"Well, it's bleeding now. We've got to find water, wash it. You need a doctor."

"Right." His eyes narrowed. "Do you see any in the vicinity, ma'am?"

She shook her head. "You were hurt, badly, yet you saved me. Twice. I . . . Why did you risk your life for me? If you believe I'm a murderer, why not let the Indians have me?"

Seeing her falling from the saddle, in danger of being trampled to death had shaken him more than he wanted to admit. Maybe it was the fever that was affecting his thinking, but he felt oddly touched by her sympathy over his wound. He'd thought he'd rescued her to use her to catch Cannon, but he didn't want to tell her that. Maybe it wasn't even true. But if it wasn't . . . then why had he?

"I thought about letting them have you," he said.

"Comforting," she replied. She glanced anxiously back toward the boulder-strewn trail. "The Cheyenne?"

"A goat won't make it over that path for the next hundred years," he answered gruffly. Her nearness made him want to put an arm around her and lean his head on her breast. He was tired. He wanted to sleep, and he wanted these crazy feelings about Tamsin to go away. "If they want us, they've got to go around the mountain and find another pass. And that will take half a day, at least."

The chestnut mare nudged Tamsin with her nose, and she ignored the horse as she tore a strip from her petticoat to tie around his waist. "I told you my horses were tough," Tamsin said as she bound his wound.

Ash gritted his teeth. "You tell me a lot of things."

She stepped back and rubbed her hands on her skirt. "That's all I can do for you without water."

"It's good. Thanks."

"It's not good. You need hot food, medicine and soap, a bed."

He wished she wasn't so damned concerned about him. He had to keep reminding himself that she was Cannon's woman, that he couldn't trust her.

"I know of a trader who has a cabin near here," he said. "Six hours that way." He pointed. "Maybe less."

"Six hours? You can't ride in your condition."

Ash shrugged. "Got a better plan?"

It was a long six hours. Sweat soaked Ash's shirt and vest, and his hair clung to back of his neck. The pain in his side had become a steady throbbing ache, and the sun made his eyes squint.

Still, he stayed in the saddle and kept his wits about him, which was what mattered. And he didn't miss the nearly invisible trail that led through a zigzag ravine with steep walls into a tiny box canyon.

A split-rail fence blocked the mouth of the quarter-acre paddock. Tamsin let the horses in, then slid the logs across to keep them from escaping.

Ash watched as she unsaddled the animals. A gush of water cascaded down the sheer cliff to pool in a natural rock basin. Eagerly, the animals crossed the grassy area to drink.

"They may be overheated," Tamsin said. "Maybe I shouldn't let them —"

"Leave them," Ash replied. "We've a climb ahead of us, and you don't want to do it in the dark."

"Are you up to it?"

He didn't bother to answer. As thirsty as he was, he knew the source of the water was a spring beside the cabin. He was afraid that if he sat down, he wouldn't get up again. Taking the rifle from Shiloh's saddle scabbard, he led the way to a crack in the rock face hidden by several pine trees.

"Follow me," he ordered Tamsin. "Put your hands and feet where I put mine, and don't look down."

"I'm not afraid of heights," she said.

But I am, he thought. Even with a clear head, the thought of climbing Jacob's Ladder had made his stomach lurch. There were no wooden rungs, only tiny ledges chiseled in the rock.

Tamsin looked up at the narrow passageway. "I don't think this is such a good idea. Why don't you stay here by the pool and I'll—"

Ash started up. "Jacob's wife goes up this with a baby on her back." He didn't bother to tell her that Jacob's woman was a Hopi Indian, who'd scrambled up and down cliffs since she'd been old enough to walk.

Halfway up, with his knuckles bleeding, his fingers numb, and his head giddy, he almost wished he'd done as Tamsin suggested. Only the thought of a real bed and Jacob's real coffee made him keep going—that and having to admit to Tamsin that he'd been wrong.

When they reached the top, Ash saw at once that Jacob Stein wasn't at home. The corral on the far side of the cabin was empty, the door was shut and barred from the outside, and no smoke came from the chimney.

The cabin, surrounded by trees, sat in the fold of a mountain. Ash didn't suppose that more than a hand's count of men knew it existed. Even the Utes didn't come here. The peak above was usually shrouded in clouds, and the Indians thought that it was the realm of malicious spirits.

"No one's here," Tamsin said as she pulled herself over the edge.

Ash took a deep breath, circled the spring, and went to the door. He pulled back the bar and pushed open the door. The inside was shadowy but neat. Foodstuffs hung from the ceiling rafters, and blankets and trade goods were stacked along the back wall.

He ducked his head, braced himself against the door frame, and counted the steps to the raised shelf-bed. Pushing back the blankets, Ash laid his rifle against the wall and stretched out on the clean mattress. His eyes closed the instant his head hit the pillow.

Vaguely, Ash was aware of drinking from a cup and, later, sipping something hot and delicious. But mostly, he knew only relief that he wasn't moving and that he could sleep.

When he woke the following morning, Tamsin was dripping lye soap and warm water over his wound.

Ash's oath echoed off the rafters. "Ouch! Damn it, woman! Are you trying to murder me in my bed?"

"Hush, don't be a baby," she admonished. "I've got to keep this clean. I washed it last night, and you never made a peep."

He swore again and sat up. "I can get on my feet. I'm not an invalid," he said testily. "You'll ruin Yoki's mattress, and then we'll both catch hell."

"Who?"

"Yoki. Jacob's wife. She's a Hopi Indian and the reason this cabin is as neat as a pin. Jacob was never this clean when he was a bachelor."

Noting that the rifle still lay where he'd placed it, Ash got up and made his way unsteadily to the table. He settled into a chair and removed what was left of his shirt. "There, do your worst," he grumbled. "Is there anything to eat around here?"

His nose told him that there was. He smelled beans and biscuits, and something else that might be stew.

"I've been giving you willow tea all night. I found a tin of bark and sweetened it. I think your fever's nearly gone."

"I'm hungry."

He heard a clatter of plates as she went to the fireplace. Glancing down at his side, he saw that the place around the wound was red but not putrid. "I told you there was nothing to this. A bullet can go clear through you. An arrowhead, now, that's different. Take an arrow and chances are you'll need to burn out the—"

"I don't want to hear about it," she said as she put a bowl of soup in front of him. "That's onion, barley, and dried something. Venison, I think. Eat it. It will give you strength."

"I want some of that bread. With molasses. Yoki always has molasses around. She has a sweet tooth."

She returned with two lopsided biscuits and a crock of molasses. "I saw a trail going down this side. Why did you bring me up that cliff yesterday?"

"A two-day ride to get here." He sniffed. "Coffee? Is that coffee brewing?"

"I'm a prisoner," she said. "I'm not your mother. Where does it say a prisoner is supposed to wait on a bounty hunter?"

"I need coffee, Tamsin."

"Say please."

"Please, damn it." She flashed him a smile as she poured a steaming cup. Her fingers brushed his as she handed it to him. He drank without waiting for the strong coffee to cool. It burned his tongue, but he could feel the energy seeping through to the marrow of his bones.

"Thank you," he said, covering her hand with his own. "Why didn't you run?"

She pulled away, went to the hearth, and returned with a bowl of soup and a biscuit for herself. "I didn't want to climb down that cliff alone."

"Not even to check your horses?" He didn't believe it for a moment. Hell, he wouldn't put it past her to tie blankets together and lower herself down to the pasture.

"The animals are fine. I laid on my belly and looked over the side."

"I was dead to the world," he said. "You could have taken the livestock and been miles away by the time I woke."

"You're hurt. I couldn't leave you alone and helpless." She crumbled her biscuit, pushing away the burned pieces. "Your friend Jacob picked this spot well. You can see forever up here."

Ash took another sip of coffee. His side hurt like hell and his head still ached, but he knew he was on the mend.

"Where is he?"

"Jacob? Off trading, I suppose. He might have gone to Denver to buy more goods, or they might be visiting Yoki's folks."

"I hope he doesn't mind our staying here, eating his food, and—"

Ash shook his head. "He won't. Jacob figures he owes me a favor. I'll pay for what we use, but we're more than welcome to his hospitality." He looked at Tamsin without being obvious. She'd bathed and washed her hair. Her shirt was a bright yellow, and her skirt seemed hastily fashioned from a length of canvas.

"Do I look awful?"

"What?" He smiled at her. "No, why should you look awful?"

"My clothes were filthy. I had to wear something while I waited for my own things to dry." She shook her head. "I tried to stitch up my blouse, but that's beyond repair. This . . ." She spread her hands in a gesture of helplessness.

"Nothin' wrong with what you're wearing. Take what you need. I'll see that Jacob doesn't lose out." The shirt gaped open at her throat. He could see just enough of the rise of her breasts to make him think about what was hidden. Her skin, where the sun hadn't kissed it, was fair and slightly freckled. He took another gulp of coffee and tried to keep his gaze on his plate.

A pool of sunlight spilled in through the open doorway and laid a pattern on the scrubbed pine floor. It was peaceful here, Ash thought. Sitting here at the table, having breakfast with an attractive woman, without worrying if someone was about to put a bullet in his back.

But thinking like that could get him killed. Tamsin MacGreggor was a puzzle, and every time he thought he had her figured out, she surprised him.

Why hadn't she left him when she had the chance?

Why hadn't she killed him? Was she using him to get her out of these mountains the way he intended to use her? And what if she was telling the truth about everything? What if Cannon wasn't anyone special to her? And suppose she was innocent of Sam Steele's killing?

"How long will we stay here?" she asked, breaking into his reverie.

"A few days," he replied, finishing the last drops and holding the cup up for a refill. "Long enough to get my strength back. Until the storms pass."

"What storms?"

"Coming down out of the north. Can't you smell it? Cold and rain, maybe hail. The last blast before summer."

"Ridiculous. It's a sunny day. There isn't a cloud in the sky."

Chapter 15

By evening of that day, rain beat against the shingles and poured through the cracks in the cabin chinking. Gushes of water streamed off the roof and pounded on the shuttered window.

Ash sat close to the crackling fire while Tamsin knelt beside him and applied ointment to the wound along his side. They had already eaten, grilled rabbit that Ash had killed with a slingshot, corn bread that she had baked, and wild greens.

"You've still got a few things to learn about weather out here," he teased. "And about cooking over an open hearth."

She ignored his reference to the rain. "At home, we had servants."

"Servants." He chuckled. "I thought all ladies learned how to bake and sew."

"Most do." She applied a little more pressure to her task and he winced.

"Ouch! I should have traded you to the Utes. You enjoy torture." His fingers grazed her shoulder and neck, lingering there until she felt her face grow warm.

"Don't," she protested halfheartedly.

"Why?"

She carried her nursing supplies to the table and washed her hands in a wooden bowl. The day had passed

163

quickly, without the usual sparring of cross words. Tonight, the cabin seemed filled with tension.

The downpour closed around them, shutting them off from the mountains and sky. With the rain, the single room should have felt stuffy. Instead, the air seemed too rich for her lungs. She was restless, her mind churned, and her body felt lighter than bird feathers.

"How long are we going to play this game?" The deep timbre of Ash's voice played along her spine and made her giddy. "Tamsin?"

"What?" She liked the way he said her name.

"Come here, woman."

She shook her head. Getting too close to him was dangerous. Not that she was afraid of him . . .

All right, she was . . . just a little, she admitted to herself. "Don't do something you'll regret," she said.

"Are you speakin' to me?"

Ash's smile would tempt an angel. It lit his face and made his eyes glow with an inner sparkle.

She cleared away the bowl and wiped the table vigorously. And all the while she was acutely aware of the scents and sounds around her, the hiss of the fire, the bite of the herbs that hung from the rafters.

She wanted to remember this night, these hours. She didn't want to think about what was right or wrong or what tomorrow might bring. She wanted to live this time . . . to know what it would be like to lie in the arms of this man.

"You know what you're doing to me," he said.

She swallowed and touched her bottom lip with trembling fingers. He could be mine, she thought, mine for tonight, at least.

And why not? What was there to lose? Her reputation? She was a widow, not a starry-eyed virgin. Once she reached California, no one would know or care whether or not she'd spent a single night in Ash Morgan's bed.

Hadn't she spent a lifetime trying to do what other people told her she should?

He rose and came to her as though it were the most natural thing in the world. Firelight played across his taut, bruised features, and she read the naked yearning there.

"Tamsin MacGreggor, you are something fine," he murmured. She didn't say a word when he raised a hand to slowly pull the pins, one by one, from her hair. Her thick knot came undone and tumbled loose around her shoulders.

With a catch in her throat, she whispered his name.

Dark eyes gazed into hers questioningly as a smile curved his lips. "I want you. I think you want me. Do you, Tamsin?"

She sighed and leaned against him as the strength flowed out of her limbs. "I don't know . . . what I want," she lied, but her fingers skimmed the sensual lines of his mouth and the chiseled angles of his cheekbones and battered brow.

She traced the length of his strong nose and the dark bristles of his unshaven cheek. As though she had all the time in the world, she savored the curves of his strong, squared chin and bronzed throat, committing every feature to her forever memory.

"Tamsin." He groaned, and his arm tightened around her. She tilted her face so that her mouth met his.

She needed him, needed to hold him closer and shut out the bad things that had happened. She didn't care if it was just for now. She wouldn't waste this precious gift of time.

His mouth fitted to hers, searing her with a kiss that

told her more than words. She clung to him, crushing him to her, and opening her mouth to draw him in.

His tongue filled her, but it wasn't enough. She could feel his hands seeking, possessing her in a way that no man had done before.

He backed her step by step until they reached the bed. Vaguely, she was aware that he'd pressed her down against the blankets and that his long, horseman's legs were wrapped around hers. She could smell rain and pine needles and woodsmoke, and above all the elusive male odor that was his alone.

She wanted more—had to have more.

"Tamsin."

"Yes."

"You're sure?"

"Yes, damn it," she cried. "Yes!"

He didn't hesitate. With a swiftness that both thrilled and terrified her, he responded to her need with a naked hunger of his own. With a sound more growl than groan, he thrust a hand beneath her skirts. Lean, callused fingers moved up her leg and thigh, scorching her skin with a welcome fire.

She arched under him, spreading her legs for his touch, thrilling to his weight and the hard proof of his arousal pressed against her heated flesh.

His kiss devoured her, and she reveled in the taste and texture of him. Wholeheartedly, she gave as good as she got, kissing him as she'd never kissed another man. But as wonderful as this was, it wasn't enough. She kneaded and caressed his neck and shoulders, caught his lower lip between her teeth, and shuddered at the wild sensations that shattered her reason and dared her to act on her innermost fantasies.

Ash's head moved lower. He kissed and bit her neck and the hollow of her throat, then buried his face between her breasts, all the while stroking and pinching her inner thighs. "Is this what you want?" he asked. "And this?"

"Yes, yes," Tamsin urged him. She'd sensed a smoldering passion in Ash that matched her own hidden desires. She'd imagined what it might be like to have him make love to her, but she hadn't dared to believe it could come true.

Reality was better than her fantasies.

Tamsin was conscious of a throbbing ache and a growing moisture between her legs that both shocked and aroused her. Sex with her husband had been an uncomfortable duty. What was happening here in this lonesome cabin was wild and primal and wonderful.

Ash fumbled with his trousers, and she gasped as his swollen member pressed against her bare thigh. She knew that any decent woman would put a stop to this, but she couldn't. Brazenly, she reached down to touch him, and her eyes widened as she brushed the tumescent length.

He was so hot . . . so alive. All virile male, she thought, and she had never felt so feminine.

Ash groaned again. "I want you wet for me," he murmured. "Wet and silky sweet." Then he probed the source of her need with one long finger.

"You're wicked," she whispered hoarsely. The feel of him inside her was maddening. She bucked against him, feeling herself nearing the delicious brink of some great precipice.

"Am I?" He tantalized her with two fingers and chuckled. "I can be even worse."

She clenched her teeth to keep from crying out with pleasure, and heard the sound of fabric tearing. Then Ash's mouth closed on her breast. "Oh . . ."

Hungrily, he licked and sucked her nipple, worrying at

her breast until she could not contain her growing hunger. "Please," she begged him.

"Please, what? Do you want me to stop?"

"No." She groaned. "Don't stop."

"Tell me what you want me to do, Tamsin," he whispered. "Do you want this?" He pressed himself into her hand, filling it and making bolts of flame sear up her spine.

"Yes, yes," she gasped.

She waited for his thrust, but to her surprise, he braced himself with his hands and lowered his head. She felt the length of his hair brush against the sensitive skin of her inner thigh and she caught her breath. He wouldn't! He didn't mean to—

"Oh!" She dug her fingers into his shoulders.

"You're sweet, Tamsin, sweet as wild honey," he murmured.

Her eyes widened as ripples of tantalizing pleasure rolled through her. "What are . . . you . . . Oh!"

She thrashed her head from side to side, unable to lie still, unable to think. His mouth was on her. His tongue teasing, licking . . . driving her to the point of no return.

He clamped a hand over her mouth to stifle her cry as she reached the peak and tumbled off into nothingness amid a shimmering rainbow of iridescent colors. The earth fell away beneath her as she drifted in delicious waves of rapture.

She hardly realized that he'd turned over onto his back and lifted her so that she was astride him. "Now it's your turn to do the work," he said.

It seemed the most natural thing in the world to settle over him, opening for his deep, full thrust. There was barely an instant of hesitation on her part as she adjusted to the odd but pleasant experience of being in control. Then she moved with him, giving and taking, letting her primeval instincts take control until her passion rose again with an even greater heat.

This time Tamsin held back her climax until Ash reached his. His stifled moan of satisfaction was all she needed to push her over the edge again. Knowing that she had pleased him was an added happiness to her own fulfillment. And this time was no disappointment. She clung to him while her mind spun out into the heavens and her body convulsed with pure physical joy.

For long minutes they lay together, still joined, sheened with sweat and utterly spent. Then he turned on his side so that she curled beside him, fitting perfectly into the curve of his shoulder.

"Is it always like that for you?" she asked.

He chuckled and kissed her lower lip tenderly. "No, but then I've never made love to a Tennessee woman before. I can see what I've been missing." He brushed the tangled hair away from her face. "You're something, Tamsin MacGreggor. With talents like yours, why the hell did you take up a life of crime?"

She was too contented to argue with him. "It wasn't like this with my husband," she said shyly. "I've never been with anyone else."

"This is a hell of a time to discover you like it."

"Are you complaining?"

"Hell, no." He sighed and lifted her hand to his lips. Gently, he kissed her palm and the place at her wrists where her veins showed blue. "Have I ever told you how beautiful you are?"

She averted her eyes. "Don't," she begged him. "Don't say what you don't mean. I know what I am. I'm too big and too tall to—"

"Hush . . ." He covered her mouth with a forefinger. "You've skin like milk where the sun hasn't dusted you with freckles. You've breasts to drive a man to drink, and hips meant to give pleasure."

"My chin is too firm," she replied. "And my mouth—"

"Your mouth is perfect for kissing." To prove his point, he kissed her love-swollen lips. "If you were a lady of fortune, you'd be rich in—"

"But I'm not, Ash," she said, suddenly sounding serious. "I'm a backsliding Methodist, and what we've done will have me on my knees praying for forgiveness, if I live long enough."

He pushed back and studied her rosy cheeks and troubled eyes. "You think what we've done is a sin?"

"Isn't it?"

"Who are we hurting? My wife is dead, and so is your husband. Considering the circumstances, I'd say we've not strayed so far from the path of righteousness."

"Don't make a joke of this," she said. "What we did—what I did, I chose to do. All my life I've tried to follow the teachings of the church. I've fed the poor, and I've tended the sick. Until I came to Colorado, I never stole so much as an apple from someone else's orchard. Now I'm a horse thief and a murderer."

He tensed. "You admit killing Sam Steele?"

"No! Not him," she insisted. "But I did kill an Indian, maybe two. Three if you count the one Dancer stomped on. And now I've just slept with a man not my husband."

He chuckled. "Since the Cheyenne were trying to murder you, I hardly think that counts against you with the Man above."

"But I did sleep with …"

"Honey, we weren't doing much sleeping. Are you sorry?"

She shook her head. "No, I'm not. If I burn in hell for what—"

He silenced her with a kiss. "If taking comfort from each other is a sin, it must be a small one."

"Comfort?" she asked in a small voice. "Was that what it was for you?"

He stroked her hair and raised a lock of it to brush his lips. "Red as a mountain sunset," he murmured. "You're a hard one, Tamsin. You back a man against a rock and give him no place to run."

"It was more than comfort to me."

"And me," he grated. "I still don't trust you as far as I could throw you, but . . ."

"But?"

He chuckled. "But you've made me break my rule about keeping business and personal feeling separate."

"You don't think I'm a soiled dove?"

"Far from it, woman. You couldn't have given me a more precious gift. Under the circumstances, I think even your God would understand."

"He's yours, too," she replied.

"There's small sin and then there's real sin, Tamsin. I think I've seen enough of the bad kind to know the difference."

She exhaled softly. "I hope so."

He pulled her closer, cradling her in his arms.

"Be careful of your wound," she reminded him.

He laughed softly. "Now you think of it?"

She pushed her tangled skirts down over her legs and sat up. "Will we get out of these mountains alive?"

He ran a hand through his damp hair. "I expect to give it my best effort."

"And you're dead set on turning me in to the sheriff at Sweetwater?"

"Afraid so, darlin'."

His feelings for Tamsin were hard to sort out, as complicated as she was. On the one hand, he felt a duty to do what he was being paid for, to take her in. On the other, he felt responsible for her.

He laced his fingers behind his head and leaned back against the pillow. Part of him wanted to believe in her innocence. And another part wanted only to repeat what they'd just done.

"Ash."

"What?"

"Could you just hold me?"

"Sure, darlin'."

"I like the way it feels."

"Me, too."

"I feel safer with your arms around me."

"Good."

"And one more thing," she whispered.

"Yes?"

"Will you try to believe me when I tell you that I haven't done anything wrong . . . that I didn't kill Sam Steele?"

"I'll try," he answered, hoping he hadn't promised more than a reasonable man could give.

Ash lay awake listening to the rain as Tamsin dozed in his arms. The fire had burned down to coals on the hearth and it was dark in the cabin, but he could see lightning flashes through the cracks in the shutter and hear the rumble of thunder moving in from the west.

His side ached where the bullet had plowed along it, but making love to Tamsin had soothed the deep hurt that throbbed in his soul.

He'd never thought to become involved with a woman like Tamsin. Sleeping with one of his suspects hadn't been in his plan.

Not that he had a real plan. His dreams had died with the cooling ashes of the cabin he'd built for Becky. He'd done what he thought he did best—hunt down outlaws and turn them over to the law. That didn't require a long-range course of action. He'd lived day by day, kept sharp by the knowledge that stupidity or a slow gun hand would see him dead before he caught up with Jack Cannon and his remaining brother, Boone.

Once he'd seen justice done, he meant to give up bounty hunting and look for some decent woman and a life that didn't mean looking over his shoulder or listening for the click of a gun hammer in the night.

But he hadn't kept his promise to Becky yet. He still had unfinished business with the Cannons. This was the wrong time and the wrong woman. There were too many complications. It was better if he didn't ponder on it too much . . . if he took what Tamsin offered and was satisfied with tonight.

She whimpered in her sleep and stirred restlessly as a loud growl of thunder rolled down from the mountain peak. Instantly, Ash felt a warm rush of emotion. Wrong time, wrong place, he thought wryly, but she did feel good next to him.

He tightened his embrace and gently kissed the crown of her head. Her hair bore a faint scent of flowers. He wondered how that was possible.

Old memories crowded around him in the darkness as the rain locked them in a private world. He found himself thinking about Becky, but oddly, he had trouble picturing her face. He'd been little more than a boy, years ago, when he'd first laid eyes on her and had fallen hard. Life had changed him since then.

Funny how a man could be attracted to two such different women. They were as different as a rose and a wildflower. Delicate, sweet Becky had been his yellow rose, blooming so long as she was carefully tended and kept safe inside a garden fence. Tamsin was the fireweed, strong and self-sufficient, as beautiful as any cultivated flower and too tough for even a forest fire to destroy.

He'd never forget Becky. She'd always have a special place in his heart, but that part of his life was over. Common sense told him that little Becky wouldn't have been happy with the man he was now.

"Fireweed," he whispered under his breath. Somehow, he had the strangest notion to find a cluster of fireweed and fill Tamsin's arms with it.

Chapter 16

Ash eased out of the low bed, picked up his rifle, wrapped himself in a length of oilcloth, and ventured into the night to relieve himself. Once in the downpour, he circled the cabin looking for any sign of visitors. He didn't see a living thing, hadn't expected to, but old habits died hard.

He was sure that they'd left the Cheyenne behind, but not so certain about Cannon. He had an uneasy gnawing in his gut that the outlaw wasn't too far off. He'd chased Jack for so many years that it seemed as though he'd developed a sixth sense regarding his whereabouts.

He hoped Tamsin would be the key to catching Cannon, but he was torn between his feelings for her and his doubts about her innocence.

Devil take him, he didn't believe Tamsin had murdered Sam Steele in cold blood, but if she killed that Cheyenne, she might have shot the rancher. And regardless of his doubts, he still had to take her in.

He'd chased down enough suspects to know that a man's past, or a woman's, had a way of catching up with them. Tamsin would never find happiness if she couldn't clear her name. California wasn't far enough to run. Sooner or later, a lawman or another bounty hunter would see her face and remember an old wanted poster.

Rather than try to arrest her, he might shoot her down like a rabid dog.

Trouble was, Tamsin wouldn't understand why his way was the only way. His daddy wasn't an educated man, but he was smart. He'd always said that a person couldn't twist and turn the law to suit themselves. Once a man started down that road, he was apt to lose sight of right and wrong.

It would be a hell of a lot easier if he hadn't been born Big Jim Morgan's boy, but it was too late to change that now. His father's sense of right was part of him, and he had to follow that trail whether it was easy or not.

Drenched by the icy rain, Ash dashed back to the cabin. He opened the heavy door to see Tamsin sitting up in bed with a worried expression on her face. "It's the middle of the night," he said, throwing off the oilcloth and shaking himself like a wet dog. "Go back to sleep."

Her eyes were large and frightened. "I woke up and you were gone."

"Just outside."

Damned if she wasn't a fine sight, wearing nothing but a blanket. Her soft Tennessee accent poured over him like warm honey, making him forget the damp chill. If she kept staring at him like that, she'd have him on top of her, making promises he couldn't keep.

"Nature called," he said gruffly, trying to force down the rising ache that rose to tempt him from reason.

What had happened between them was physical, good sex between two lonely people, nothing more.

The argument didn't sit right, and he tried to justify the notion as he threw his makeshift cloak over a chair and went to the hearth to dry off. By the time he'd built up the fire so that the bigger sections of log caught, she was standing beside him, her naked body wrapped in a blanket.

"I was afraid you'd left me," she said, draping another blanket over his shoulders.

"Afraid I'd left you?" He grinned and let his gaze linger on the swell of her breasts beneath the worn patchwork squares. "After chasing you over half the Rockies?"

Her cheeks flushed pink in the firelight, and she stared at the floor. "I thought maybe the Cheyenne war party . . ." She shivered and pulled the blanket tighter around her. "I've never felt such hate before."

"They have reason."

"How can you say that? You killed—"

"I killed them. Yes." He nodded. "I cut a man's throat and shot another to keep them from murdering us. But I've seen more savagery out of whites than Indians. At Sand Creek, the Colorado militiamen crushed children under their horses' hooves. They shot them like rabbits, and—"

"Stop." She raised the blanket to cover her ears. "It's too horrible. I don't want to hear it."

" 'Vermin,' John Chivington called them. The good colonel led seven hundred men with howitzers down on Black Kettle's sleeping village. 'Kill and scalp them all,' John said. 'Little and big. Nits make lice.' Can you imagine how grapeshot cuts through a buffalo hide tepee?"

Tamsin's pale face grew white, but Ash continued, as much for himself as for her.

"The militia destroyed every living thing, dogs, ponies, and infants. The warriors fought all day, soaking the earth with their blood, selling their lives dearly to protect their women and children. And when the last Cheyenne brave fell, Chivington's troops slaughtered the wounded and mutilated the dead."

"No more," she pleaded. "For God's sake, no more."

"I don't imagine the Lord had anything to do with it.

Chivington was a Methodist minister, a hero at Glorieta Pass, during the war. I didn't like John much, but I respected him . . . then. No more. I've always wondered what could make a decent man forget religion when it comes to someone with a different skin color."

"Come back to bed," she urged.

"Yes, ma'am." He went to the door and dropped the heavy wooden bar. "A little damp outside for travelin', but that should discourage unwanted guests."

She lifted the covers for him and slid over so that he could settle into the warm hollow in the mattress. He stretched out his legs and put his arm around her, pulling her against him. She came willingly and laid her face against his chest.

"I guess I sound foolish," she murmured. "When I woke up and you were gone, I thought . . ."

"It's all right, Tamsin. I'm here, and I'm not going to leave you." *Not unless I have a chance to go after Cannon,* he thought.

Why the hell was this so difficult? How was it that being near her, hearing her voice, touching her soft skin, drove him to distraction? She was tough as rawhide. He'd seen her courage in situations that would have had gritty cowboys soiling their chaps. But right now, she seemed as fragile as the pink-and-white-flowered porcelain Aunt Jane used to set the Sunday supper table.

He'd always been afraid to handle those fancy dishes. He hadn't wanted to break one. That's the way he felt about Tamsin at this minute. He wanted to wrap her in goose down and keep her safe . . .

. . . from him as well as from what waited for her in Sweetwater.

She inhaled deeply. "This is such a magnificent country, but it's so hard. The violence . . ."

"There was bloodshed aplenty back in your Tennessee

during the war, wasn't there?" He stroked her hair and massaged the back of her neck and her shoulders until he felt her tension ease. "Even in your little town, you must have heard of neighbors—even family—turning against one another."

"Yes, of course." She shivered and crept closer to him, laying a hand on his chest. "I wanted to get away from all that. I wanted to start over in California. It's a new place, new and clean."

"So is Colorado Territory. You've seen a lot of the bad, but there's good as well. There's nothing so pretty as the sun coming up over the mountains or the smell of the air after a rain."

She caught his hand and brought it to her lips. Tenderly, she kissed each knuckle in turn. "There are golden sunrises in California, I hear. The sun goes down over the ocean. It's never cold there. There are giant trees and valleys knee-deep in grass. My horses—"

"You set a passel of store on those animals."

"I have to. They're all I have left of what was good in my childhood. My home . . . Granddad. Dancer and Fancy are all I have to build a future." Her eyes glistened with emotion. "I raised them from foals, both of them, halter broke them, trained them to saddle."

"You should have taken ship for California or joined a wagon train. Those horses might have cost you your life."

She raised her head and looked into his face. "There are some things worth risking everything for."

Her warm body took the chill from his bones, and he molded his hand to the hollow of her back. Outside the cabin, the rain showed no sign of letting up, and the steady cadence against the shake roof was strangely erotic.

"You're right. There are things worth dying for," he murmured just before he bent and kissed her. Then he asked her the question that weighed heaviest on his mind. "Tell me about Jack Cannon."

She stiffened. "There's nothing to tell."

"Leave that for me to decide. I want to hear it, all of it. No lies, Tamsin. I want the truth, if you can tell it."

"I told you, it was nothing. I was working my way west, staying in this little town in Nebraska, Wheaton. I was a clerk in a general store, very little pay, but there was a clean room in the back of the building where I could sleep. And Mr. Harvey let us eat at noon and six. We could take cheese, crackers, dried fruit, even bread and pies that hadn't sold and were starting to go stale. He didn't charge me, so long as I ate in my quarters and didn't tell his wife."

"What does this have to do with Cannon?"

"He came into the store, and I sold him ammunition and a pair of expensive boots that Mr. Harvey had been trying to get rid of for a year. Jack told me that he was a rancher in town to purchase livestock. He seemed pleasant enough, but I'm no fool. He asked me to have dinner with him, and I refused."

"You refused?"

"Yes. I was a woman alone without friends or connections in the town. I felt that I had to guard my reputation."

"So you didn't let him take you to eat?"

"Not then, not until he'd asked every day for nearly a week. Then he asked me if I was a churchgoing lady. I said that I was, and he suggested we attend services together."

Ash felt a wave of disbelief sweep over him. "You're telling me that Texas Jack Cannon, train robber, thief, and murderer, took you to church?"

"No, he didn't. He stopped at the store on Saturday evening and told me that he couldn't make church. Would I accept his apology and have Sunday night supper with him? We did. He was charming and funny, even a little old-fashioned. He bought my dinner a few more times, and then we went to a church social, and we rode together. My animals needed exercise."

"After-church suppers and apple pie. This sounds better and better."

"You wanted the truth," Tamsin said. "I'm telling you."

"Go on."

"While we were riding, we stopped to water the horses, and he became . . . ungentlemanly. He implied that I had given him reason to expect more than friendship. We argued, and he tore my blouse. I slapped his face. He frightened me, and I drew Granddad's pistol and told him I'd shoot him if he didn't back off. He did, I mounted Dancer, and rode back to town. The next day, when he came to the store to tell me that he was sorry, I wouldn't accept his apology."

"Don't imagine that went down well with Cannon."

"It didn't. He got very quiet, but I knew he was angry. He said that he wasn't used to being refused, and that I'd regret it. That night, I delivered an order to a lady on the far side of town. We talked, and I didn't get back to the store until after dark. Someone had forced their way into my room. Nothing was disturbed, but the latch was broken, and a meadowlark lay on my bed. Its neck was broken.

"I was terrified, and I went to my employers' home and told them what had happened. They laughed and said the cat must have killed the bird, but they let me sleep there. The next morning, I left town. That's it, that's all there was to my association with Jack Cannon."

"You never slept with him?"

"No! What do you think I am?"

"Did you kiss him?"

"No. Yes . . ."

"Yes or no?"

"That's what we argued about. He tried to kiss me. He did kiss me, but I turned away. I wasn't ready for that kind of attention from a man. And I wasn't about to be forced into . . . into trading that for a few suppers."

Ash exhaled softly. "You spin a fine tale, Tamsin. You want me to believe in your complete innocence, yet you defended Cannon soundly enough when I first—"

"I didn't want you prying into my affairs. I was ashamed that I'd been taken in by him. I had no proof that Jack broke into my room. The cat might have killed the meadowlark. And I wasn't sure that he wasn't right, that I had led him on by riding out unchaperoned." She paused. "I can understand why you can't accept my explanation . . . after letting you . . ."

"Us, you mean?"

She nodded. "It wasn't the same with Jack. He's attractive, but . . ."

"He's a sight prettier than me, if my memory serves me well enough."

"He's handsome, but almost too much so. It's still hard for me to believe that a murderer and wanted outlaw would come into town and walk around as though he were an honest citizen."

"But he frightened you."

"Yes, when he kissed me."

"And I don't?"

"Not now," she whispered.

"Maybe you should be afraid of me."

"I don't think so." She sighed. "I don't want to fight with you, Ash. Not tonight. Maybe not ever again. I don't want to think about Jack Cannon or the Cheyenne or even about California. I just want to lie here with you and listen to the rain on the roof."

"Just listen?"

"Talk to me. Tell me about you when you were a child. Before your father died."

"Was murdered."

"Was it all violence? Don't you have any good memories?"

"Once I rode a calf and won ten cents at a barn raising."

"That's better." She closed her eyes. "Hold me, please."

"I can do that."

"Tell me something else. Something warm and happy. Something good that happened to you when you lived with Aunt Jane."

"Hmmm, not school. I didn't like that much. Or church, too much preachin'. Sam Houston."

"Who?"

"Not who. What. Sam Houston was my cat. Aunt Jane gave him to me for Christmas one year. He was so tiny, he could fit in the palm of my hand."

"A kitten? I thought children who grew up to be gun-slingers had wolves for pets. At least a mean dog."

"I like cats. Always have. They're independent."

"What color was Sam Houston?"

"About the shade of your hair. Maybe more orange."

She laughed and traced tiny circles on his bare chest with her fingertips. He cupped her breast with his hand and was rewarded with her sigh of pleasure.

"Keep that up, and you'll wake the dead."

"You mean, we could . . . again? So soon?"

He chuckled and brushed the cleft between her breasts with the tip of his tongue.

"Don't laugh at me," she said. "I didn't know. Once my husband . . . I didn't know a man could . . ." She left the rest unsaid and began to massage his shoulders and neck.

His loins tightened. "A man can do a lot when he's with you." He rubbed his thumb over her swollen nipple and felt her growing arousal.

"I want to make you happy," she murmured. "Tell me what to do."

He groaned as her exploring hand slid down to caress his loins. "You're doing fine on your own," he managed.

"Make love to me again."

She twisted so that she was sitting upright on top of him. Blood pounded in his head. "Woman," he groaned.

She moved slowly, sensually, teasing him, heating the part of him that was already throbbing with need.

He wanted to tell her that he cared about her, that he believed her, but the words stuck in his throat. Instead, he let his hands and willing body speak for him. Touching her, feeling her body against his filled him with hot urgency.

"Tamsin . . . Tamsin . . ."

"I'm here," she replied. "I'm here for you." She slanted her mouth against his, scorching his flesh with a heated joining that left him breathless and aching.

Arching her back, she traced the outline of his nipples with her tongue, laving each one, then nipping at it until small bursts of pleasure rocketed through his veins.

"How do you want it?" he asked her. "Quick or slow?"

She laughed softly and nibbled on his left earlobe. "Slowly," she teased. "Slow and sweet."

"Witch."

Sweat broke out on his forehead as he fought to control his response, giving her what she'd demanded, loving her with lazy deliberate caresses. And all the while she moved sensually against him, whispering and stroking his most sensitive spots, prolonging the exquisite pleasure until nature could no longer be denied.

Later Ash fell asleep and Tamsin lay awake in his arms

still trembling inwardly with an excitement she never dreamed existed. She knew that what she was feeling had to be far more than a physical attraction.

Foolish, impossible thoughts tumbled in her head. She wondered what it would be like to bear Ash's child, to grow old with him. She could almost picture the two of them sitting on a porch in California in the twilight, drinking lemonade, while their grandchildren chased lightning bugs in the garden.

Did they have fireflies on the west coast? Or was that another illusion, as far from reality as her horse farm? Ash had taken what was offered. They had not spoken of love or marriage, and she was worse than a fool if she expected more.

Her jaw tightened. Stubbornness had gotten her this far. She'd find a way to get to California, and she'd find someone like Ash to love her. She'd take her wedding vows in a church with flowers growing around the door, and she'd have her horses and her babies. Somehow . . . somehow she'd make her dreams come true.

Henry Steele stood by the window of his late brother's bedroom and stared at the flashes of lightning on the western horizon. A small storm had passed over earlier in the evening, dropping a little rain on the pastures. They needed more water. It had been a mild winter and a dry spring. If runoff from the mountains was less than usual, the Lazy S stood to lose livestock.

That didn't sit well with Henry, especially since he'd been left Sam's entire estate in a will made years before Sam and Sarah had married. Even if he decided to sell the ranch and move to St. Louis as Sarah wanted him to, drought would bring the asking price of the land way down.

Throwing a robe over his naked torso, Henry walked

quietly out into the hallway, taking care not to wake Sarah. The next door led to another bedroom and beyond that a parlor that had also served as Sam's ranch office. He went in, struck a match, and lit the painted globe lamp on the oak desk.

A stubbed-out cigar lay discarded in an ashtray. Henry lit that from the lamp wick and rested his reading glasses on his nose. Settling onto a high-backed chair, he picked up the copy of the *Rocky Mountain News* and began to reread the headline story about the robbery and murders committed by Texas Jack Cannon and his gang of cutthroats. He'd gotten to the second page when he heard the door creak and glanced up.

Sarah stood in the doorway wearing a white linen gown with a high neck and long embroidered sleeves. "It's late, Henry," she said. "Why are you up?"

"I couldn't sleep. I'm sorry, did I disturb you when I got up?"

"Haven't you read enough about those awful outlaws?" She came to him and put her arms around his neck. "I can't sleep alone. I keep having nightmares about Sam . . . about his death."

"You must think of your health, dear . . . yours and our son's. You'll catch your death of cold walking around the house in bare feet."

"I hate this house. I hate the ugly floors and the brown walls. When are you going to take me away, Henry? You promised."

He patted her back. "I didn't promise, Sarah. I said I'd think about it. This ranch is a profitable business. If we do sell, and I say 'if,' it will take time to find the right buyer."

"I know it's crazy, but when I got up, I forgot that he was dead. He used to come in here at night and work on his accounts." She shuddered. "I smelled the cigar smoke, and I thought . . ."

"You thought I was Sam."

"Yes, no . . ." She sighed and turned away to stare out the window. "I'm glad he left the ranch to you, Henry. He lied to me about it. He did. He told me that he'd changed his will two years ago, that he'd made me his beneficiary. But I don't care. I never wanted any of it. I hate cows. They're smelly, horrible beasts. I need to be around people and shops. My own church. Parties and socials. Do you have any idea how long it's been since I've been to a dance?"

"Sam loved this ranch. All the more reason to be cautious with its disposal. I don't know why my brother didn't leave everything to you, but that doesn't matter, my dear. It will be ours, whether we sell or keep it. Fifty-fifty, a legacy for our child."

She lifted a lace handkerchief to her mouth. "Our child will never set foot on this land if I have anything to say about it." She twisted the bit of cloth. "Take me away, please. I can't stand it here. I won't stay here."

"You were happy here once."

"No." She shook her head. "Never. I was never happy here." She turned and looked at him. "I knew I'd made a mistake from the first days of our marriage. Sam changed after the wedding."

Henry scoffed. "Sam didn't change. He was always a son of a bitch. He was good at covering it, when he wanted to."

"If you won't come with me, I'll go to St. Louis alone. I want to have my confinement there."

"Not yet," he said firmly, crossing the room to take her in his arms. "As soon as Morgan brings back the Mac-Greggor woman, as soon as she's tried and found guilty, then we'll go."

"Can't you forget her?" Sarah demanded. "Can't you just let it go?"

"It will follow us. We need to close this part of our lives first. Then I'll take you wherever you want to go. And we'll be married as soon as a decent interval has passed."

"You swear it, Henry. You promise?"

"Absolutely, Sarah. As soon as Tamsin MacGreggor hangs for my brother's murder, we'll leave Sweetwater together."

"All right," she agreed. "I'll wait a little while longer. But if your bounty hunter doesn't find her, then I'm going. Do you understand? I will not have our baby born here in the shadow of Sam's ghost."

"We'll go as soon as the matter is settled, Sarah. We owe that much to my brother. You know what the Bible says: 'An eye for a eye.' We can't let the guilty woman go unpunished."

"You're right, I suppose," she murmured. But her eyes glistened in the lamplight, and a single tear rolled down her pale cheek.

Chapter 17

Gunfire blasted through the heavy night fog as a crowd of shouting, howling men and women stormed the Sweetwater jail. "Bring her out!" Judge Steele shouted as he edged his horse to the head of the throng. "Bring out the murdering back shooter!"

"Hang her!" shrieked a slovenly saloon wench waving a torch.

"Yes!" cried the black-veiled widow from the seat of a buggy. "She murdered my husband! Give her hemp justice!"

Illuminated by the yellow glow of a kerosene lantern, Walker stepped out onto the stoop in front of the jail, a shotgun cradled in his arm. "Tamsin MacGreggor's my prisoner," he bellowed. "Do you want her?"

"Yes!"

"Hand her over!"

"Hand over the murdering whore!"

Laughing, Walker yanked off his tin star and tossed it into the dirt. "Take her!"

As he stared in horror at the mob, unable to move, Ash heard Tamsin scream. "No! No!" he tried to say, but the words wouldn't come. His throat was dry and aching, as though a rope were tightening around it.

Two cowboys appeared in the doorway with Tamsin between them. Her calico dress was torn down the front,

*exposing her breasts. Her face was bruised, her mouth
bleeding.*

"Ash!" she cried. "Ash, help me!"

*Henry Steele threw a rope over her head and kicked his
mount. Tamsin tried to grab the rope, but she was yanked
off the edge of the wooden walkway into the street. She
screamed again as Steele spurred his horse and dragged
her down the street toward the gallows.*

*"No!" Ash said, struggling against the bonds that held
him. "No! She's innocent."*

*Somehow, he reached the foot of the steps. Above him, a
noose swayed in the fog.*

"Hanged by the neck until dead!" Henry Steele said.

"Until dead," echoed the mob.

*"Ash . . ." Tamsin whimpered as the judge settled the
noose around her neck and pulled a black hood over her
face. For the barest instant, her frightened gaze met his.
And then he saw nothing but blackness.*

*Ash felt cold sweat running down him as the trapdoor
snapped open and the crowd roared.*

He felt himself fall and jerk upright. He blinked the
sweat from his eyes. His heart pounded against his chest
wall. He sucked in air as though he were drowning.

Dazed, he looked around. It was pitch-black, and it took
him a few seconds to realize that he was still in Jacob's
cabin with Tamsin sleeping peacefully beside him.

"Woman, what have you done to me?" he whispered.

Devil take him, he didn't care if she had murdered
Sam Steele. All he wanted to do was take her away and
protect her. He tightened his arm around her, telling
himself that he'd tear up her arrest warrant, ride south to
Mexico, go anywhere so that they could be together.

But even as he formed the silent vow in his heart, he
realized he couldn't keep it. He knew only one code, his

daddy's. He had to live his life in the way he'd been raised, or there'd be no peace for him, ever.

"What's wrong?" Tamsin asked sleepily.

He looked down at her, wanting nothing more than to tell her that she'd won, but the words wouldn't come. "Nothing, hon, go back to sleep."

"The rain's stopped, hasn't it?"

"Yeah, the rain's stopped."

"What now?"

"We wait until the ground dries; then I take you back to Sweetwater for trial."

"Just like that?" The quaver in her voice turned him to jelly. "As though we hadn't . . ."

"No, darlin', not just like that." He kissed the crown of her head, inhaling the sweet, clean scent of her hair. "I'm going to get you a lawyer," he promised. "The best damn lawyer west of the Mississippi. And I'm going to stand with you, every step of the way until we get through this."

She made a small sound of distress. "All right, Ash. Have it your way. I'm just too tired to fight you anymore."

"I won't let you down," he promised.

"You'd better not."

A horse whinnied, and Ash reached for his gun.

"Hello the cabin!" a voice called from outside.

Tamsin rose and began to pull on her clothing as Ash motioned her to stay clear of the door.

"Be ye friend or foe?" the stranger demanded.

Ash lowered his weapon. "Jacob, you old grizzly, is that you?"

"And who else would it be in the middle of the night? Who be you, pilgrim? God-fearing or one of the wicked?"

"Not as wicked as you," Ash shouted back. "I'm opening the door. Don't shoot me." He glanced back at Tamsin to be certain she was decent. She'd given up the attempt to dress and had covered herself with a blanket.

"Ash Morgan! You son of a polecat! What are you doin' up this way?" the buckskin-clad trader demanded as he ducked his head to enter the cabin. "And not alone, I see." He snatched off a shapeless hat decorated with a beaded hatband and an eagle feather. "Evenin' ma'am."

She blushed. "How do you do, Mr. . . . Mr. . . ."

"Jacob will do, ma'am. Proud to make your acquaintance." He leaned a Hawkin rifle against the wall and took Ash's hand. "Good to see you, son."

"And you, Jacob," Ash replied. "This is Tamsin Mac-Greggor. We had a run-in with a Cheyenne war party a few days back and came by to take advantage of your hospitality."

"Did ye, now? I heard some bunch of young bucks was liftin' hair around here. Glad it wasn't yours."

"Or yours," Ash said. "Is your lady with you?"

"Land 'o mercy, no. Had to haul her south to visit her people. She's in the family way, and nothin' would do but what I take her to her mother until the mite gets here. To tell the truth, son, I'm thinkin' of movin' my whole operation south. Utes gone, Cheyenne turned hateful, and white folks got no patience with an old-timer like me."

"Hungry?" Ash asked him. "We've got some stew and biscuits left." Ash glanced back at Tamsin. "You may as well go back to sleep. If I know Jacob, he'll have me up until dawn talking."

"I just might have a bite," Jacob agreed. "Nothin' like a bowl of hot stew, a little Taos lightning, and good company."

"I'm sure this is your bed," Tamsin said. "I can—"

"No." Jacob scratched his beard. "I can sleep when you folks have rid on. Me and Ash haven't swapped stories in what—nigh on to a year?"

"At least." Ash pushed the kettle over the coals and

stirred the pot with a long-handled iron spoon. I should offer congratulations on being a father."

Jacob grinned and settled cross-legged on the floor. He pulled off his high moccasins and warmed his feet at the fire. "Had to marry her, all legal like. Times are changin', boy. Used to be a man could do what he wanted in these mountains, long as he watched his back. No more. Civilized folk movin' in. It will be tough enough on that mite of mine, being half-Indian, without being born on the wrong side of the blanket."

"She deserves marriage, to put up with you," Ash said.

"Yep, yep, that she does." The mountain man took a long-stemmed pipe and tamped it full of tobacco, then lit it and took a long, slow puff. "Talked to a mule skinner, south of here. He claimed his partner was shot and two horses stolen last Wednesday. Says he saw five gunhands. Described one of the shooters as Texas Jack Cannon down to the gray horse and fancy boots."

"How did he say he lived to tell of it?"

"Claims he was in the woods, taking a crap, when he heard the shootin'. Crept up, seen the odds, and laid low." Jacob grimaced. "Can't vouch for the mule skinner. Never seed him afore. He might of got drunk and killed his partner hisself. But I remember you had a special dis-likin' for Jack."

"I was thinking of riding down to Leon Cannon's place. Is he still alive, do you know?"

"Haven't heard of him dead. 'Course, him being Jack's uncle, Leon ain't got too many friends in these hills. It ain't like he has neighbors in for Sunday dinner."

"I wanted to take a look at the house and see if Jack was layin' low there, but—"

"But you didn't want to drag Miss Tamsin into a beehive?"

"What are you talking about?" she demanded. "Drag me where?"

"Nothing," Ash said. "Go to sleep." Actually, he'd been planning to take her to Leon's cabin and use her as bait. Now he'd changed his mind. If she was lying about Jack, he didn't want to know it. "Will you be here for a few days, Jacob?"

"Want to leave the little lady in my care while you have a look-see?"

"No one's leaving me anywhere!"

Ash dipped stew into a clean bowl and handed it to Jacob. "She will be trouble, I promise you. She's as tricky as a Mississippi gambler. Turn your back on her and she'd hit you over the head with a chunk of wood."

"You lying weasel!" Tamsin cried. "If you leave me here, I won't be here when you get back."

"I'll tend her for you, boy, but if she murders me, you owe me a Christian burial." Jacob took another puff on the pipe and grinned. "And digging a grave in these rocks ain't a chore to be sneezed at."

Thirty miles of hard riding brought Ash to a ridge overlooking a two-story log house and a ramshackle barn. Years before the war, Texas Jack's uncle, Leon Cannon, had built this place.

The word was that Jack, Vernon, and Boone had been raised near San Antonio by an aunt and uncle after Comanches wiped out the rest of the family. Leon came to Colorado after he'd stolen so many of his neighbors' cattle that they banded together and set a price on his head.

The place didn't look lived in to Ash. Maybe Leon was dead or had moved on. The cabin roof had patches on it and the barn leaned heavily to one side, but the corral looked in good shape. If Jack Cannon had a home this side of hell, Leon's old place was it to Ash's way of thinking.

Ash had hoped that Jack and his boys might be hiding out here after all the excitement they'd caused in Nebraska. But it seemed Ash had had a long ride for nothing. No smoke came from the chimney, and the weeds around the back door were waist high.

He'd been careful not to leave fresh signs of his own. He'd crept near enough to water Shiloh and fill a canteen from the spring a few hundred yards behind the house. Then he'd climbed up on the roof and covered the chimney hole with sticks and boards. Finally, he'd backtracked, hidden his horse in a gully, and climbed up here to this overlook to consider whether he'd guessed wrong again.

If Jack Cannon wasn't here, he could be anywhere from Kansas City to Mexico. He'd hoped for a little luck. Finding the outlaw, capturing or killing him, would have made explaining to Tamsin why he'd left her at Jacob's cabin a lot easier.

He was sure that she'd be safe with Jacob until he could get back to her. Whether she'd understand why he had to ride off on a hunch was something else. He'd chased Cannon so long that he wondered sometimes what his life would consist of once he caught him.

And he would find Jack. It was just a matter of time. Which of them killed the other one would be the toss of a coin. The outlaw was a crack shot, and he was smart. Ash only hoped he was smarter.

Ash stretched his legs and rubbed at the healing bullet wound. Dusk had fallen. Far off to the west a coyote howled at the moon. Other than crickets and the occasional hoot of an owl, it was as quiet as a Quaker funeral.

His belly rumbled, reminding him that he hadn't eaten since noon. There was bread and dried meat in one of his saddlebags, but going down to where Shiloh was tied would mean leaving his lookout, and he wasn't ready to chance that yet.

He took a sip of warm water from his canteen. It tasted tinny, but it was wet. Most folks thought that a bounty hunter's life was exciting, one chase after another. Truth was, a lot of what he'd done these past years was to sit and wait. It developed a man's patience.

Tonight that quality would be put to the test.

"Patience, Boone," Jack Cannon advised his older brother. "You'll never get ahead if you don't learn that. We don't want to be the first ones in. The vault may not be open yet." He tipped his hat to an elderly woman walking by. "Morning, ma'am."

"I don't like standin' around, is all," Boone replied, tugging at his starched shirt collar. "And I don't like wearin' these fancy duds."

"Clothes make the gentleman. You walk in the Goldsborough Trust in dirty work clothes and scuffed boots and already they're suspicious. What's an owlhoot like that doin' in our bank? Maybe he's up to no good."

"No need to talk to me like an idjit. That crap gets old. If we wasn't blood kin, I'd of put you in the ground a long time ago."

Jack smiled and ignored Boone's insult. He had no doubts about whether or not his brother could be trusted. There were just the two of them left, and Boone felt the same way about family as he did. They were a team. Boone might be woolly around the edges, but Boone would walk through hellfire and pull the devil's tail if Jack said so.

Two horsemen rode slowly into town and reined in across the street from the bank. Billy dismounted and pretended to check his pony's left foreleg while Tom looked on.

Jack could just see the brim of Carlos's hat above the false front of the blacksmith's shop. The big Texan was too slow on the ground, but put him on a high spot with a clear shooting range, and Carlos was worth any three men with a rifle.

Jack hoped Goldsborough's bank wouldn't be a disappointment. He'd read an article in the Wheaton newspaper about the growth of the new Colorado town, but the dirt streets were nigh on to deserted this morning. The door to the saloon was still shuttered, and only a half dozen customers had gone in and out of the general store. He'd seen an old prospector with a mule, two cowboys, and the blacksmith.

Billy glanced at him anxiously. It was time. If he held off much longer, the boys would begin to get edgy. Jack nudged Boone and walked across the street and into the bank.

He paused just inside the door, letting his eyes get accustomed to the shadowy light after the bright sun outside. The main room was small. One corner of the building had been partitioned off to make an office for the manager. The metal safe was built in to the back wall, and it stood open.

"Good morning, sir," a mustached teller called. "Can I help you?"

"Yes, indeed," Jack said. "I'd like to speak to the manager about opening an account here."

The clerk hurried forward. "I can help you with that."

"No, I have a large sum to deposit."

"Mr. Dresser! A customer to see you, sir!"

A portly, balding man appeared in the office doorway. "I'm Mr. Dresser, the bank manager. Can I help you?"

"You can," Jack said. Boone whipped a sawed-off

shotgun from under his coat and pointed it at the bald man. Smiling, Jack opened his leather satchel. "We've changed our minds, gentlemen. We want to make a withdrawal."

Billy rushed in from the street with his forty-five drawn and ready. "Street's clear," he said.

"Grab a handful of clouds!" Boone ordered.

The clerk blubbered and reached for the sky. Dresser's face turned red, and he glanced back toward his open office door.

"Now." Jack didn't raise his voice. Shouting made Boone nervous, and bad things happened when Boone got spooked.

"Robbery!" Dresser yelled. "Get out, Mrs. Rivers! Run!"

Jack threw Boone a warning glance, but it was too late. Boone's shotgun roared, deafening them and cutting down the manager in the expensive suit.

A woman screamed.

"Damn it all. Didn't I tell you not to go and do that," Jack said. He pushed past the trembling clerk and began to scoop money off the vault shelf as Billy plunged into the dead man's office and dragged out a heavily rouged woman by the hair.

"Let me go," she wailed.

"Please." The teller's eyes were big, and he was sweating. "Here. Take my wallet," he began as he reached inside his coat. "Take the money and—"

Boone's second barrel silenced him.

Jack began to swear as he grabbed the last of the bills and started for the door. Billy put his pistol to the female's head, and Jack slapped it away. "Bring her along," he ordered. "We may need her."

Outside, the horses were waiting, and Tom was already in the saddle, eyes scanning the street for trouble. A rifle fired from inside the saloon as someone took a shot at them through the window. Glass shattered, but the slug went wild.

A small man came out of an alley, both pistols blazing. Bullets flew around Jack's head like angry bees. Then Carlos's rifle cracked, and the shooter toppled facedown.

Billy tossed the shrieking hostage in the red dress over his saddle horn and swung up on his horse. Dust rose as Tom spurred his pinto down the street with Jack and Boone right behind him.

At the first corner, they turned left and circled to meet Carlos. They were out of Goldsborough before half the citizens dared to show their faces.

A mile away, Jack signaled a halt. "Split up. We'll meet where I told you tomorrow night."

"What about her?" Billy demanded, shoving his sobbing captive onto the ground. "Want me to finish her off now?"

Jack looked at his brother. "Boone? What do you think?"

"No!" the woman moaned. "Don't kill me."

"She ain't nothin' but a whore," Boone said.

Jack glanced down at her long legs and low-cut dress. Her scarlet cheeks and too yellow hair proclaimed her trade. "Are you?" he demanded.

"Yes, yes. I am." She sobbed. "Don't hurt me. I'll do anything you want."

"What were you doing in a bank so early in the morning?"

"Mr. Dresser was . . . was a customer," she gasped. "He was a regular every Tuesday morning."

Boone laughed. "Got his self blowed away for you, didn't he, bitch?"

Billy slid a pistol from his holster. "She seen our faces, Jack. What's your rule? No witnesses."

The woman covered her eyes and sobbed hysterically.

Jack shrugged and looked at his brother. "Up to you."

"Hell, let's take her," Boone replied. "We can always kill her tomorrow."

Jack smiled. "My thoughts exactly. You keep stretchin' that brain of yours, and there's hope for you yet, big brother."

Chapter 18

When Ash appeared at Jacob's cabin four days after he'd left her, Tamsin didn't know whether to kiss him or push him off the cliff. "Damn you," she shouted at him. "Damn you! I thought you were dead. I wish you were dead."

Ash grinned at Jacob. "Told you what she was like."

The trader chuckled. "Spoke the truth, too. Thought I'd have to chain her to a tree to keep her here. 'Course I'm use to that. My woman's either lovin' me or tryin' to kill me."

Ash went to the spring and splashed cool water over his face and head, then drank deeply.

"Well?" Tamsin demanded. "Did you catch your outlaw?"

Ash shook his head. "Didn't see hide nor hair of him."

Jacob drew a long puff on his pipe. "Some days is like that, son. Reckon you had a long ride for nothin'."

"At least I found out where they weren't."

Jacob laughed. "Truth to that, too."

Ash and Tamsin rode away from Jacob's cabin the following day. The horses were rested and full of ginger as they rode east down the mountain. They found a stream and followed it until dark. Ash was afraid to risk a fire, so they ate cold rations.

It was an uneasy night. Tamsin dozed fitfully in his arms, often tossing and crying out. Once, she woke, soaked with sweat and trembling, but couldn't remember what had frightened her. And despite his fatigue, Ash snapped awake at every rustle of brush or call of a night bird.

Morning broke soft and misty. They ate and were in the saddle in minutes. They drove the horses hard all that day and the next, stopping only to skin and dress a deer that he shot in midafternoon.

That night, Ash was too restless to sleep. The hair on the back of his neck prickled, and his skin stretched drum tight over his body. Once, he thought he heard a cougar cough, but it was far off and he couldn't be certain enough to worry Tamsin about it.

Ash was concerned about her. She didn't complain, but dark shadows formed under her eyes, and she seemed unnaturally subdued. The long days in the saddle sapped strength from a man, let alone a woman, and he knew she was tired. But he wouldn't rest easy until he'd put the wilderness behind them, and they reached the white settlements.

Late the following afternoon, Ash called a halt at the sulfur springs where Tamsin had stolen his supplies. "We both could use a hot bath and some rest," he said. "The horses need a day or two to graze. They're getting thin."

Tamsin wrinkled her nose as she stared at the rising columns of steam that dotted the rocky meadow. "You expect me to wash in that scalding water?"

He laughed. "It's not that hot. You'll love it, I promise."

Tamsin looked doubtful.

"Think of the horses. Their feet are sore. Fancy threw that shoe this morning." The animals were bone weary. Of the five, the stallion seemed the strongest. Despite what he'd said about the thoroughbreds not being able to take rough country, Dancer had thrived on the high game trails and stony ground. "Suit yourself, woman," Ash said with what he hoped was an endearing grin. "But I intend to scrub myself to some semblance of a human being."

"Meaning I'm not?"

He shrugged.

Once the animals were unsaddled and hobbled to graze, Ash led Tamsin across a sloping green field strewn with multicolored wildflowers: purple prairie smoke, pink and white cat's paws, brown-eyed Susans, and golden-tinged broadleaf yucca. They circled a half-dozen rock outcrops and bubbling springs to reach a larger pool near the edge of the pine forest. Here the mineral water was clear enough for them to see the clean sandy bottom and the natural stone ledge along one side that formed a perfect bench.

Tamsin felt the blood rush into her cheeks as Ash stripped and lowered himself in. As the sulfur water rose over his legs and hips, he groaned with pleasure. He closed his eyes, lay on his back, and let himself float.

"You expect me to take off my clothes and swim stark naked?" A true Tennessee lady would have refused to join him in such a shocking venture. But it was hard to re-member what a Methodist girl should do when a man like Ash Morgan wore nothing but a self-satisfied smile.

He opened one eye and grinned devilishly at her. "Is there anything I've haven't seen, darlin'?"

"I guess not." She chuckled. He was right, she thought. After what they'd been through, there was no need for false modesty.

And Ash was a stirring sight with his coal black hair floating around him, and his shoulders as wide as a farrier's.

She loved him, she realized. She loved this beautiful,

dangerous man who wanted to take her back to face a hangman's noose. But how far could she trust him? And how long before he ran off on her again?

Ash had promised that they'd camp here tonight. She'd be a bigger fool than she was to give up what he was offering her here and now because of what might happen tomorrow.

"Are you coming in, or are you chicken?"

"We'll see who's chicken." Quickly, she pulled off her clothing and leaped in.

The water closed over her head, not icy cold like all the creeks she'd bathed in for the last few weeks, but deliciously warm. "Oh," she sighed. It was heaven. "I thought it would be boiling." Reaching down, she picked up a handful of sand and began to scrub away the sweat and grime.

"Some of the pools are," Ash said, "but this one has two springs feeding it, one mineral, and another surface water. That keeps the temperature from getting too warm."

"It's perfect," she answered. "Perfect." When every inch of her skin that she could reach was pink and glowing, she rinsed her hair over and over again. "All I need is soap for my hair."

"I can fix that," Ash offered. He climbed out of the pool and walked a short distance away to pull up several flowering plants by the roots. "These are yucca," he explained when he returned and began to crush the roots on a rock. "Native shampoo and soap in one."

When she looked hesitant, he beckoned her closer.

"Let me," he said. She jumped in over her head and let him rub the sudsing plant material into her tresses. "It feels good," she murmured. What felt better was Ash's strong fingers massaging her scalp, lathering, and rubbing her hair, her neck, then her shoulders, breasts, and belly. And all the while he washed, his dark eyes never ceased to caress her.

Somehow, once he'd rinsed out the shampoo, it seemed only fair that she do the same for him. Her initial shyness faded away as they laughed and touched and swam together beneath the vast blue Colorado sky.

She had known from the first moment Ash entered the water that he wanted to make love to her. She'd expected him to kiss her and pull her down under the soothing water. But she'd not guessed at how the bright sunlight would add fuel to her desire.

One kiss and she was lost. The second . . . oh, the second kiss . . . They clung together, rolling underwater, embracing, wrapping arms and legs around each other, then rising to catch a breath and begin all over again.

Something about the water and the sunshine and the dangers that they'd lived through in the past few days drove her to a height of passion she'd not realized possible. She wanted to run her hands over his shoulders, neck, and chest, and down over his flat belly to tangle in the mat of hair below. She wanted to feel the power in his length and breadth. She wanted to taste him and give him the rapture he'd shown her.

And deep inside, she knew that this would be the last time. She'd given him her word to turn herself in, but with her life in the balance, what difference did one more lie make?

I'll love you now, she thought with bittersweet determination. But later . . . later, Ash, my glorious man, I'll do whatever I have to do to survive.

Ash was not content to let her do all the work. He gave as good as he got, and finally, when she'd lost all sense of time and place, they came together in the way that men and women have since the beginning of the world.

I want to remember every touch and every kiss, Tamsin thought when she lay floating in the water wrapped in his arms. With a contented sigh, she opened her eyes and stared into his face.

I think I'm in love with you, Ash, she thought. I hope you never forget me.

"Why that worried look, darlin'? I said I'd take care of you, and I will. My lawyer is the best. No one is going to hang you. And . . ." His dark eyes narrowed. "After I finish what I have to do, I want . . ." He shook his head. "I can't make you any promises, Tamsin. Not yet."

"I've never asked you for any," she said, but the hurt she felt kept her from falling under his spell again.

"You'll just have to trust me."

"I do, Ash," she lied. "I have to."

He kissed her again. "Hungry?"

"Always."

"I'll take care of that."

She swam over to the underwater slab of rock and sat on it while Ash dressed and went to see about dinner. The warm bubbling spring eased her sore muscles and drained away her fatigue, but nothing could heal the ache in her heart.

All her life she'd dreamed of a strong, loving man like Ash. And now that she'd found him, she knew that for her, there'd never be another.

She didn't know if it was her imagination, but here in this magical pool, at the moment of fulfillment, she'd felt a spark of life. She hoped they'd created a child today. Then she'd have a piece of him to hold close and cherish forever. And if it was true, that was all the more reason she had to make certain that she didn't die for another man's crime.

If she was pregnant, Atwood MacGreggor would do more for her dead than he ever had alive. He'd provide a name and respectability for Ash's babe. No one needed to know when she had been widowed. She'd concoct a sad tale of her husband's demise on the journey to California. Something courageous would do nicely, so that her son or daughter would have proud memories.

As I will, she thought. No matter what happens, I'll always cherish Ash's memory and this time we had together.

Her reverie was broken by his return with firewood and a handful of false Solomon's seal, a lilylike flower that grew along the edge of the wood. Tamsin recognized the plant as one Ash had picked before. The leaves and shoots were not unpleasant and made a welcome addition to the venison.

She started to climb out of the water, and he waved her back. "No, stay where you are," he ordered. "I'm preparing this meal. Grilled deer steaks, green stuff, and—" Dramatically, he produced a dead bird resembling a partridge. "Roast chicken!"

She laughed. "That's close enough, I suppose, but don't expect me to pluck feathers. That's one job I hate worse than chopping their heads off."

He raised a dark eyebrow suspiciously. "I doubt you chopped many chickens—with all those servants around the plantation."

"It wasn't a plantation. I lived on a horse farm." She sighed. "Yes, the cook did do the chopping and the scalding. But I didn't like watching."

He chuckled. "Sounds more like it."

"I didn't hear gunfire. How did you acquire our main course?"

Ash grinned. "For your information, Mrs. MacGreggor, I am the best stone thrower west of Austin. I once threw a stone that killed a grizzly bear, bounced off the bear's skull, and brought down an antelope, then stunned the biggest trout—"

"The biggest liar, more likely," she teased. Pushing her sorrow to the farthest corner of her mind, she resolved to make the most of this precious time together. She'd not spoil it for either of them by sulking over things that couldn't be changed. "Will you bake buttermilk biscuits to go with that chicken?" she teased him. "And I'd dearly like fresh churned butter, strawberries, and—"

"Strawberries, I can do. I saw some ripe ones back near where the horses are grazing. Just let me get the fire going and—"

"I'll build the fire. You prepare the bird and pick the berries," she replied. "If I stay in here any longer, I'll shrivel up and float away." She rose and held out her hand to him.

Ash helped her up the bank. "Hmmm," he said with an admiring gaze. "Maybe I'm not as hungry as I thought." He bent and kissed her. "Have you ever made love in a berry patch?"

"No." She laughed. Then he whispered something so wicked in her ear that she gave him a small shove. "Ash Morgan! Wherever did you . . ."

He dropped the bird and swung her up into his arms. "Best try it before you complain," he said. He kissed her again, and this time she forgot everything but the sweet sensation of his lips against hers, and her naked breasts pressed so tightly against him that she could feel the beating of his heart.

It was dark before they shared the partridge and the rest of the meal. Then, when they couldn't eat another bite, they swam again in the mineral pool to wash off the sticky remains of crushed strawberries. Afterward, as they dried off, Ash doused the fire.

"By daylight, it's safe," he explained. "Any hostiles who saw the smoke would assume it was steam from the hot springs. But in the dark, the flames will show a long way. I'm sure that Buffalo Horn's friends have given up on us and returned to their camp, but they aren't the only hostiles in these mountains. There's no sense in taking unnecessary chances."

I can't understand you, Tamsin wanted to say. You insist you want to protect me from the Indians, but you're willing to turn me over to a crooked sheriff and a murdering judge.

She swallowed the lump in her throat. Tonight, she'd have to make her move. Somehow, she'd escape Ash. She couldn't go back toward the Cheyenne, so she'd have to backtrack, ride near Sweetwater, and take another route. She might even have to go north and join one of the wagon trains moving west.

"Ready for bed?" he asked her as he kicked dirt over the coals.

"Ready for sleep. I think I could—"

Without warning, Ash's hand closed around her arm. "Good. Then you won't mind if I take a few simple precautions to make sure you don't do to me what you've done before."

"What? Let go of me!" she protested as Ash brought her wrists together at her waist and tied them tightly with a length of rawhide.

"No! You can't!" Fury boiled up inside her, and she kicked at his shins. "I won't let you!"

Dancer stamped his feet and snorted in alarm. Another of the animals whinnied nervously.

"Darlin', this hurts me worse than it hurts you," Ash said.

"You don't trust me." Trembling with anger, she sucked in ragged gulps of breath.

He laughed. "Should I?" With one motion, he knocked

her legs out from under her, caught her before she hit the ground, and pinned her feet.

"No! No! You can't do this to me!"

Ash wrapped another cord around her ankles. "I just want to make certain you're here to eat the breakfast I'm going to cook for you in the morning."

"Damn you! You tricked me!" Tears of anger ran down her cheeks. "You made love to me while all the time you—"

A ferocious roar ripped through Tamsin's protest. From the corner of her eye, she saw a green-eyed shadow lunge out of the trees. "Cougar!" she screamed at Ash. "Cougar!"

Chapter 19

Ash leapt for his gun. Tamsin couldn't see him, but she knew that's what he was doing. He wouldn't leave her. Unarmed, he stood no chance against the slashing claws and teeth of an enraged cougar. Bound and helpless, she couldn't fight back. She couldn't even run.

If he didn't get to his weapon, they were finished.

Strangely, in the split second it took to recognize the mountain lion's roar and realize that the cat was attacking them, Tamsin's fear burned away, leaving her with the taste of Ash's mouth and his clean scent imprinted on her mind. Ash, she thought. Oh, Ash, I do love you.

Cool certainty and the knowledge that she was about to die settled over her with the calm of an evening mist. It seemed to her that the horses' terrified whinnies and the puma's scream faded until all she could hear was the rustle of wind through the trees and the gurgle of the spring.

The puma snarled again, so close that Tamsin was sure she could feel the beast's hot, fetid breath. Then two gunshots blasted.

"Ash!" The sound of racing blood hammered in her ears.

"It's all right." Ash's face loomed over her. "It's dead."

Blackness threatened to smother her. A faint buzzing started in her head and grew louder and louder.

"Tamsin? Tamsin? Speak to me, damn it!" Ash seized

her shoulders and shook her. "You don't have to be afraid. The cat's dead."

She heard the hiss of his knife slide out of his sheath; then the leather ties binding her fell away. Ash gathered her in his arms and rocked her, whispering her name over and over.

Gradually, the humming receded. "Ash?" she murmured. A sweet sickly smell seemed to surround her. She knew what it was. Blood.

"It's a female," Ash said. "Big. She must go two hundred and twenty pounds."

"A real cat? Flesh and bone? Not a ghost?"

"As real as I am. The one I killed before must have been her offspring. Pumas don't hunt with another animal unless it's a mother and her young."

"It's dead? Really?"

"Yes," he answered softly. "It's over. I'm sorry, Tamsin. So damned sorry."

"You should be." She pushed free and cautiously approached the dead animal. "How could anything so magnificent be so terrible? Did she hate us . . . like the Cheyenne? Did she track us all this while out of—"

"Not hate, darlin'." He pulled her away from the cat. "She turned outlaw, a man killer."

"Like Jack Cannon."

Ash nodded. "Maybe, but that's not a wild animal's nature. Men prey on others for money, but a mountain lion's needs are simpler. All a cat wants is to be left alone, to hunt, to mate, to raise their cubs in peace. Usually, a puma keeps as far from a human as possible. Something went wrong inside this one, something that twisted her."

"Grief for her offspring?" Tamsin suggested.

He shrugged. "It's not something we'll ever know."

"But to trail us so far . . . I don't understand."

"Not so much distance the way a lion hunts. This one's hunting territory could easily cover a hundred miles."

"She wasn't so different from the Cheyenne, was she? So long as we stayed away and left her alone."

"Maybe, maybe it's the way things happen. Nothing stays the same, Tamsin. Not Tennessee, not Texas, and not Colorado. One of these days the wild Cheyenne and the mountain lions will be gone. It will make life easier for some folks, but something special will go out of these mountains with them."

"And the desperadoes? Will they be gone as well?"

"No," he replied huskily. "They'll just change their hats and wear fancier clothes. Believe me, Tamsin, as long as there are people, the outlaws will be with us."

At dawn, they rode southeast, entering more-civilized country. Tamsin was torn, waiting for a chance to escape, but not wanting to leave the man she'd come to cherish more than her own life.

The canyon widened, and Tamsin guided Fancy close to Ash's gelding. Ash had rolled up his hunting shirt and tied it behind his saddle.

He'd told her he didn't want to be mistaken for a hostile and shot by one of his own kind. With his long, dark hair and sun-bronzed skin, she wondered that anyone would recognize him as a white man.

The buckskins he'd found in Jacob's cabin suited him as well as his long coat and neatly tailored vest and trousers, she decided. Ash Morgan had an unpredictable streak that marked him as a mustang. It could be that no woman would ever bridle his temper or train him to a tame way of life.

"We don't have to do it this way," she said to him. "You could forget the bounty on my head and come to California with me."

Ash didn't answer for several minutes, then stroked his stubbled chin. "It's a fair offer, Tamsin. I've never been that far west, and I've always had a hankering to see the sun set over that rolling blue ocean."

Her heart pitched into the pit of her stomach. "But you won't, will you?" Stubborn. He was as stubborn as a Missouri mule. "Does the reward mean that much to you?"

He scoffed. "You know better than that, woman. Don't be scared. I promised you a top-notch lawyer. I've known Henry Steele for some time. I believe he's an honest man, but in case he's not, I'll make certain you don't come to trial in his courtroom."

"I'm sure that's supposed to make me feel better," she replied. But it didn't. She was terrified of being arrested and dreaded the disgrace of being behind bars. No one in her family had ever been jailed, other than a great-great-grandmother who was suspected of spying on the British for the Americans during the War of 1812.

What if Ash's lawyer wouldn't represent her or wasn't as good as Ash thought? Suppose the jury believed Henry Steele's word over hers?

She was a stranger accused of horse theft and murder, a southerner in Union territory when emotions still ran high from the war. What if Ash was forced to testify against her? If he told them that she had stolen his horse, would that make them think her guilty of the killing?

Tamsin shivered. It was all well and good for Ash to talk about obeying the law and upholding a moral code of right and wrong. He wasn't the one facing a death sentence.

"You know I didn't commit that murder," she said.

"Yes, woman. I suppose I do. I can't figure how the hell you managed to get yourself knee-deep in this much trouble without being guilty as sin, but I believe you."

"It's about time!" She gave a sigh of relief. "Then, if you do believe me, you can understand why I can't go back. Come to California with me."

Ash reined in and stared at her. "Don't be stupid, Tamsin. I'm not going—"

"I'm not stupid. Don't ever call me that again." Atwood had called her stupid, and it had ended any hope of their making their marriage work.

She knew Ash thought she should trust him. In his eyes, he'd never done anything to make her think that he wouldn't keep his word. But she was afraid that he was asking more than she could give.

"I promised you I'd take care of you," he said, reining his horse close to hers. "Stop worrying, and let me do it."

She sighed again. If only it were that easy.

Four days later, on a side street near the Denver courthouse, Ash escorted Tamsin into a freshly painted office. The small gold building with white trim was so new that carpenters were still nailing cedar shingles to the roof. "This is the lawyer I told you about," Ash explained. "Dimitri's the best."

An elegantly dressed, middle-aged man with prematurely gray hair and gold-rimmed glasses peered over the top of a desk stacked high with books. "Ashton? Is that you?" He rose, replaced a quill pen in an inkwell, and came around the desk to meet them.

"Dimitri." Ash extended a hand and the little man shook it vigorously. "I'd like you to meet someone," Ash continued. "Dimitri Zajicek, this is Mrs. Tamsin MacGreggor."

Dimitri nodded, pulled an embroidered handkerchief from his coat pocket, and wiped at the smeared ink stains on his fingers. "It is my honor, Mrs. MacGreggor. Forgive the mess; it's usually far worse, but I've just moved into this office and I haven't had time to complete my customary clutter." The lawyer rattled on as he escorted her to a chair, cleared a small tea table of heaped papers and folders, and produced a steaming silver pot and delicate cups and saucers.

Dimitri Zajicek was a far cry from her Tennessee lawyer, but his manner inspired confidence, Tamsin thought as she sipped the sweetened tea. She hadn't known Dimitri for more than five minutes, and here she was explaining her dilemma without the least hesitation.

Ash stood behind her, his hand on the back of her chair. She could feel his gaze on her, and even though he didn't speak, his being there gave her confidence. "So, you can see that I was afraid to go into the Sweetwater jail," she said. "I'm certain that the sheriff and Judge Steele are both dishonest. And I truly believe that the judge murdered his brother and plans to put the blame on me."

"I can't believe that Henry Steele is that kind of man. But right or wrong, I couldn't take the chance of her being tried in Sweetwater, Dimitri," Ash said. "Can you help us?"

"There was a cowboy, too," Tamsin put in. "I think they called him Broom or Brown. He was there at Steele's ranch the day I heard Sam and Henry argue. Sam became furious with the man when he wouldn't throw Henry off the place. They exchanged words, and Sam fired him. The cowboy threatened Sam. He could have returned later and done the killing."

Ash's face darkened with suspicion. "You never mentioned this cowhand before."

"It didn't seem important. It all happened so fast that I just remembered what Broom said to Sam. I was so sure that the judge was the killer . . ."

"That you didn't tell me." Ash's knuckles whitened as he gripped the chair back.

"That's certainly something to look into," Dimitri soothed as he continued taking notes. Then he paused and glanced up at Ash. "You did hear that Jack Cannon committed another bank robbery south of Pueblo?"

Tamsin's hand trembled, spilling amber liquid over the side of her flowery blue porcelain cup into her lap.

"No." Ash's features hardened. "I hadn't."

"In Goldsborough. It's a small town, but developing into a mining center. A deputy was killed during the robbery as well as the bank manager and a teller. The Cannon brothers are also suspected of that stage robbery in Pueblo, and at least two bank holdups in Nebraska."

Ash swore softly. "I heard Jack was on the move. A friend told me Cannon murdered a mule skinner and stole his horses. I rode down to Cannon's uncle's old place to see if they'd gone to ground, but I didn't find any sign of them."

"No." Tamsin set the cup and saucer on the table. "Stay out of this, Ash. You promised you'd stand by me if I gave myself up."

A muscle twitched along the length of his left forearm. "I made another promise to Becky that I'd make sure Cannon paid for his crimes."

Tamsin seized his arm. "She's dead, Ash. She's dead, and I'm alive. Has it all been lies between us? Don't I mean anything to you?"

"You mean everything, woman. But I've got to finish what I started."

"They took a hostage," Dimitri continued. "A woman customer. The countryside is up in arms, but they haven't found any trace of them. I hear they're calling in federal marshals."

"They won't catch him. Cannon knows these mountains like the back of his hand."

"I can look after Mrs. MacGreggor if you want to join the search. I'll be happy to post her bond."

"Ash, no." Tamsin's voice took on a shrill note as she clung to him. "You can't do this to me."

"It would mean a lot if you'd look after her, Dimitri. I'll guarantee your bond."

"You don't have to do that," Tamsin said angrily. "Take your bounty money and go. After all, you are the great Ash Morgan. The marshals, the posse, they're wasting their time. You're the only one who can capture these outlaws and save the hostage!"

Ash flushed under his tan. "I know Cannon better than anyone else. I know his habits and his tricks. I won't let him lead me into an ambush."

Dimitri laid down his pen. "Of course, Helen and I will welcome Mrs. MacGreggor into our home," he continued smoothly, as though he hadn't heard what she'd said, as though Ash's running off alone after Jack was the most natural thing in the world.

"That's settled, then." The lawyer got to his feet. "Helen and I have had other accused ladies stay with us before, and I'm sure Judge Marlborough will agree. There's really no provision for women in the jail, and no reason for Mrs. MacGreggor to remain behind bars if she'd give me her word not to try and escape." He glanced at Tamsin.

"Why not? No one's going to listen to anything I have to say." Suddenly tired, she sank into the chair.

"Tamsin." Ash put a hand on her shoulder. "I have to do this. I'll be back before you go to trial."

She raised her head and stared at him through tear-misted eyes. "Will you at least form your own posse, take armed men with you?"

"I work better alone. Besides, I was wrong before when I thought he'd gone to his uncle's cabin. I might be pulling good guns off on another wild-goose chase."

"And what if Jack kills you? What then?"

He shrugged. "Honey, I've got to—"

"I don't want to hear it!" She rose to her feet and backed away from him. "If you're going, then go— straight to hell, you bastard!"

"Maybe I will," Ash said softly before turning to stride out of the lawyer's office, leaving her numb and heartsick, already regretting the bitter words she'd flung at him.

Ash's determination lasted as far as McNarr's dry goods store, where he bought ammunition, a new rifle, and food to last him a week. It stayed with him as he made arrangements to sell the mule and leave Tamsin's horses at the livery stable. It even held firm as he thrust a foot into the stirrup and swung up on Shiloh's back.

As he reined the gelding in a tight circle, Fancy raised her head and uttered a plaintive whinny. Instantly Tamsin's image formed in his mind, and Ash's steely resolve cracked.

He swore a foul oath. "I can't do it," he muttered. "I can't abandon her."

Dismounting, he handed Shiloh's lines to a stableman. "Put him with the others," Ash ordered gruffly. "I've changed my mind. I'll be staying in Denver."

"How long?"

"As long as it takes."

Swallowing his pride, he started back for Dimitri's office and what he guessed would be a whole lot of apologizing.

It was late afternoon by the time Dimitri, his wife Helen, and a well-chastised Ash accompanied Tamsin across the creaky floorboards into Judge Marlborough's chambers. In Dimitri's home, she'd bathed, washed, arranged her hair, and dressed from the skin out in Mrs. Zajicek's fashionable clothing.

Jolly Helen Zajicek was three inches shorter than Tamsin and a good two stone heavier, but the good wife's whalebone-and-elastic corset crushed, pinched, and squeezed every inch of Tamsin's flesh from hip to collarbone. Side-button cloth boots, a size too small, cramped her toes. And the flannel-covered steel-cage crinoline, two petticoats, and dove-gray, shot-silk taffeta gown with its lined bodice and tightly cuffed three-quarter sleeves smothered her.

The day was stifling hot without a hint of a breeze, but Mrs. Zajicek wore gloves, hat, and cape, and had insisted that Tamsin top her outfit in the same manner. "A lady cannot be too careful not to allow her standards to slip on the frontier," she'd said with twinkling eyes and a merry laugh.

Tamsin felt that the widow's hair brooch at her collar was too much, but Mrs. Zajicek would not be swayed.

"You're going before Judge Marlborough. He is extremely conservative. Under the circumstances, you must make the best possible impression."

The judge's secretary, a dour young gentleman in a wool pin-striped suit, showed the four of them into the inner chambers, opened a heavily draped window, and let himself out through a side door.

Tamsin sat gingerly on the edge of a chair, relieving the ache in her pinched toes, and tried to compose herself. Dimitri seemed certain that the judge would allow her to remain as their houseguest and that the trial could be moved here to Denver. She hoped the lawyer was right. But greater than her apprehension of what would happen was the fear that Ash might change his mind again and go off chasing the outlaw Cannon.

She glanced at him for reassurance. He was a far cry from the rough bounty hunter who'd ridden into town with her. He wore an elegant, black woolen coat, a pin-striped shirt, a cravat, and a gentleman's hat. Someone who didn't know him might guess at his occupation, but no one would take him for a lawyer or a banker. Proper clothing, stylish haircut or not, Ash Morgan stood out as the dangerous man he was.

A drop of sweat trickled down between Tamsin's breasts. She felt wrung out, limp. Even having a repentant Ash here with her didn't restore her usual optimism.

Overhead, a fly buzzed noisily. The purple drapes hung motionless. The only sound in the room was the loud ticking of a clock on the mantel.

Bookshelves lined two walls of the chamber. A large mahogany desk and high-backed chair dominated the room. Not a single paper, not even a pen holder, marred the polished expanse of shining wood. The odor of cigars hung heavily in the still air.

Mrs. Zajicek sat in a chair beside Tamsin. Dimitri stood rigidly erect, hands clasped behind his back. No one spoke, and the fly continued to drone.

Then the door opened and a portly black-haired man entered the room. His plump, florid face seemed too small for the huge black mustache, and his small, spectacled eyes peered out from under equally black brows.

Tamsin remained silent, as Dimitri had instructed her, while he explained the situation. Judge Marlborough listened without interrupting while the lawyer asked for a change of venue and an impartial judge to hear the case.

When Dimitri finished, Judge Marlborough removed his glasses, rubbed them with a starched handkerchief, and balanced them on his nose. He opened his top desk drawer and removed several papers. Then he rummaged in another drawer for pen and ink.

I have a bad feeling about this, Tamsin thought. Butterflies fluttered in the pit of her stomach, and an unbearable itch had started on the right side of her back under her corset.

Ash's gaze met hers, and he winked, offering silent comfort.

The judge cleared his throat, then blew his nose loudly into his handkerchief. "You are Mrs. Tamsin MacGreggor?"

She stood. "I am. And I want to say—"

He cut her off. "Sit down, madam. Answer what I ask, no more. You'll have every opportunity at your trial." He opened the top drawer again, removed a bell, and rang it before beginning to write on the official-looking document with large bold strokes.

Tamsin started to speak again, but Dimitri cleared his throat and motioned her to silence. The clock ticked, competing with the scratching of the judge's pen. Finally, the door opened, and Tamsin's knees went weak as Sheriff Roy Walker entered the room.

Judge Marlborough raised his head. "Sheriff, you'll take Mrs. MacGreggor into custody and hold her in the Sweetwater jail until her trial," he ordered.

"Like hell!" Ash leapt to his feet.

"Hold your tongue, Mr. Morgan, or I'll find you in contempt of court."

"This isn't a trial," he fired back. "You haven't listened—"

"Don't tell me how to manage my courtroom!"

"This isn't a courtroom!"

"Any place I say is a court. One more word from you, Mr. Morgan, and you'll find yourself behind bars."

"Sir—" Ash began.

"Is that clear?"

"Crystal clear, your honor," Dimitri put in. He motioned Ash to sit down.

"Good," Judge Marlborough said. "It's fortunate for us all that Sheriff Walker was already in Denver on prior business."

"Please, your honor," Dimitri protested. "My client has voluntarily surrendered herself, and she's willing to post a high bail. She's no threat—"

Walker's boot heels clicked on the polished floor as he walked toward Tamsin. "You're coming with me, lady."

"No." She recoiled but made no attempt to flee. In these clothes, in the middle of Denver, where would she go?

"Your honor," her lawyer argued. "Mr. Morgan—"

"I'll take full responsibility for her appearance in your court," Ash said. "My reputation speaks for itself."

Judge Marlborough's artificially black eyebrows came together in a forbidding frown. "This woman is accused of a heinous crime. Samuel Steele, an honest rancher and respected member of the Sweetwater community, was shot in the back. There will be no bail for your Mrs. Mac-Greggor. She's a citizen of Tennessee. She's already run once. I'll take no chance on it happening a second time."

Ash leapt up again. "Don't touch her, Walker!"

"Ashton!" Dimitri grabbed his arm and moved to block him. "This won't help our case."

Tamsin trembled as Walker snapped a handcuff around her wrist. "She'll not get away from me, Judge." Then he brought his face so close to hers that she could smell sweat and a woman's cheap perfume lingering on his shirt. "You're under arrest for the murder of Sam Steele."

I won't cry, Tamsin vowed as the sheriff clamped the cuff. Hopelessly, she glanced at her Ash.

"The jail at Sweetwater isn't fit to house a gentle-woman," Dimitri said. "Surely, Denver—"

The judge stood. "Denver is no more prepared to deal with her than Sweetwater and has less reason to bear the expense." He gestured impatiently to Walker. "Take her away, Sheriff. And I remind you that I'm holding you personally responsible for her safety until that day."

"She's innocent!" Ash shouted.

"I didn't shoot Sam Steele."

"For your sake I hope you are," the judge replied sternly. "For if you're found guilty, the Territory of Colorado will exact the highest punishment. Your sex shall not help you. You'll hang by the neck until you are dead, and God have mercy on your black soul."

Chapter 20

In two days, Tamsin was in the Sweetwater jail and found herself the object of great speculation by the residents of the town. Two ministers, the widow Fremont who ran the boardinghouse, three members of the Methodist Women's Society, a prominent shopkeeper, and Rabbit Hawkins, the town drunk, had all found excuses to come into the jail and stare at her.

Ash, Dimitri, and Helen had followed the sheriff and prisoner to Sweetwater. Ash rode Shiloh and tied Tamsin's horses and the Appaloosa behind Dimitri's carriage.

By the first afternoon, Ash had found a private barn to shelter the livestock and paid a visit to Shelly at Maudine's Social Club.

The black-haired lass welcomed him with open arms, if a little sleepily. "It's good to see you, Ash," she said, covering a dainty yawn with her hand. "Come in, but be quiet. Maudine's still sleeping."

He followed her down the shadowy hall and into a handsome parlor furnished with velvet-covered settees and thick, rich drapes closed tightly to keep out the sunshine.

The bawdy house was just coming alive. From the kitchen, Ash could smell baking bread and hear the soft laughter of the black cook. A calico cat curled around his leg, and Shelly scooped it up in her arms.

"You know you've got no business in this room, Silky," she cooed. She rubbed her artificially red cheek against the cat's fur and threw Ash a saucy look. "Still cold in the mountains? Heard you tracked down that back-shooting woman that murdered Sam."

Shelly was barely dressed, her voluptuous figure adorned with lacy drawers, black stockings, and a corset beneath her dragon-red Chinese robe. The scent of jasmine clung to her hair and silk wrapper.

She opened a sliding door to another room and pushed the cat in. "Polly," she called softly. "Come get Silky. Maudine warned you about letting him in the front parlor." Then she turned to Ash with a professional smile. "I suppose you'll be wanting a bath."

"And a little of your time, darlin'."

"Official time, or friendly time?"

He passed her a handful of silver dollars. "I'd like to talk to you, just talk, nothin' more. I need some answers, about an old customer of yours."

"Wouldn't be Sam Steele, would it?"

"And Edwards at the livery."

Shelly glanced over her shoulder to see if they were alone. "Sam was a regular, but you know we don't talk about gentlemen friends. Edwards never came here. He likes his pleasure cheap."

"You don't discuss business. I know that. What I want to hear is gossip. There isn't much that goes on in Sweetwater that Maudine's ladies don't know."

"Isn't that the truth?"

Ash turned toward the new voice. Maudine LaFrance was standing in the doorway that led to the entrance hall. "Good afternoon, ma'am," he said. "I was just—"

"Looking to get me and my girls in trouble?" Maudine was barely five feet tall, somewhere between fifty and eighty, with the complexion of an English dairymaid and the eyes of a tiger. Once stunning, she was now, in Ash's eyes, merely elegant. Her voice for all her air of authority was surprisingly high and girlish.

"You know me better than that, Mrs. LaFrance." He flashed her what he hoped was an endearing grin. "I'm trying to help a lady out of a bad spot. I need information, and I'm willing to—"

Maudine waved her hand. "No, Mr. Morgan. It's not necessary to mention an amount. I know you'll be more than generous. But you must understand that anything you learn here must never reflect on me or my ladies."

"No, ma'am, it won't," he promised.

"And none of us will testify in a court of law. You do understand that?"

"Yes, ma'am."

Maudine smiled. "Then I see no problem." She looked at Shelly. "Take Mr. Morgan to the bathing room and give him whatever he requires."

"That's what I like about you, Mrs. LaFrance," Ash replied. "You're a sensible woman."

"Save your compliments for Shelly." Maudine paused, touching her cheek lightly with one painted fingernail. "And, after your bath, leave your cash donation in the blue ginger jar in the front hall on your way out."

Later, Ash visited Tamsin at the jail. "I won't be here in the morning," he said. "I have some things I have to do, but don't worry, I'll be back by evening."

"What things? Does it have anything to do with Jack Cannon?" she asked.

"No, it doesn't. It has to do with clearing you. Trust me, Tamsin. You're not getting rid of me so easily."

She'd passed a sleepless night in the bare cell and was

still bleary eyed when Dimitri appeared early in the morning.

In one hand the dapper lawyer carried his black leather briefcase. Under the other arm he balanced a tray with a teapot, cups, sugar, cream, and hot cinnamon scones.

"I thought perhaps a decent cup of tea would cheer you up. Lemon wasn't available. I hope you like milk."

"It's fine, thank you. I don't understand why you're doing all this for me," Tamsin said as Dimitri set the tea tray on the wooden stool in her cell and removed several hard-boiled eggs from his pocket. "You don't know me. You don't know if I'm lying about the murder. You have no reason to trust me, yet you've left your home and other clients to come here and concentrate on my case." She chuckled. "And you've brought breakfast."

Pleasantly embarrassed, Dimitri tugged at his high collar and cleared his throat. His black coat and waistcoat were immaculate, his white shirt was starched, his trousers bore a knife-edge crease, and his shoes were shiny enough for Tamsin to see her reflection.

He looked totally out of place in this dingy jail cell that smelled of stale urine and despair. Yet, he managed to appear undaunted by the bleak surroundings.

"Ashton trusts you," he said. "I've never known him to be wrong about a person's character." He smiled. "And I do have some aptitude in that area myself. I'm convinced you're not a murderess."

"Even believing in my innocence, you're going beyond your duty as my lawyer. Not that I don't appreciate it. I do, it's just that I don't have any money to—"

"You must not be concerned with finances. Ashton has generously guaranteed all my expenses. He offered to pay my fee, but I'll accept none from him, ever." Dimitri gestured grandly. "Ashton saved my wife's life. That's how we met him. My dearest Helen was coming west from Baltimore to join me. She and Ashton were on the same train traveling through Missouri when it was attacked by Confederate sympathizers."

"During the war?"

"Yes." Dimitri nodded. "Yes, in '62. When the rebels entered the car, demanded all the passengers' valuables, and began shooting, Ashton threw himself over my wife and took a bullet to protect her. Wounded, he killed two of the marauders and drove off the others. Neither of us will ever forget that gallant deed." He chuckled. "Besides, Ashton plays a tolerable game of chess. And you have no idea how difficult it is to find a decent opponent west of Baltimore."

"Ash is a good man, isn't he?"

"The best," Dimitri agreed. "Smart, absolutely fearless, and honest to the bone. He should have taken up the study of law. He'd have made a fine judge." He smiled, revealing a silver filling in an eyetooth. "I'm not blind, Mrs. MacGreggor. It's clear what the relationship is between the two of you. And you needn't fear; Ashton has none but the most honorable intentions toward you. I'm certain of it."

"I wish I had your faith." Tamsin rose to pace nervously. "Have you spoken with Henry Steele?"

"Yes, I have. He's quite adamant about what he found in the barn. He'll be a good witness for the prosecution. I always advise my clients to avoid being found standing over a body whenever possible." Dimitri chuckled at his bit of humor and adjusted the knot of his perfectly tied cravat.

Tamsin nibbled her lower lip and studied the little man. Had she seen Dimitri Zajicek on the street, she would have passed him without suspecting that beneath that graying cap of hair, with its center part and heavy layer of Acme Hair Oil, nestled a steel-trap mind. Strange that two such different men as he and Ash should have developed such an obvious respect for each other.

She smiled. So Ash played a good game of chess, did he? He was full of surprises. If she survived the rope and Ash his outlaws, she'd have to challenge him to a match. Her grandfather had taught her chess when she was eight, and it had been a passion ever since.

"A trial date has been set," Dimitri announced, pulling her back to her present situation. "Monday, a week."

"You can't let Henry Steele preside," she replied. "I'm certain that he killed his own brother. What other reason could he possibly have for being in that barn that late at night? I heard Sam order him off the ranch that day. They were furious with each other. Apparently it wasn't enough for Henry to covet his brother's wife. He must have hated Sam enough to shoot him in the back."

"Henry Steele cannot judge this case. It's illegal and impossible. Leave that to me. But if you hope to cast suspicion on a judge, we must have more evidence than his being there," Dimitri reminded her. "You were there, and you're innocent. It could have been a third party who committed the crime. A disgruntled employee? A passing horse thief?"

"If it was, then there were two of us there to steal horses that night." She shook her head. "It makes no sense. Unless Sam Steele was the horse thief. Someone took Dancer and Fancy from the livery stable the night before, and they weren't the first horses to go missing in this town according to the boy who mucks up for the hostler."

"You mentioned the lad before." Dimitri whipped out

a pencil and a small leather-bound notebook. "Give me his name and his exact words."

"I'm not sure of his name, but he was about fourteen with olive skin and black hair. He said, 'Sam Steele trades in horses. Some people say he's not particular whose they are.' "

"You're certain that's what he said?"

"Yes. And you should question Mr. Edwards, the livery stable owner. He seemed a dishonest sort to me. Either he sold my horses to Sam, or they were in league with each other. Sam insisted he had bills of sale for both animals, but I didn't see them. They could have been false."

"Or the papers never existed," Dimitri suggested. "I'll put *bills of sale* at the top of my questions for the widow Steele. If there are such papers, she should be able to produce them."

"If Sam Steele's widow, Sarah, I believe I heard him call her, was behaving improperly with the judge—"

"Then she may be a hostile witness as well," the lawyer finished. He pursed his lips. "Leave Mrs. Steele to me, Mrs. MacGreggor. I've questioned deceitful witnesses on the stand before." He moistened the pencil point with the tip of his tongue. "Can you remember anyone, other than this Mr. Edwards, who saw you ride into town with your horses?"

She shook her head. "There may have been a cowboy outside the feed and grain store." She nodded. "There was, but he mounted up and rode out. I don't think he ever looked in my direction, so I couldn't give you a description."

"Very well. Let me follow up these leads. You're not to worry, Mrs. MacGreggor. Criminal law is my favorite aspect of the justice system. I'll do my best for you and Ashton. I promise you that."

"And you won't let Henry Steele preside over my case?"

"If he tries it, we'll scream loud enough to bring the governor running."

"Just as long as he runs fast enough to get here before I go to the gallows."

"Let's hope it doesn't come to that."

"Amen to those words."

Dimitri finished his cup of tea and departed, leaving Tamsin alone in her cell until noon, when Helen Zajicek appeared with a basket lunch. She took one look at the plate of beans and the dry biscuit that the deputy, Joel Long, had provided and shook her head in disgust.

"I wouldn't feed that to a dog."

"Thank you for your thoughtfulness, but I'm really not hungry," Tamsin protested as Helen began to unpack her hamper.

"Tish, tish. You need to eat to keep up your strength. You must not become downhearted. Have faith in Mr. Zajicek. He is an excellent barrister, and he will stop at nothing to provide you with the best defense."

"I'm sure he will," Tamsin replied. But her real faith lay in Ash. She kept hoping he'd relent, break her out of jail, and force Henry Steele to confess he'd committed the murder.

Helen leaned close and whispered, "Mr. Zajicek wrote down everything you told him about . . ." The plump woman stopped and silently mouthed *Sarah Steele and Judge Steele*. "He intends to question the widow Steele at great length."

"Thank your husband for me," Tamsin answered. "Thank you for everything. I don't know what I'd have done without you."

Helen smiled. "Stuff and nonsense, Mrs. MacGreggor.

You would have done what you've done all along. Any woman who can survive being captured by hostile natives is strong enough to face a jury."

"Time's up," Long called.

Helen murmured a few words of consolation and let the curtain fall across the cell door. Tamsin heard the woman's footsteps recede and a brief exchange as Helen passed through the outer office.

Despite the smell of chicken drifting from the basket, Tamsin left the food untouched and sat on the metal bunk along the far wall. Outside the window, boys threw stones and shouted catcalls. She ignored them as well. Both her stomach and her mind were uneasy.

Ash had told her that he wasn't going after Texas Jack, but that didn't keep her from imagining Ash wounded and bleeding along some lonesome trail, or worse, lying dead. Images of Shiloh trotting into sight with an empty, blood-soaked saddle formed in the back of her mind and made her crazy.

Dimitri's statement haunted her: "Ashton has honorable intentions toward you."

Ash hadn't promised her anything beyond what they'd had. She couldn't expect more than his friendship. Certainly not marriage. If he'd wanted things to be different, he would have said so by now, wouldn't he?

If she got out of this mess, she would have to go on to California alone. Doing that would be hard, but not impossible. What she couldn't face were her fears of never hearing his deep voice or seeing his wicked grin again.

Hours passed. Night fell, and the moon rose.

Ash promised me he'd be back, Tamsin thought as she paced the cell. He wouldn't break his word. But he had when he left her at Jacob's cabin. Why would this time be different?

Then she heard the sound of a horse and ran to the window. She pushed the toe of her shoe into the cracked plaster and pulled herself up to peer out through the bars.

A single rider waited there, a tall figure in a plains-man's hat.

"Ash?"

"Who else were you expectin'?" He chuckled. "Sorry I'm late, darlin', but I've been talking to that cowboy you told me was fired from the Lazy S, Broom Talbot."

"You found him?"

"Workin' on a spread east of here. He pretty much backed up your story of what happened that day. He said he threatened Sam but he wouldn't have killed him."

"See? It happened just like I told you."

"I tried to ask Henry Steele, but he won't talk to me. Either he's protecting himself or his brother's wife."

"Widow."

"Yeah, widow."

Tamsin's fingers ached from holding on to the plaster. "Can you come inside?"

"Not until morning. The office is locked tight as a drum. Joel Long is the deputy on guard duty, but he's probably asleep."

"Oh." She wanted to touch Ash . . . to have him hold her in his arms and tell her everything would be all right. She would have traded this cell for a mountain campsite, Indians, cougars, and all.

"I brought you something," he said.

She peered through the shadows, but it was impossible to see more than his silhouette. "A hacksaw?"

He laughed softly.

She heard Shiloh take a few quick steps, and then flowers rained around her face. Surprised, she dropped down to the floor and sat there.

"Tamsin?"

"Yes?"

"Are you hurt?"

"No."

"What's wrong?"

"You brought me flowers?"

"Fireweed and candytuft."

She swallowed, trying not to cry, as she picked up the scattered wildflowers.

"What's wrong, Tamsin?"

"Nothing." Tears stained her face.

I love him, she thought. I really love him.

"Don't you like them?"

"I can't see them. It's dark."

"The fireweed is about the color of your hair." His voice was husky, full of emotion. "Candytuft has a yellow center with white petals."

"Thank you." She gathered them against her breast.

"We're going to get you free," he said. "One way or another, Tamsin. You're not going to hang."

"That's what my lawyer tells me."

"He's a good man, darlin'."

"He said the same about you."

"Well, I'd best get Shiloh to the stable. He's had a long ride. I'll check on Dancer and Fancy for you."

"You didn't put them in Edwards's barn? After what happened before?"

He laughed. "No, I didn't leave them there. Good night, woman."

"Good night, Ash." She waited for him to say the words she wanted to hear more than anything. And when he didn't, she did. "I love you."

He didn't answer.

"I love you," she called again. She pulled herself up

and looked out onto an empty alleyway. "Oh, Ash," she murmured. Then she dropped to the floor and gathered her flowers again, watering them with her own abundant tears.

Chapter 21

"Ash!" Tamsin sat bolt upright on the wooden bunk. Her heart was racing, and she was visibly trembling. Rubbing her eyes, she got up and went to the barred jail window. She could have sworn she heard a shot, but it was barely light out.

No one seemed to be stirring in the town.

She returned to the bunk and began to unplait her hair. She was fully dressed, which made for a decidedly uncomfortable night. She'd slept poorly, but she couldn't remember any nightmares, not until the awful dream that woke her.

Tamsin pulled the scratchy wool blanket around her. She felt icy cold, despite the already rising temperature outside. She couldn't shake off an uneasy feeling that something bad had happened to Ash.

She brushed her hair and pinned it into a knot at the back of her head. She poured water from a tin pitcher into the matching bowl and washed her face. Soon Walker or Deputy Long would come to escort her to the boardinghouse to use the ladies' bathroom and outhouse. She hoped there wouldn't be a repeat of the first day's ordeal.

People had stared at her and called her names. A little boy, no more than eight years old, had spat at her. Back shooter, they'd called her. Murderess!

It seemed the townsfolk weren't waiting to hear her side in a court of justice. They'd already convicted her in their minds. She hoped none of her accusers would sit on the jury.

Tamsin heard the door to the street open. Shaking the water from her hands, she turned hoping to see Ash or Dimitri.

"Are you comfortable?" Henry Steele's angry gaze met hers. "We usually don't go to such pains for a horse thief and murderer."

"You know I didn't kill your brother!" Tamsin balled her fingers into fists and glared through the bars at the judge. "Not only didn't I commit the crime, but I think you know who did."

Henry Steele scowled. "Your lies are growing thin, woman. And your lawyer's tricks won't help you on the stand. You shot my brother in the back for those horses, and you're going to pay dearly for it."

She stiffened. "There's really no point to this conversation, is there? I'd prefer you spoke to Mr. Zajicek until we meet in court."

"That suits me as well."

He was barely out of the sheriff's office before Ash, Dimitri, and Helen came in. Tamsin knew by one look at their faces that they had bad news. "What is it?"

"Simply appalling," Mrs. Zajicek murmured.

"Henry Steele is going to preside over my case?"

"Not that either," Dimitri said. "We've heard no word on our request for an unbiased—"

"What, then?" Tamsin persisted.

"It's that poor boy," Mrs. Zajicek said. "The one from the stable."

Tamsin glanced at Ash.

The barrister continued: "I spoke at length with the

boy yesterday. He was terrified, but he seemed sympathetic to our case. I'm afraid Javier Chispero won't be able to testify on your behalf. He's been found dead."

"Dead?" Tamsin felt sick. She remembered the boy's plain brown face and his dark, frightened eyes. "I thought I heard a shot about dawn."

"The stable owner, your Mr. Edwards, found him this morning in one of the stalls," Ash said. "It seems there's been an accident."

Tamsin sank onto the cot. "What kind of accident?"

Ash's eyes were hard. "According to Sheriff Walker, the boy fell from the hayloft onto a pitchfork."

"Poor Javier," Tamsin said. "Oh, God, I hope it's not my fault that he's dead. First Sam Steele, now the boy."

"But how could you be responsible?" Mrs. Zajicek asked. "You were here in jail. It's simply a terrible coincidence."

"It's no coincidence," Ash said. "Somebody killed Javier to keep him from telling what he knew about the missing horses."

"My thoughts exactly, Mrs. MacGreggor," Dimitri agreed. "All we have to do now is find out who murdered Javier, and that may tell us the identity of Sam Steele's real killer."

"If the murderer killed this child, Mrs. MacGreggor may be next," Helen said. "She's in great danger."

"I'll spend the next week sitting outside this cell," Ash replied. "No one will get past me to harm her."

"No," Dimitri said. "You're both wrong. Mrs. MacGreggor is as safe as in God's hands."

"How so, my dear?" his wife asked.

"The killer wants Mrs. MacGreggor alive and well to stand trial for the crime. Without her, the blame might fall elsewhere."

"You're right," Ash agreed. "I hadn't thought—"

"If you want to help, I suggest you follow Henry," Dimitri said. "Shadow his every move. See who he talks to and where he goes."

"That makes sense to me," Tamsin said. "I've known all along who killed Sam. I just couldn't convince any of you."

The day dragged into afternoon and finally evening. Dimitri and his wife brought her supper and told her that Ash was watching the judge as they'd planned.

"I don't care what they think," Helen said. "I'm still worried about you."

"I'll be fine," Tamsin replied. "At least until the trial. I can't say that the accommodations are the finest I've ever enjoyed, but no one has bothered me."

"And let's hope it stays that way," the older woman said. "Court day can't come too soon to suit me."

Sometime after midnight, Tamsin was awakened by coarse male voices and the stamping of feet. Curses and laughter followed, and shortly the deputy entered the cell area carrying a kerosene lamp. "Got company for you, woman."

Tamsin shielded her eyes from the sudden light as Deputy Joel Long set the lamp on a shelf across from her door.

Sheriff Walker and several loud strangers surged into the hall. Between them, they supported a prisoner in handcuffs. His clothing was torn, his face bruised and bloody. He seemed barely conscious.

Long unlocked the door to the cell across from Tamsin, and Walker shoved the beaten man inside. He fell forward on his knees, retched, and collapsed on his face.

"Reckon you two know each other," the sheriff said sarcastically to Tamsin.

One of the hard-faced group muttered a crude remark as Long turned the key in the lock. "Don't get too comfortable in there, Cannon," the deputy said. "You won't be there more'n a few hours."

"Yeah, then we'll hang the bastard," one of Walker's companions said. He was short and stocky with muscular arms and a full black beard. "Maybe both of them."

"None of that talk," Walker replied. "This is my jail. Cannon stays here until the proper authorities come up from Pueblo to fetch him. They can hang him down there."

"What about the woman?" another demanded.

"She's bound over for trial here. I'm sworn to uphold the law in this county, and by God I'll do it or know the reason why."

"Save us a hell of lot of money and time by stringin' 'em both up tonight," the bearded man argued.

Tamsin stared at the injured prisoner. Cannon? That wasn't Cannon. The sheriff had arrested the wrong person. This cowboy was too big, and his hair was too dark.

He moaned, spit out a tooth, and pushed himself up to a sitting position. Blood streamed from his shattered nose, and one eye was swollen shut.

"Who are you?" Tamsin asked.

He swore an oath so foul that it turned her stomach.

"You're not Jack Cannon."

"Listen, bitch, when I want something from you, I'll ask."

She retreated to the far side of the cell, away from the sickening smell of vomit. "You're an outlaw, aren't you? If you're not Cannon, who are you?"

He raised his head, glaring at her with a single bloodshot eye. "Oh, I'm a Cannon, all right. Jest not the pretty one. I'm his big brother, Boone." He hawked and spat again. "I know you, woman. You're that bitch what did Jack wrong back in Nebrasky. I seen ye with him once."

Frightened, Tamsin turned her back on him and tried to keep down the nausea rising in her throat. She'd put Jack Cannon behind her, and she didn't want any reminders of her foolhardy association with him.

"Jack'll be glad to see you, bitch," Cannon taunted. "He don't like fancy pieces turnin' their backs on him."

She clenched her teeth and tried not to listen.

"He'll be right pleased."

"He has nothing to do with me."

"Tell him that. My little brother'll be comin' fer me. He'll be comin' soon."

Tamsin shivered and prayed that Boone was wrong.

An hour before dawn, the urgent ringing of an iron bell startled her from a light doze. She'd slept in brief stretches, crouched in a corner of the cell as far from Boone Cannon as she could get.

"What's that?" she cried, not realizing that she'd spoken aloud. The lamp had burned out, and in the blackness it took her a moment to realize where she was.

"That'll be Jack," Boone cackled. "Told ya he'd come, bitch."

Tamsin tried to see out the window, but clouds covered the moon, leaving the alley pitch-dark. She felt her way to the front of the cell and began pounding on the bars. "Deputy! Deputy Long! Come here! Quick!"

Outside, the bell pealed frantically.

"Fire!" a man bellowed. "Fire in the church!"

Footsteps clattered past the jail windows.

"Hurry! The school's goin' up, too!"

Tamsin continued to shout for the guard. "Long!"

Banging echoed from the front office. "Fire! Open the door! The whole town could burn. It's real bad! We need more hands!"

"No!" Tamsin screamed.

Joel Long's sleepy voice was barely audible as the door hinges squeaked. "What can I—"

The deputy's words twisted to a surprised gasp and then a gargled choking. Something heavy sagged against wood, then hit the floor.

Footfalls grew closer and the inner door to the cell area swung wide.

"Brother? You in here? Light a lamp, damn it. How am I supposed to see anything in here."

Tamsin went numb.

"Jack! I expected ya to throw a rope on the winder bars and yank 'em out," Boone said.

"No need, was there? Bring the light, Billy! Billy and me just walked in the front door, all friendly like."

A circle of yellow light illuminated Jack's smiling face. "You owe me for this, Boone. Didn't I warn you about whores and whiskey? If you'd listened to me and stayed out of that saloon, you wouldn't be in here looking like a slab of beef, would you?"

"Shut up and open the door," Boone growled.

The second outlaw dangled a ring of keys in one hand, a drawn Colt in the other. "Guess you're lookin' for these."

Tamsin backed to the far wall of the cell.

"Reckon you'll be glad you come fer me, brother," Boone said. "Look-ee here."

Jack's accomplice, the one he'd called Billy, undid Boone's lock. Jack came toward Tamsin. "Well, well." He motioned for Billy to open her cell, too.

"Leave me alone," Tamsin said.

"Come down in the world, haven't you, Miss High-and-Mighty?"

"Take him and go," she pleaded.

"And leave you here to face all the trouble?" He pushed back the door. "Come on, Red."

"No."

"Damn it, Tamsin. We haven't got all night. I've got a dead lawman out there, and we can't wait all night for you to make up your mind."

"Just go, please."

Jack shrugged. "That's your last word?"

"Yes!"

He glanced at the outlaw with the gun. "What's the rule?"

Boone laughed. "No witnesses."

"Sorry, Tamsin. I'd like to make an exception for you, but . . ." He motioned to Billy. "Kill her."

Tamsin's heart skipped a beat. "No! I'm coming. Don't shoot me."

Jack advanced on her. She shivered but forced herself to come toward him. "You're certain this time?" he asked.

She nodded. "I'll come."

He grabbed a handful of her hair and pulled her close. She gasped but didn't cry out as he slapped her hard across the face. "I owed you that one," he reminded her. "That's your first lesson."

Blood trickled from Tamsin's split lip, and it took all her willpower to keep from throwing herself on him and trying to pound his nose as flat as his brother's.

"Jack!" Boone urged. "Yah waitin' for the swivin' posse to come back?"

Jack released his grip on Tamsin and started for the door. Billy looked at her questioningly. She took a deep breath and hurried after the outlaw leader.

Outside, two silent men on horseback waited. At the far end of the street, pandemonium reigned. Tamsin could see people crowding the street. Flames shot through the roof of the Methodist church, engulfing the schoolhouse and turning the sky red. Shouting townsmen ran through the smoke and confusion with buckets of water amid crying women, barking dogs, and panicked livestock.

Jack swung up onto a gray horse, sidled it over to the high wooden walkway, and offered Tamsin his hand. She took it, and let him pull her up behind him.

"Don't fall off," Jack warned. "If you do, Billy will put a bullet in you. He's a good man. I never have to give him an order twice."

"Hey, there!" Sheriff Walker ran toward them. "What do you think—"

A rifle cracked from a rooftop across the street, and Walker dived for cover. Jack put spurs to the horse, and they galloped away from the fire and out of Sweetwater.

"Morgan! Ash Morgan!"

Ash handed his water bucket to the next man in line and turned toward Sheriff Walker. Ash's eyes stung with smoke, and his face felt scorched by the heat of the flames. Coughing, he walked back toward Walker.

The sheriff held his arm clutched against his chest. "Your woman just broke out of jail," Walker said. "And she took Boone Cannon with her."

"What?" Ash stared at him in disbelief. "Tamsin broke out of jail? That's not possible. And what the hell is this about Boone Cannon? She was the only prisoner in—"

"Boys from south of here brought Cannon in after midnight. Seems the rest of the gang came after him. I'd lay odds they set the fire as well."

Ash pulled his shirttail out of his trousers and wiped his eyes. He heard what Walker said, but the words didn't make sense. "Tamsin's gone? Cannon's bunch took her? Where was your deputy? Why didn't he protect her?"

"Long's dead. Knifed to death." Walker grimaced. "I'm bleedin' like a stuck pig. I came on them while they were makin' their getaway and caught a slug in the arm."

"Jack? Was he with them?"

"Couldn't make out faces. Doubt if I'd recognize him if I had. But I saw your woman. She's part of this, Morgan. She shot Sam Steele, and she's as guilty of Joel Long's killing as any of the rest."

"You're wrong," Ash shouted. "They must have taken her as a hostage. She wouldn't—"

"Shit, I saw her. She didn't try to run. One of them called to her, and she took his hand and climbed up behind him. Face it, bounty hunter. She made a fool of you."

Ash's gut cramped as though he'd taken a bullet. Fear for Tamsin's safety squeezed his chest and made it hard to draw breath or think straight.

Walker was out of his mind! Nobody could make him believe Tamsin capable of such a crime or of going willingly with the outlaws. He had to go after her—had to get her away from Jack before what happened to Becky . . .

Cold fury replaced the confusion in Ash's mind. Years of hunting dangerous men had made him methodical. "You forming a posse to go after them?"

"Hell, yes. Soon as I get the doc to sew up this arm. You volunteering?"

Ash shook his head. Other searchers would only slow him down. "I work best alone."

"Still defending her?" Walker spat on the ground by Ash's boots. "You're bad as she is. Get in my way, and—"

"If Boone Cannon was in your jail, you should have set more than one man to guard him. Did you think Texas Jack would let you hang his brother? Joel Long was nothin' but a kid. He didn't have the experience to deal with the Cannons, but you should have. Long's blood is on your hands, Walker."

"How the hell was I supposed to know Jack Cannon would set Sweetwater on fire?"

"You should have known he'd do something crazy. You're not fit to wear that badge."

Walker took a step toward him. "And you are?"

"I don't want your job. I just think this county deserves better than it's gettin' for its money."

The sheriff's angry retort was lost in the commotion as Ash headed for the boardinghouse and his gear. Minutes, even seconds, counted. But if he ran off halfcocked, he'd end up dead, and Tamsin would pay the final price.

In his room, Ash gathered ammunition, strapped on his gun belt, and picked up his rifle. Shouldering his bedroll, he moved out into the hall. Dimitri and his wife were there.

"I heard what happened," the lawyer said.

"Cannon took her. She didn't go on her own."

"No," Dimitri agreed. "I didn't think she would."

"Bring her back safely," Helen called after Ash. "She loves you."

"And he loves her," Dimitri said softly. "He just hasn't admitted it yet."

In the stable, Ash saddled both Shiloh and Dancer. The stallion rolled his eyes and tossed his head, but Ash yanked the girth tight, strapped on his bedroll, and led both horses out of the building. Max Spence, the barn owner, waited outside in the yard.

"I don't think the fire will come this way, Mr. Morgan, but if it does, I'll get your other animals to safety."

"You'd better." Ash took a firm hold of Dancer's bridle, thrust a boot into the stirrup, and mounted the big bay stud. "That mare's worth more than your house."

"You're going after the escaped outlaw, aren't you?"

Ash grabbed Shiloh's lead rope and kicked Dancer hard in the sides. "I'm going after my woman."

He followed the road west, away from the scattered houses, toward the mountains. He didn't know how long Cannon would keep to the trail or what direction Jack would take if he left it. When dawn came, there might be tracks to follow.

They had a start. On a horse like Dancer it would still take time to gain on them. If they stopped to take their sport with Tamsin, there was nothing he could do to help her.

But he didn't think Jack would be so careless. Jack hadn't lived as long as he had by being stupid. He had to think like the outlaw. What would he do if he were Texas Jack? That was easy. He'd push hard until the horses faltered. He'd slow the pace, but he wouldn't go to ground until dark.

And when he called it quits, he'd need grass for the horses and water for the animals and himself.

If he were Jack, he'd go to his uncle's cabin and stay there a few days before cutting south to Mexico.

Old Leon's place lay northwest, a long journey if Ash retraced his path southwest through the pass to Jacob's cabin and followed the canyons north. But it wasn't that far from Sweetwater, maybe a hard day's ride.

"He's headed for the cabin, damn it," Ash shouted.
Jack had to be, because if he wasn't . . . Ash blinked the
dust and wetness from his eyes and lashed the stallion
into a dead run.

he right...ack d the ...ridle round ...vo started
shoe ...he had wanted it he won't ... Ash untied the
...net and women from ...the ...rse and placed the saddle
...his own horse.

Chapter 22

Tamsin's thoroughbred was still running hard at daybreak when Ash reined him in and switched to Shiloh's
back. With an inner hunger that food wouldn't quell, he
knew that it was too late to search for tracks. Either he'd
guessed right and Cannon was headed for his uncle's or
he'd lost them entirely.

Lost her forever.

The trail he'd followed since he'd left Sweetwater had
become fainter and fainter, ending in the charred remains of a house, burned out like his own hopes.

For hours Ash had tried to think of a rational plan to
get Tamsin away from Cannon without putting her life in
jeopardy. So far, he had none. All he could think was that
if he'd been with her when Jack came to break Boone
out of the county jail, Jack would be dead and the young
deputy alive. Most of all, Tamsin would be safe.

He'd made the wrong choice when he'd decided to follow Henry, and guilt plagued him with the throbbing
agony of a broken tooth. He'd sworn to take care of
Tamsin, and he'd let her down as much as he had Becky.
If he didn't get Tamsin back alive . . . But that wasn't a
possibility he could let himself consider.

It seemed that he'd been a loner most of his life, grasp-
ing at something shining and having it slip away . . . his
daddy's hand . . . Aunt Jane's warm kitchen . . . the acres

he'd cut out of raw Colorado land. He'd never wanted much, a sense of justice and a place to share with someone who cared whether or not he came home at night.

He'd let rigid duty and an old code keep him from seeing that Tamsin MacGreggor glittered brightest until she'd slipped through his fingers.

Circling ahead of Cannon's gang and arriving at Leon's first would give Ash an advantage. When he'd gone there before, he'd stuffed the chimney so that if they lit a fire, the house would fill with smoke.

That idea was no longer an option. Jack held Tamsin hostage. Ash couldn't let them reach the cabin. Cannon wouldn't hesitate to trade Tamsin's life for his own. Worse, he might kill her out of pure spite if he found out who was chasing him.

The odds were still in Jack's favor. Walker had seen four outlaws, but Ash wasn't sure that there hadn't been another. In three of his earlier robberies, Jack had put a shooter on a high spot. And Jack Cannon was a man who liked to perfect a scheme and stay with it.

By midmorning, both of Ash's horses were thirsty and showing the effects of a hard ride. He stopped long enough to let them drink the contents of the two canteens he'd brought with him, saving none for himself. When they finished, he remounted and rode until the sun was high overhead.

When he topped a high bluff, he edged the horses into the shade of a grove of pines and used his spyglass to search the valley.

Far below he saw four horses and riders following a game trail. One animal carried double. Ash's heart leapt in his chest. Tamsin was alive, and he had time to right the wrong he'd done her.

He scanned ahead of the leader, then right and left, hunting for a scout. He located the fifth man, his horse plainly played out, lagging several hundred yards behind the others.

Ash stroked Shiloh's sweaty neck and murmured to him softly. The roan's sides were damp, and he was breathing hard. Tamsin's stud was fresher, but the route Ash figured to take down this ridge hill was fit more for mountain goats than horses. When push came to shove, he had to put more trust in the stocky gelding's agility than in the racehorse's speed.

An hour later, still riding Shiloh, Ash got within range of the fifth gunman. "Stand," Ash ordered the weary horse as he slid his rifle from its sheath.

"Lord, forgive me," he whispered. He took careful aim, leading his target, and squeezed off a perfect shot. The crack was still echoing through the valley when the pistolero dropped.

Tamsin clung to the outlaw in an exhausted daze. She'd ridden all night and into the day without a drop of water or a morsel of food. Jack had slapped her hard enough to make her ears ring when she hadn't dismounted fast enough a few hours back.

When his horse had begun to tire from carrying two, he'd ordered her up behind Billy, a man cut from the same devil mold. Billy never spoke a single word to her, but his flat amber eyes watched her from a compassionless face. Touching the desperado, putting her arms around his waist, made her skin crawl.

Each hour took her closer to nightfall, a time when she knew Jack would call a halt to his ride. And if Ash didn't come before then, Jack had promised her that he would have her in every way that a man could violate a woman.

And he had promised the others that they could use her in turn. . . .

So Tamsin had watched and waited as her strength

slipped away, knowing that if she made her move too soon, she would pay the ultimate price.

She had no doubt that Ash would come after her. She knew it in every drop of blood, in her bones, and in the far corners of her soul.

If only he didn't come too late.

The sound of the rifle shot wrenched Tamsin from her trance. She released her grip on the bandit's waist, slid off the horse's rump, and hit the ground running.

Billy cursed and yanked his horse away.

"Catch her!" Jack yelled.

Bullets whined past her head, but she didn't stop. Without looking back, she dived into a clump of thick brush and clawed her way through the tangle.

Jack shouted and Boone laughed. Horses snorted and spurs jingled as one of them leapt out of the saddle mount and tried to force his way into the bushes after her.

Briars tore at Tamsin's hair and clothes, but she pressed on, heedless of the pain. A pistol fired again, behind her.

Something stung her arm, and she cried out as the force knocked her down. Shocked, she realized that she'd been hit. Blood soaked her sleeve, but strangely, she felt numbness rather than pain.

She got up and staggered out the far side of the thicket. Shielded by scrub pines from her pursuers, she dashed down a narrow, rocky ravine.

"Get her, you fools!" Jack yelled.

Sparks of color spiraled in front of Tamsin's eyes. The ground beneath her feet seemed to be shifting, and sounds echoed in her head. She kept running, dodging from one clump of cover to another.

Ash heard the shots and turned Shiloh loose. Leaping into Dancer's saddle, he whipped the bay stallion into a flat-out run.

Tamsin had made it as far as a gully that cut into the wooded hillside. Ash reined the stud to a trot as he zigzagged through the stunted pines, dodging boulders and leaping rocks and fallen logs.

"Ash!" He could tell from Tamsin's scream that she was still running, but hopelessness rang in every shrill note.

"Where do you think you're goin', bitch?"

The hard thud of a man's fist hitting human flesh followed.

Tamsin gasped in pain, then began to sob.

A few yards away, another man uttered a scornful guffaw. "Save a little for me, Billy."

Ash heard cloth rip.

Tamsin's shriek of fear sliced through him.

The stallion burst through the cover of trees into the glaring sunlight. Ash saw Tamsin on the ground ahead, struggling with a man while another jeered and urged his partner on.

The startled *forajido* slapped leather, but Ash shot him full in the chest before his pistol had cleared the holster.

Tamsin's assailant let go of her and went for his own Colt. Ash jacked another shell into the rifle chamber, but didn't fire for fear of hitting Tamsin. Fiercely, she clung to her assailant's arm, spoiling his aim.

The first shot went wild, almost shattering Ash's rifle stock and sending chips of wood and metal flying. Ash felt the sting of a dozen hornets, but it took all his skill and concentration to stay in the saddle as the squealing stallion fought the bit and reared.

Ash launched himself out of the saddle. He hit the earth and rolled, coming up on his feet to see Tamsin clinging like a burr to the outlaw's back.

Dancer plunged past, and his left rear hoof caught Cannon's man in the knee. He staggered back just as Ash drove his fist into the man's midsection.

Tamsin fell as Ash's opponent whipped his pistol up. Powder and heat scorched Ash's cheek, but he came in hard with a strong right fist.

It caught the pistolero on the chin and dropped him like a poleaxed steer. Spooked by the pain and gunfire, the bay horse bolted away down the draw.

Tamsin sat white-faced and breathless, holding her bleeding upper arm. "It's not my fault. I didn't go with them—"

"Come on!" he said, grabbing the fallen bandit's pistol. "Before the reinforcements get here."

He slipped an arm around her and helped her up. She leaned against him, struggling to stay on her feet.

The gunman was regaining consciousness. Ash knew that he should kill him. He lifted the weapon, but was stopped by the frightened look in Tamsin's eyes.

"That's murder," she said.

With an oath, Ash lowered his aim, putting a bullet into the fallen killer's injured knee. "Does that suit you, woman?"

She turned her face away. "I'm all right. I can walk."

"Like hell." Gathering her in his arms, he plunged into the trees, ran a hundred yards, then stopped. Sitting her down, he pushed her to the ground and crouched over her, protecting her with his body. "Don't make a sound," he whispered.

Two horses trotted up the ravine and stopped. The rock walls echoed with curses.

"Jack! Carlos is dead!" Ash would have bet his daddy's spurs it was Boone's voice.

Ash had heard the story that Jack Cannon had tried to hang his brother Boone when the two were boys. Whatever the reason, Boone spoke in a harsh rasp.

A volley of shots peppered the trees.

"Save your ammunition!"

Ash wondered if that was Jack. It had been years since he'd heard the outlaw speak, and he couldn't be sure. He leaned close to Tamsin's ear. "There were five of them, weren't there?"

She nodded, trembling under him like a wounded bird. "Jack, his brother, and Carlos. You shot Carlos."

"I killed two of them. Who was the fifth man, the one whose horse went lame?"

"I don't know. I never heard them call him by name." She shuddered. "The other one—the one who tried to rape me. He's Billy."

"You should have let me finish him when we had the chance."

She drew in a ragged breath. "That would make you as bad as him."

"It might make me alive."

Her lower lip quivered. "Jack said he was going to do things to me . . ." She jammed a hand against her mouth to keep from crying. "I didn't think you'd come in time."

"You're all right. I have you." Tamsin's hair was tangled with twigs and leaves, but beneath the dust, she still smelled as sweet as he remembered.

Alone, he would have gone after the remaining three, but with Tamsin to worry about, it seemed wiser to run.

She twisted to look up at him. "I didn't want to go with them. They threatened to kill me."

He nodded. "I guessed as much."

"You did?"

"Shhh, darlin'." He allowed himself to touch her cheek for just an instant. "I'm going to get you out of here in one piece, but you've got to help me."

"There's tracks from a single horse," Boone called.

"Just one animal?"

"That's all I see, Jack."

"You asshole! If there's only one horse, then there's only one shooter. Find him!"

Black hatred thickened Ash's throat, and he forced back the killing rage. When it came to besting human vermin like the Cannons, anger was a man's worst enemy. Ash knew he needed to use his wits. The odds were three to two, and Tamsin was weak from loss of blood. Jack was a crack shot. Given half a chance, he would kill them both.

Ash grabbed Tamsin and ran uphill, not stopping until he was out of breath. Then he drew her down into a hollow behind a rock. "Keep your head low," he told her. "I'm going to get us a mount."

She clung to him. "Don't go," she said. "Dancer will find me."

Ash brushed her mouth with his. "You're hurt, darlin'. You need to lay still and let me worry about Cannon."

"But Dancer—"

"He's scared. We can't wait for him to lead them to us." He ripped off his scarf and bound it around her arm. "It looks bad, but I think the bullet missed the bone."

"No. Don't go. They'll kill you."

"Be brave a little longer, darlin'. We can't get out of here without a horse."

"Promise me you won't let them catch me?"

He tilted her chin and looked into her eyes as icy dread seeped through his gut. "Did they abuse you?"

She shook her head. "A slap or two, nothing more."

"It doesn't matter. You can tell me the truth."

"I am telling the truth, you idiot," she snapped at him. "You stopped them." Tears filled her eyes. "I'd rather be dead than have those monsters—"

"Alive is better, woman. Always choose life. But it won't come to that. I swear to you." He stood up. "Wait here, and don't make a sound."

"Don't leave me."

"I'll be within earshot. You just call out if you need me."

Pistol ready, Ash moved from tree to tree, scanning the forest for any sign of movement. The shooting had stopped, and he could no longer hear voices below.

He'd turned Shiloh loose after he'd killed the first of Jack's gang with the rifle. The gelding wouldn't roam far, but the trick was to get him before Cannon's boys did.

He needed to get Tamsin safely away to wash her arm before it swelled with infection. And he needed to finish off Jack and his two remaining accomplices. If he didn't, he knew Cannon would track them down.

Maybe Tamsin was right, he thought. He should have brought along a posse. Maybe, for once, he'd bitten off more than he could chew.

Chapter 23

When Ash returned to the spot where he'd left Tamsin, he found Dancer standing beside her nuzzling her shoulder. "I told you he'd come back."

"If you don't mind, woman, I'm not in the mood for your reminders."

"All right." Her face was bloodless, but she smiled at him. "Have they gone? The outlaws?"

"Maybe. Maybe not." He looked at the sky, gauging the hour and how long it would be until dark. He didn't think they were far from Leon's cabin. He hoped Cannon would decide to go there rather than chase Tamsin through the woods all night.

"Dancer's hurt," Tamsin said. "I need to wash those cuts on his side and rump. I must have pulled out a dozen splinters. I hope they don't get infected."

"What about you?"

"I'll be all right."

She didn't look all right to him.

"You didn't find Shiloh."

He shook his head. "I did locate a spring higher up the ridge. We can camp there tonight."

"And in the morning?"

"Sweetwater is east of here."

"You're taking me back." She nodded. "Jail looked pretty good to me a few hours ago."

He didn't lie to her. He just couldn't tell her the truth, that he'd have to leave her and go after Cannon. His rifle was almost destroyed; they had two pistols and one horse between them. They couldn't outride Jack's gang, and they couldn't outshoot him. As long as they stayed hidden, they might be safe. But when they started back toward Sweetwater, he knew Jack would come after them.

He put her on the stallion and led Dancer uphill to the spring. They couldn't risk a fire tonight, and they were without food, but they could survive with water.

It took a half hour to reach the spot. He helped Tamsin down and let her drink her fill before he led the horse to the small run-off pool between the rocks. Tamsin sat stoically while he tore up a clean shirt from his bedroll to cleanse the bullet hole and stanch the bleeding. Next he packed the wound with moss that he scraped off a boulder and bandaged it tightly.

"You might have brought us some dry biscuits or bacon in that pack of yours," she chided when he was finished with his doctoring. "And you need to take care of Dancer's injuries."

"I'll wash the damn horse's scratches."

"They aren't scratches. They're puncture wounds. He could get lockjaw."

"Maybe I should have put a vet in my pack as well."

"Fried chicken would have been nice. Or apples, ripe red apples."

"Would have if you'd given me notice you were runnin' off again." He grumbled as he cared for Dancer's cuts.

"You can't blame that on me. I was kidnapped."

"So you say." He grinned at her and spread a blanket on a pile of pine needles, then gestured for her to sit on it. "You're more trouble than any owlhoot I've ever gone after."

"Sorry."

Carefully, he reloaded Billy's pistol and placed it within reach. "This one's for you. Use it, if you need to." He settled down beside her and put an arm around her shoulder. Tamsin's head fell naturally against his chest as though that was where it belonged.

She looked up at him, and he winced at the sight of the dark circles under her eyes. "What happens in the morning?"

"I told you, let me worry about that," he said. "You sleep. You look like you need it." He pulled her close, mindful of her injured arm. "I've got no intentions of dyin', Tamsin. Once this is done, we can start living."

Gray smoke billowed from Leon's chimney in the early morning light. Ash lay on his belly near the house spring and thought about Tamsin while he waited for Texas Jack to show his face.

She'd be fightin' mad when she found out that he'd gone off without her again, but he figured she'd forgive him once Jack was permanently out of the way.

It seemed impossible to him that they'd only known each other such a short time. She was part of him now, as close as his right hand, as necessary as his lungs for giving him life.

Horses, cows, or kids, he didn't give a tinker's damn what she wanted to raise or where she wanted to raise them. He could turn his hand to just about anything, and he was tired of hunting men.

It was time someone else tracked down the Texas Jack Cannons and the James boys. His belly was empty. His arm hurt like hell, and he had blisters on both heels from walking half the night. Damned if he wasn't getting too old for this business.

He'd left a note for Tamsin under Billy's pistol. He'd drawn a map showing her the way back to Sweetwater and left instructions to get to Max Spence's place and have Max contact Dimitri.

If he didn't make it back, she could take Dancer and ride. He'd have to put his faith in Dimitri to get her out of trouble with the law. Nobody else could do what he had to do this morning.

The back door opened and Billy limped out, using a barrel slat for a crutch. He had a thin mustache, wore bloodstained rags wrapped around his head, and carried a shotgun.

"Three left," Ash muttered under his breath. He hadn't expected the injured man to be able to walk this morning, let alone carry a weapon. It showed that outlaws had grown tougher than they used to be. Or that he was a complete fool for letting Tamsin talk him out of killing Billy where he'd found him.

A trickle of sand rolled down from the bluff above him, and Ash tensed. Had Jack or Boone slipped out and come up behind him?

A cold sweat broke out on his skin. He didn't dare move and give away his position, but neither could he lie here and wait for a bullet through his back.

Slowly Ash turned his head. No silhouette of a man loomed above him. The grass and wildflowers that sprouted from the overhang seemed undisturbed. What then could—

He froze as something heavy slithered over the back of his calves just above his boot tops. His breath caught in his throat, and his heart bucked against his chest. A long second passed, and then another.

From the corner of his eye Ash detected motion. At the same instant, a dry buzzing turned his gut inside out. Ash's mouth shriveled as though he'd eaten a green peach when the rattlesnake's diamond-shaped head appeared inches from his right elbow.

The serpent's body slid over Ash's legs, and the flat expressionless eyes gleamed with moisture as the snake flicked a long, thin tongue. Ash remained motionless. He knew it wasn't possible, but he would have sworn he could smell it.

The rattler smelled of death.

Sweat dripped into Ash's eyes. His lungs began to burn for lack of oxygen, and his fingers cramped on the damaged rifle stock. Somewhere high above, he heard a hawk shriek a plaintive cry. Ash's parched mouth tasted of lead.

Slowly the scaly, gray-green patterned body coiled and sounded another lethal warning, a dull vibration like the rattle of seeds in a dried gourd.

The snake turned its huge striped head to stare at him with frigid, glassy eyes, and Ash's bowels clenched. When he was twelve, he'd seen a boy bitten by a big diamondback. His leg had swollen to gigantic proportions and turned black. And all his parents' prayers hadn't been enough to save him from a screaming death.

A prairie rattler wasn't as volatile as a diamondback, but one this size packed enough poison to kill a horse.

Ash didn't know how much longer he could hold his breath, but instinct told him that any movement could trigger a deadly strike.

Then something rustled in the grass. The snake's head snapped around as a white-bellied deer mouse popped into sight. The tiny rodent rose on its hind legs and sniffed the air.

The rattler blinked.

Emitting a faint squeak, the mouse darted off. The snake leapt after it, and both vanished from view. Ash inhaled deeply, remembering Billy and his shotgun just before the weapon blasted.

Ash snapped his rifle up, preparing to return fire, then realized that the outlaw hadn't been shooting at him.

Ash's breathing slowed and his heart quit jumping as he watched the man walk into the tall weeds and lift up the rattlesnake.

The back door flew open, and Boone Cannon showed his face. Boone had aged a lot since Ash had last seen him. His blond hair had darkened and thinned, and one side of his face bore an ugly scar. "What the hell you shootin' at, Billy?"

"Thought it was a rabbit," the man with the shotgun answered. "Ain't nothin' but a damned ole rattler." He heaved the headless body of the twitching reptile over the top rail of the corral, and the horses shied and crowded to the far side. Billy laughed. "Skittish, ain't they?"

"Jack don't like being woke up this early by you actin' the ass," Boone said. He walked out a few steps from the back door, scanned the valley, and fumbled with the front of his trousers.

As Boone relieved himself, Ash's finger tightened on the trigger. If he fired now, he could drop both of them before they could shoot back.

Common sense told him that's just what he should do, but he couldn't. He'd killed more men than he wanted to remember, but he didn't like the way he'd felt when he'd shot that man out of the saddle yesterday.

"You'd be no better than they are," Tamsin had said.

Maybe he'd lost his taste for killing when he thought that trash like these two deserved more than being mowed down with no more thought than Billy had destroyed the snake.

"Drop your guns! You're under arrest!" he shouted.

Billy jerked the shotgun to his shoulder, and Ash drilled him through the heart with a single bullet.

Boone drew his Colt and started firing as he backed toward the house. Ash's bullet caught him in the groin.

Boone staggered back and fanned the hammer, spraying the ground near Ash with lead. Ash's next round caught him through the throat. He fell, half in and half out of the open doorway.

Ash leapt to his feet and ran for the house. Then Jack Cannon appeared at the front corner of the cabin with a rifle in one hand, a pistol in the other.

Bullets whizzed past Ash's head like angry bees. One shot. He dived for the ground and rolled as Jack kept up a steady hail of lead.

Sand exploded in Ash's face as he scrambled to find some shelter from the bullets. He hunkered down behind a pile of rotting fence posts, and got off a shot at Jack as he dashed for the corral.

Jack was already over the corral fence. Ash took careful aim and fired. The bullet plowed through a railing and drove into Jack's left knee. He swore, fell, dropped the rifle, and struggled to his feet. Panicked horses milled around him, and Ash saw him grab Shiloh's saddle.

Jack twisted and tried to get off another shot. When the pin clicked on a spent shell, Ash was up and running toward him. The outlaw swung up onto Shiloh and lashed him toward a low place in the fence. Then Ash saw something out of the corner of his eyes. He glanced in the direction of the spring and saw Tamsin riding toward him on Dancer.

Swearing, Ash whirled back toward the corral as Jack galloped toward the broken rail. Ash's final bullet hit him in the right breast.

Jack sagged forward and dropped the reins. Ash whistled. The gelding turned hard to the left, nearly throwing the outlaw out of the saddle. Jack grabbed a handful of horn and stayed with the horse as he shied and came to a trembling halt halfway between Tamsin and Ash.

"Don't shoot me!" Cannon yelled. "I give up! Don't shoot!" He slumped forward and raised one hand over his head. "I'm dropping my gun. See." He let the empty pistol fall.

Ash's finger tightened on the trigger of his Colt. He'd never wanted anything so badly in his life as he wanted to put two shots into Jack's belly and watch him die slow and ugly.

The outlaw with the pretty-boy features had aged since Ash had seen him last.

He wanted to kill him just the same.

"You don't deserve to live," he said. "Give me one reason, Jack, why I shouldn't—"

"'Cause I know you, Morgan. You ain't got the balls to kill me. Just like you didn't have the balls to satisfy that pretty little wife of—"

Cannon's eyes widened as a crimson flower blossomed on his chest. "I . . . I . . ." Blood spilled from his open mouth, and he toppled out of the saddle.

Tamsin lowered Billy's smoking pistol. "He had a derringer hidden in his boot. He would have murdered you, Ash."

He stared at her, still unable to believe what he'd seen. "You killed him."

"What was I supposed to do, let him kill you?"

"Hell, woman," he said as he lifted her down off Dancer. "I'm glad you did. I just can't believe you made that shot from the back of a horse. Do you know how many marksmen would miss—"

"I couldn't miss." She tilted her face up to kiss him. "I was the only hope you had."

He held her for a long time, until she stopped trembling, and his heartbeat returned to normal.

"I suppose we need to take them back to Sweetwater for a Christian burial."

Ash shrugged. "It would be the only decent thing to do." Then he added, "Of course, we could dig graves ourselves. If we had a shovel." He buried his face in her hair and hugged her again. "But since we don't, I'd say it's best we leave them to the coyotes."

Chapter 24

It was hot enough to fry eggs on the wooden sidewalks of Sweetwater the afternoon of Tamsin's trial. Not a breath of air stirred in the Rooster's Den, the town's largest saloon.

Judge Buckson Marlborough, presiding justice, had taken one look at Henry Steele's chambers and appropriated Howie Knight's thriving business establishment for the proceedings. So much attention had been raised by the trial among the good citizens of Colorado Territory that seating was at a premium and the street outside was crowded with gawkers. One enterprising woman had filled the back of her wagon with a barrel of sweet cider, gingerbread, and pies, and was selling slices faster than her husband could count change. Across the street from the Rooster, a Baptist minister stood on a packing crate and preached the gospel to one aging Ute Indian, a German immigrant in lederhosen and steel-toed clodhoppers, and three heavily rouged ladies currently on holiday from their positions at the Rooster's Den.

Children, dogs, and poultry wandered amid the throng of noisy onlookers. Horses whinnied, chickens scratched, dogs barked, and babies wailed. Shopkeepers had moved their goods to the sidewalks in front of their establishments and were doing a brisk trade.

Inside the saloon, Tamsin fought a rising nausea in her

stomach and tried to make eye contact with the jury as Dimitri had instructed. Twelve stern-faced men sat on hard wooden benches and stared at her with varying degrees of contempt as Henry Steele completed the final minutes of his damning testimony against her.

The splintery floorboards were sticky under her feet, and the overpowering stench of years of spilled beer, vomit, blood, and stale tobacco made her light-headed. Since her grandfather had always insisted Tamsin had the strength of a workhorse, her physical weakness made her believe that her suspicions were a certainty.

In the last harried weeks, her woman's time had come and passed without a show of blood. She'd tried to remember the last time she'd had her flow. It was definitely before Sam Steele's death. But after—she couldn't remember.

She strongly suspected that her intuition had been correct when she'd felt that she and Ash had made a child that glorious day at the hot springs.

"Tamsin?" Ash laid a hand on her bandaged arm.

"Mrs. MacGreggor. Are we boring you?" Judge Marlborough asked.

His sarcasm sliced through her reverie, and she jerked upright. To her shock, she saw that the witness chair beside the justice's table was empty. Henry Steele had already taken his seat with the prosecutor to her left. The lawyer representing Colorado Territory, Russell King, was a big man with a paunch, gray sideburns, and a double chin.

"Will you honor us by taking the stand, Mrs. MacGreggor?" King asked sarcastically. The crowd loved his remark. Even two of the jurors snickered.

"I'm sorry," she murmured as she got to her feet.

"It's all right," Ash said quietly.

She really did feel unwell. The room seemed to be pitching. She wondered if they had earthquakes in Colorado.

Dimitri took her arm and helped her up the two steps to the bottom landing of the staircase where Judge Marlborough presided. Today the doors to the social chambers above, which Tamsin supposed to be usually well oiled, remained firmly closed. According to her friend and lawyer, the upper floor of the Rooster was given over to lodging for gentlewomen. Tamsin doubted that there was a genuine lady among them.

Russell King asked question after question, all styled in a manner to make her look guilty. Dimitri had received letters from her hometown assuring the judge that Dancer and Fancy were legally hers. Unfortunately, statements from strangers in Tennessee didn't hold much water here in Colorado.

Tamsin tried to remain calm. She answered each accusation fully and with dignity. Some truths rang harsh in the courtroom.

"You admit to this jury that you went to Mr. Steele's stable with the express intention of stealing two valuable thoroughbreds?" the prosecutor asked.

"You don't understand," Tamsin began. "These were my—"

"Answer the question," King said.

"It's not possible to steal my own—"

Judge Marlborough rapped his gavel on the table. "Yes or no, Mrs. MacGreggor."

Tamsin bit back a peppery reply and said, "No. I did not."

King smiled. "Then why, may I ask, were you trespassing on property you had specifically been ordered to stay—"

"I think you should ask Judge Steele what he was doing there in the middle of the night," she replied.

"Objection," King protested. "The defendant is evading my questions."

Tamsin felt hotter and hotter inside the layers of clothing and boned corset Dimitri's wife had insisted she wear. The black silk taffeta folds of the flounced dress with its high collar and tight waist smothered her. Sweat beaded on her face and collected in the hollow of her upper lip. If she didn't get off this witness stand soon, she'd faint.

"Mrs. MacGreggor. Mrs. MacGreggor, you will answer the questions put to you by . . ."

The judge droned on, but Tamsin forced herself to sit straight and keep watching the members of the jury. She shifted her gaze from one to another with what she hoped was an honest demeanor.

"Your honor," Dimitri said. "I believe my client is unwell. Could you grant a short recess?"

"Objection," King said. "This is my witness. There's no need to delay this jury—"

"It's all right," Tamsin said. "I'm fine. I'm ready to proceed."

King continued with his grilling for nearly an hour; then finally she took her seat at the defense table and Ash clasped her hand.

"Good work," he whispered. "You'd have my vote for innocent."

Dimitri put a finger to his lips, warning them to silence as Sam Steele's weeping widow took the stand.

King's demeanor toward Sarah Steele was totally different from his manner with Tamsin. He spoke softly, sympathetically. He asked only a few questions, then excused her.

As she stepped down, the widow Steele's gaze met Tamsin's. Quickly Sarah looked away, but not before Tamsin saw her flush.

"She knows more than she's saying," Tamsin whispered to Dimitri.

Next, King called Edwards from the livery to testify as to Tamsin's behavior the day she found her horses missing.

Tamsin listened in disbelief as Edwards described two totally different animals that she supposedly left in his care. "He's lying!" she cried.

"Order!" Judge Marlborough declared. "Hold your tongue, woman, or you'll be removed from my court."

"Like I said," the stable owner continued, "that woman left an old mare and a black gelding, neither one worth spit. The kid what worked for me, Javier, claims she came back that night with a man that matches the description of the outlaw Jack Cannon and took the horses away. Next day, she starts yellin' she had blooded stock. . . ."

Ash stared at Edwards, then whispered in Dimitri's ear.

Tamsin's lawyer jumped to his feet. "Your honor, this man isn't—"

King turned and glared at Dimitri. "This is my witness. Mr. Edwards—"

Ash stood up. "That's the problem, Judge. That's not Edwards on the stand. At least that's not his legal name. He's really Ed Jackson out of Kane's Crossroads, Missouri. He's wanted by the authorities there for horse stealing, extortion, and barn burning. I also believe he should be charged with Javier's murder."

The witness leapt up, overturning his chair, and fled up the steps behind the judge's table. Pandemonium erupted as Sheriff Roy Walker and Ash both tore off after him.

The livery owner ducked into one of the rooms on the second floor. Seconds later, Tamsin heard glass breaking, then a gunshot.

The entire jury produced pistols and joined the chase. Women screamed, King cursed, and Sarah Steele laid her head on Henry Steele's chest and began to sob loudly. Judge Marlborough shouted for order, but no one paid him the slightest attention. Some of the onlookers pushed past the judge and ran upstairs; the rest spilled through the saloon doors into the street.

Dimitri pulled a derringer from his satchel, took Tamsin's arm, and escorted her through the confusion into a back office.

Buckson Marlborough followed, a Colt .45 in one hand and a bottle of good whiskey in the other. "Don't think your client's going to escape," he said sternly.

Dimitri motioned Tamsin to a chair and took two glasses from a shelf in the corner. "Your honor—*Bucky*—does it seem to you as though Mrs. MacGreggor is attempting an escape?"

The judge muttered and poured both glasses half full of the spirits. Dimitri clicked his glass to Marlborough's and took a sip.

Tamsin chewed at a fingernail and watched the door.

Two hours later, the trial resumed with a courtroom cleared of everyone but Ash, the sheriff, the accused, counsel, witnesses, the jury, and the presiding judge.

Sheriff Walker testified. "Edwards . . . I guess his name is really Edward Jackson, is under arrest and being held in my jail for Missouri. He was apprehended by Morgan, who's claimin' the two-hundred-dollar reward. I'm also plannin' on askin' him some hard questions on the death of his stableboy, Javier Chispero."

Marlborough glanced at King. "Do you have any further remarks about that witness?"

King shook his head. "No, sir. His true identity was unknown to any of us. Edwards—Jackson—has lived in Sweetwater for three years. We had no way of knowing—"

"Yes, yes, I understand that. Do you have anything else to say about Samuel Steele's murder?"

"No, sir. Prosecution rests."

Marlborough grunted. "I hope so. Dimitri?"

Tamsin's lawyer rose. His eyes were a little brighter, his stance somewhat rigid. Other than that, Tamsin thought, no one could have guessed he'd just downed five shot glasses of sipping whiskey, one less than the judge.

Dimitri gestured toward the empty witness chair. "I'd like to call Mrs. Steele, if it please the court."

The judge frowned. "Not much, it doesn't. Can we get this over with, son?"

A pale Sarah Steele took the stand.

"Mrs. Steele," Dimitri began. "I won't make this any more difficult than it already is for you."

She brought a handkerchief to her eyes and sniffed.

"Do you see my client?"

Sarah nodded.

"Is she a lady, would you say, Mrs. Steele?"

Sarah's reply was too low for Tamsin to understand.

"Could you repeat that, please?" Dimitri asked. "Is Mrs. MacGreggor a lady?"

"I don't know."

"You don't know." Dimitri put his hands behind his back and walked over to the jury. "I'm sure these gentlemen would have no difficulty in deciding that question."

"Objection," King complained.

"What's he doing?" Tamsin whispered to Ash. "He'll antagonize them."

"Shhh," Ash answered. "Wait and see what he's getting to."

"Well, then, Mrs. Steele, would you describe yourself as a lady?"

"Objection!"

"Yes, I would," Sarah replied. She was visibly trembling.

"Do you know what the penalty for murder is?" Dimitri asked quietly.

Sarah nodded.

"And it will not bother you to see this innocent woman hanged by the neck for—"

"No. No," Sarah cried. "I can't, Henry. I just can't. I'm sorry, but—"

"What the hell are you talking about?" Henry Steele demanded, rising to his feet.

"Order! Order in this court!"

"Who did kill your husband?" Dimitri asked.

Sarah covered her face with her hands. "I did," she said. "I killed him."

"You don't know what you're saying!" a stunned Henry shouted.

"She did it?" Tamsin cried. "Sarah shot him?" Tamsin flung herself into Ash's arms.

"I knew all along you couldn't have done it," he teased.

"Did you?" She drew back and pummeled him half-heartedly in the chest. "If you did . . ." She tried to gain control of herself. "If you did," she repeated, "you sure had a strange way of showing it."

"I'll have order in this court, or I'll lock you all up for contempt," Judge Marlborough said, slamming his Colt on the table.

Henry Steele's face whitened to chalk. "You killed my brother?" he rasped.

Dimitri laid a hand on Sarah's shoulder. "Would you like to continue?" he asked. "Tell us exactly what happened."

"Shut up, Sarah!" Henry shouted. "Don't say—"

"Get him out of here," Marlborough ordered, pointing

to Judge Steele. "Sheriff! Do your duty or find another job!"

Walker hustled a protesting Henry toward the swinging doors.

"Please," Sarah begged. "Let him stay. I want him to hear. I don't know if I can tell it again, and Henry must know why."

Walker glanced back at Marlborough.

"He can stay," the presiding judge consented. "But one word out of you, Henry," he threatened, "one word, and I'll shoot you myself."

"Sam and I," Sarah began brokenly. "It was a mistake, from the first. My mistake. Sam was a hard man, very hard. He hit me whenever I . . ."

Dimitri took Sarah's hand. "You don't have to go on if you don't want to."

"No, if I don't tell it now, I never will," she insisted. "Henry and I . . . I love Henry, and I think he loves me." She looked at him, and he nodded.

"Sam found out about us, about the baby . . . Henry's baby. He said he was going to kill Henry. He said it, and he would have." She was speaking to Judge Steele, as if they were alone in the room, Tamsin thought.

Sarah inhaled deeply and went on. "I followed him to the barn that night." She glanced at Tamsin. "They were her horses. I'm sure of it. Mr. Edwards stole horses and sold them to Sam. They always had bills of sale. Sam made them himself. It was one of the reasons Sam's ranch was so successful. He always had good horses to sell in Denver."

"Go on," Dimitri urged.

"That night, I was leaving him. I'd sent a note to Henry, asking him to come for me. But somehow, Sam found out. He let the cowboy deliver the letter, but he was waiting in the barn for Henry to come. He said he was going to shoot Henry first, so I'd know he was dead. First Henry, and then me. I couldn't let him do that."

"So you followed your husband to the stable," Dimitri supplied.

"Yes, I did. I told him I was going to stop him the only way I knew how. I had to protect Henry and our baby, you see. Who else could do it?"

"Yes," Dimitri urged. "Then what?"

"He laughed. Sam laughed. He said I was . . . He called me a filthy name. He said I didn't have the guts to shoot him. And then he turned his back on me."

"And you shot him," Dimitri finished.

"Yes."

"You intended to kill him, or you intended to frighten him. Which was it?" Dimitri asked. "Think very carefully, Mrs. Steele. Remember back to that terrible night. You were in the stable on a dark, stormy night. You were upset, frightened. Are you sure you meant to pull the trigger? Or is there a possibility that it could have gone off accidentally?"

Sarah looked up into Dimitri's face. "It could have been an accident."

"There," the little lawyer declared. "There you have it, gentlemen." He whirled on the jury. "This frail woman, a woman already traumatized by beatings and the threat of being murdered. She goes to the barn and tries to frighten her husband by pointing a gun at him."

"And the weapon simply discharged." Marlborough slammed his Colt on the table. "Sheriff. Arrest this woman. She is to be delivered to my court in Denver for trial two weeks hence."

"Marlborough—" Judge Steele began.

"Shut up, Henry," Marlborough said. He rapped the table again. "Henry Steele to pay the fine of one hundred dollars for contempt of court."

"One hundred dollars?"

"Make that five hundred dollars. Fine dismissed if Judge Steele provides this court with proof of his marriage to Mrs. Samuel Steele within twenty-four hours."

"That's blackmail," Henry retorted.

Judge Marlborough fixed him with a steely, if somewhat unfocused, gaze. "Will you or will you not do the honorable thing by this lady?"

"But you're going to try her for murder."

"I am. But that doesn't mean you don't have a responsibility toward her child."

Sarah looked at Henry hopefully.

"I will, damn it," Henry replied.

"Good." Marlborough stood up unsteadily. "Dimitri, your client is free to go."

"Which client, your honor?" Zajicek asked.

Bucky Marlborough chuckled. "Mrs. MacGreggor. You'll have a more difficult job defending the other one."

"Perhaps," the lawyer replied. "But there are extenuating circumstances."

"Aren't there always?" Marlborough slammed his Colt down a final time. "This court is no longer in session."

Chapter 25

Tamsin and Ash returned with Dimitri to the boardinghouse, where his wife, Helen, joined them for a celebration supper. The owner had set up a private table for the four of them in a small chamber off the main dining room.

"How brilliant of you to suspect Mrs. Steele," Helen remarked.

Dimitri smiled and patted his wife's hand. "Hardly brilliant. We were running out of suspects, and Mrs. Steele had as much reason to want to be rid of her husband as Judge Steele did. And she seemed entirely too sympathetic toward Mrs. MacGreggor. Naturally, if Ashton hadn't identified the livery owner as a wanted criminal using an alias, we would have been in a difficult position with that jury."

"Edwards's escape attempt didn't do us any harm either," Ash put in.

"I don't care. You're still a brilliant lawyer," Helen said. "You would have thought of something. You always do."

"Thank you, my dear. I'm glad you think so," Dimitri answered, and then went on to explain the details of Sarah Steele's confession.

"But how will you defend her?" Helen asked. "Since she's already confessed to the shooting."

"Extenuating circumstances," Tamsin put in.

Dimitri nodded. "Exactly."

Ash hardly heard a word. He was as jittery as a steer at a barbecue, and he couldn't take his eyes off Tamsin. There was so much he wanted to say to her, so much that they needed to settle as soon as they were alone together. But he couldn't be rude to Dimitri and his wife by refusing their hospitality after all they had done for Tamsin.

Supper was steak, potatoes, and gravy, with homemade biscuits, and gingerbread for dessert, better food than he'd had in a month. He couldn't help noticing that Tamsin was pushing her food around her plate, barely nibbling at her meat. He supposed that the trial had made her as nervous as he was.

Dimitri and Helen kept up the conversation during the meal, more than making up for Tamsin's unnatural quiet. Ash didn't say much either, but he managed to finish his gingerbread and hers, then washed it all down with two cups of strong black coffee.

"Would you like to go walking with me, Tamsin?" he asked when they'd finished supper, and she folded her napkin and laid it on the table. As soon as they got outside, out of earshot of eavesdroppers, he meant to ask her to marry him. He even had Aunt Jane's wedding ring in his shirt pocket. He hoped it would fit her finger.

Tamsin frowned. "I'm sorry," she said hesitantly. "I'm really feeling very tired. Perhaps in the morning—"

Confused, he rose to his feet. "What do you mean in the morning? I've got—"

She looked at Dimitri's wife and two spots burned red on her cheeks. "Mrs. Zajicek has kindly offered to share her bedchamber with me tonight."

Dimitri laughed. "I'm afraid you'll have to bunk with me in the attached parlor, Ashton. There are so many people in town for the trial, the only other rooms available are those on the second floor of the Rooster."

"Mr. Zajicek!" Helen admonished.

"Sorry, my dear. My apologies, Mrs. MacGreggor," he replied with a chuckle.

Tamsin shook her head. "No, don't apologize. After what you've done for me, nothing you could say would offend me."

"Don't be too sure," his wife remarked. "My Mr. Zajicek can be quite rowdy when he's taken a nip. And I fear he's had more than one today."

"Good night, Ash," Tamsin said. "I really am tired." She walked through the doorway into a narrow hallway lit by a curtainless window.

He followed and grabbed her arm. "Why?" Ash demanded.

Brilliant green eyes framed by thick lashes stared into his. "I'm telling you the truth, Ash. I'm not feeling well. And Mrs. Zajicek invited me to stay with her. What was I supposed to say? I'm sleeping with Ash Morgan? Announce to the whole town that no, I'm not a murderer, but I am a loose woman?" She pulled away. "We're not in the mountains anymore, are we? There is a code that good women live by, and . . . I may have strayed, but I've not fallen, Ash. I can't be that easy anymore."

"Hell, I thought you and me . . ." What had come over her? She seemed a stranger, making him suddenly at a loss for words.

"I'm not ungrateful for what you've done," she said. "I don't blame you for anything that happened. No one forced me to become intimate with you."

"What are you talking about? You know what we have together, you and me."

"No . . . I don't know. And that's what I have to think

about." Flushing, she turned abruptly and started up the stairs.

"Tamsin?"

"Tomorrow."

He didn't know whether to swear or go after her and kiss her. Having the charges dismissed should have made her happy. . . . And if she wouldn't talk to him, how was he going to tell her that he wanted to marry her?

"Women," he muttered. His arm was aching where the bullet had nicked him, and he was working on a hell of a headache. Damn if he wouldn't go back to the saloon and have a drink himself.

Tamsin closed the bedroom door and leaned against it. Her heart was beating rapidly, and she felt light-headed. Either she was coming down with the ague or she really was with child.

She went over to the bed and sat down. She'd hurt Ash, and she hadn't meant to. The moments of elation when the judge had dismissed her charges had given way to uncertainty.

California seemed farther away than ever.

Since her husband's death, her dream had kept her going. She'd been determined to prove wrong Lawyer Crawshaw and all the others who'd laughed at her.

If she told Ash that she thought she was carrying his child, she knew that he'd take care of her, might even feel that it was his duty to marry her. She loved him, but that wasn't the way she wanted to start a marriage. And suppose she wasn't pregnant at all? Her body might simply be reacting to the ordeal she'd been through. Could she say to Ash later, "Well, I thought I was in the family way, but I'm not? Sorry, my mistake."

He'd never promised her anything beyond what they had, wonderful memories that she would carry with her for the rest of her life. Forcing him into marriage by holding fatherhood over his head didn't seem to her to be the most sensible of plans.

Could she simply ride away and give him up, loving him as much as she did? That was as bleak a thought as bearing a child without a father.

Slowly, she unbuttoned the bodice of her black dress and pulled it over her head. Next she struggled with the cursed steel-hooped crinoline, removed two petticoats, her shoes, and her stockings, leaving her standing barefoot in a simple linen chemise and calf-length cotton drawers.

All these fine garments were borrowed, too loose and too short in some places, too tight and confining in others. In truth, she had less now than when she'd come to Sweetwater. Her riding outfits, her spare clothing, and all of her personal possessions were lost. She had no money and no hope of earning more if she wished to reach California before winter snows blocked the passes.

Mrs. Zajicek had offered her a loan and promised to secure her a place in a party that was leaving Denver for San Francisco. The older woman had assured her that there were two respectable ladies traveling with their husbands and small children.

One lady, a Mrs. Tourtillott, had expressed a desire to find a woman of good character to help her with her little ones on the arduous journey. Mrs. Zajicek felt certain that with her personal recommendation, Tamsin could have the position.

The thought of being in Helen and Dimitri's debt was depressing, yet Ash had already promised to supply Dimitri's expenses in defending her. That amount must certainly be repaid.

She had known Ash Morgan for a matter of weeks, not months or years. When she'd proved herself to be such a poor judge of men in the past, could she surrender all her dreams for a man who was a virtual stranger? Throw herself on his mercy simply because she thought she was in love? Would she have felt the same way about Ash if he'd simply come courting her in a yellow-wheeled buggy? Or if he was a grocer rather than a dashing bounty hunter?

The unease in her belly passed, but her mind would not stop churning. She forced herself to drink a glass of water and brushed and braided her hair. It was barely dusk through the dusty window when she climbed into bed, determined not to shed tears over her hapless state. In the morning, when this day was behind her, she would make a decision about Ash Morgan and her own future.

In the morning, she promised herself.

"The hell you will!" Ash said. It was nearly noon the following day, and Tamsin was mounted on her chestnut mare with the Appaloosa and stallion in tow. Ash had followed her out of Sweetwater onto the Denver road after a late breakfast with Dimitri and his wife.

Tamsin hadn't been out of sight of the town when she'd announced that she was joining a wagon train to San Francisco.

"Who's going to stop me?"

"I am." He reined Shiloh so close to Fancy that his duster brushed Tamsin's skirt. "You're not going anywhere without me."

She threw him a look that would have soured milk. "I think I'm in love with you," she said.

"You do? Well, that makes sense. You're in love with me. I'm about to ask you to marry me, and you're running away."

Her eyes widened in surprise. "Marriage? With you?"

"Hell, no, not with me! With my horse. What's wrong

with you? Have you lost what sense you have? I'm asking you to be my wife."

She clicked the chestnut into a trot. "It's an odd way to ask a lady, I must say." Her chin firmed. "You've said nothing about love."

He snatched off his hat and threw it onto the ground in disgust. "Damn it, woman, it's not a thing I should have to say. You ought to know how I feel about you."

"Should I? A gentleman would make himself perfectly clear."

Feeling foolish, he circled Shiloh and scooped up his hat. "You think I'm just going to let you ride out of my life? After you shot Jack Cannon to save me?"

"Not out of your life." She pulled up her mount. "This is too sudden, Ash, too fast for either of us. I'll be in San Francisco. I want you to think about this for a few months, then if you still want me, you can write to me in care of general delivery, and—"

"That does it." Jabbing his heels into his gelding's sides, he guided the horse close to Tamsin and lifted her out of the saddle.

"Stop! Put me down," she protested as he dragged her up in front of him.

He stilled her thrashing with a sound kiss.

"Marry me, Tamsin," he whispered when they came up for air. "Marry me and take me to California with you."

"Do . . . do you mean it?" she stammered. "Do you really love me?"

He kissed her again, and her arms went around his neck so tightly that he could hardly breathe.

"What will you do in California?"

"Build you that damn horse ranch you're always clamoring about. Surely you can find work for a halfway decent wrangler on it."

"How do I know you'd make a good wrangler?"

"I rode that Satan-born imp of yours, didn't I?"

"That was downhill in a rock slide and later when people were shooting at him. Dancer was too frightened to put his best effort into getting rid of you."

"He seemed to try."

"Maybe," she admitted. "But I won't have any ranch, not for years. I'm broke. I don't have anything but these three horses and . . ."

"Tamsin MacGreggor, will you never shut up. I've got enough for both of us."

"What?"

Shiloh came to an abrupt halt, and he swung down out of the saddle and lifted her down. "Look in my saddlebag."

"In your saddlebag?" she repeated.

"Are you deaf as well as addled?" He yanked open the leather pouch and filled her hands with certificates of deposit. "I never expected to live long enough to settle down, but I saved what I made, just in case. The reward for the Cannon brothers will pay our way to California, and this should buy your precious land."

"You're serious?" She swayed against him, and he held her so that her red-gold hair tickled his face and he could smell her fresh, sweet scent.

"You're the best thing that ever happened to me, Mrs. MacGreggor, and I'm not dumb enough to let you get a mile away, let alone to California."

"You really love me?"

He chuckled. "What have I been saying?"

"I'm not sure. What have you been saying?"

"You're not letting me out of this, are you?" He smiled at her. "I love you, Tamsin MacGreggor. Love you with all my heart and soul. I should have known it sooner, but I never claimed to be the smartest man west of the Mississippi."

"Will you still love me tomorrow and the day after that?"

"I'll love you as long as the sun rises in the east, woman. And if it doesn't, I'll love you just the same."

"All right," she answered softly. "I'll make you a deal. If you can ride Dancer back to Denver without him throwing you into the dirt, I'll marry you."

"I'd ride the devil's wind for you."

"Then I'd best be your wife, for I'm not likely to get an offer like that from a finer man."

"You'd better make your vows with me," he answered. "I intend for you to be carrying our first child by the time we get to San Francisco."

"I think I can promise that." And then she rose on her toes and kissed him, and he stopped thinking of anything but the woman in his arms, the woman he meant to love and cherish for the rest of this life and into the next.

Epilogue

The two outlaws tied their ponies and crawled on their bellies toward the corral beside the main stock barn on Tamsin's Hope. "Keep your head down," the first desperado said. "He's fast on the draw."

"Not fast enough," his comrade hissed.

Ash's back was to the fence, his attention focused on the bay colt. On the far side of the pound, the chestnut mare laid back her ears and gave an anxious whinny. The foal responded with a high-pitched squeal.

"Easy, Cheyenne," Ash soothed. He stroked the colt's velvety nose, ran his hand up to scratch behind the twitching ears, and buckled the halter. "You be quiet, too, Fancy. Nobody's going to hurt your new baby."

The little bay laid back his ears, quivered all over, and sneezed. Then he raised one dainty front hoof and pawed the ground.

"Shh," Ash murmured as he offered the colt a piece of apple. "By next week you won't even notice you're wearing a halter." He released the lead line, and the little horse ran to his mother and began to nurse.

"Go for your gun, bounty hunter!" the younger pistolero shouted.

"Give us all your horses and all your gold!" his amigo demanded.

Ash turned. His eyes narrowed as he stared into the green eyes of the outlaw leader. "I've been looking for you two for a long time."

"Yeah?" the smaller, dark-haired bandit said cockily. "Well, we been trailin' you, too, bounty hunter."

"You gonna draw, big man?" his redheaded partner said. "Or are you—"

Ash laughed as a hand closed on the redhead's collar.

"Mama!" David's eyes widened in surprise, and he dropped the fishing pole he'd been using for a rifle.

The littler criminal threw his pole, turned to make his getaway, and gasped as Tamsin grabbed him by the seat of his baggy trousers. His broad-brimmed sombrero slid back revealing big brown eyes, a freckled nose, and a dimple on his chin.

"Were you going someplace, Jared?" she asked.

"Hi, Mama."

"We were just foolin'—" the nine-year-old protested.

"Playing bounty hunter with Daddy," his younger brother chimed in.

"What have I told you about violence?" Tamsin asked.

"We didn't have a real gun. Just fishing poles. Daddy was—"

Ash shook his head as he climbed over the corral fence and joined Tamsin. "Don't you boys drag me into this. Where were you two when we were ready for church this morning?"

Jared flushed and kicked the dirt with the toe of his boot. "David said the fish were biting."

"So you two went fishing instead of going to church with your mama and me?" Ash asked.

"Yes, Daddy," David admitted sheepishly.

"Umm-humm," Jared agreed. "But we caught fish for dinner."

"Enormous fish," his brother said.

"I thought that's where you might have gone when I found holes in my flower bed," Tamsin observed.

"We needed big worms, Mama," Jared explained. "Big worms live in your flower beds."

"Lucky for you two there's going to be a special service this evening," Ash said. "Reverend Graham and his wife offered to pick the two of you up and take you to church with them."

"But Daddy, you promised we could ride out to the north pasture with you and bring in Dancer and the mares." David looked hopeful. "I'm awful sorry we missed church this morning, but next Sunday—"

"Next Sunday we'll be in our usual pew as a family," Tamsin said. She released her prisoners. "I want those ponies curried and turned into their stalls, and then—"

"Then the two of you can take the fish in to Maria, eat the cold dinner your mother left on the table for you, and help Maria wash the dishes," Ash finished. "Baths for both of you."

"Put on your church clothes, and you may read until it's time to go with the reverend," Tamsin said.

David sighed. "But where are you and Mama going?"

"We'll just go and get the horses ourselves. Now, you heard your mother! Get! And take Sam Houston with you. That fool cat has been after your mother's canary all morning. Next time you run off, take him with you."

Shoulders slumped, heads down, the little bandits trudged off to fetch their ponies. The big orange-and-white tomcat trotted after them, tail flicking back and forth.

Ash put an arm around Tamsin's shoulders and chuckled. "Rascals, both of them."

"All three," she said. "Sam Houston climbed up my lace curtains and left a dead mole on the back step."

Ash rubbed his face in Tamsin's hair. "Don't be too hard on Sam Houston. He's just keeping critters out of your flower garden." He tilted her chin and looked into her eyes. "Sure you wouldn't rather go to services than round up horses with me? We've got enough wranglers on this ranch."

She smiled up at him. "And Sunday's their day off. What if they want to go to church? Besides, I think I like riding off with you into the sunset. We could pack a little supper—"

"And a blanket," he added.

"I remember what happened the last time I went picnicking alone with you." She patted her rounding belly. "Another Morgan."

"Maybe it will be a girl this time."

"I'd like that," she said softly. "But I wouldn't mind another boy either. I've grown quite fond of my three men."

Ash glanced up toward the sprawling adobe ranch house sheltered beneath the flowering trees. "We've done all right for ourselves in California, haven't we, woman?"

"I've done all right since I met you," she replied.

"You just say that because it's true," he teased, then raised her chin and kissed her tenderly.

"I love you, Ash Morgan," she whispered.

"And I love you, Tamsin Morgan."

The bay colt whinnied, and Tamsin laughed softly. "You're certain you don't miss your old life," she murmured. "Free as the wind, riding wherever your fancy takes you?"

"Bad joke," he said. "More like wherever your Dancer takes me."

"Sorry." She grimaced. "It was the best one I could think of at the moment."

He pushed the brim of his hat up. "Mrs. Morgan, has anyone ever told you that you talk too much?"

"No, sir," she replied sweetly. "I don't remember that they have."

He sighed, knowing defeat when he heard it. "Fetch your picnic supper, wife. I'll saddle the horses. And ask Maria if she'll put the boys to bed when they come home from church. I've a feeling we'll be spending tonight under the stars together."

"Me, too," she murmured.

He pulled her into his arms. And this time, the kiss he and Tamsin shared was as deep and sensual as the passion they shared for each other, their children, and this big, beautiful, new land.

BODYGUARD
by Suzanne Brockmann

Threatened by underworld boss Michael Trotta, Alessandra Lamont is nearly blown to pieces in a mob hit. The last thing she wants is to put what's left of her life into the hands of the sexy, loose-cannon federal agent who seems to look right through her yet won't let her out of his sight.

FBI agent Harry O'Dell's ex-wife and son were tragic casualties in his ongoing war against organized crime. He'll do whatever it takes to bring Trotta down— even if it means sticking like glue to this blonde bombshell. But the explosive attraction that threatens to consume them both puts them into the greatest danger of all . . . falling in love.

Published by The Ballantine Publishing Group.
Available in bookstores everywhere.

SEPTEMBER MOON
by Candice Proctor

Patrick O'Reilly loves life in the Australian wilderness. All he needs is his land, his work, and the company of the children he adores. The last thing he wants is the prim and proper Englishwoman who arrives to care for his unruly children. Yet he finds himself inexplicably drawn to this proud woman and the fire he knows exists beneath her refined exterior.

Accepting a job as a governess is the only way Amanda Davenport can earn passage back to her beloved England and away from this rugged, uncivilized land that she hates. Despite her fears, Amanda gradually awakens to the shimmering heat of this wild country, to the children she can't help but love, and to this magnificent man whose raw sensuality dares to expose her own undeniable passion.

Published by The Ballantine Publishing Group.
Available in bookstores everywhere.

By Judith E. French

RACHEL'S CHOICE

Widowed, pregnant, and with acres of crops to plant, Rachel Irons is determined to save her farm. When fate sends her an extra pair of hands in the form of a handsome rebel soldier, she's willing to risk the danger of harboring the enemy.

Though this man she calls Chance finds himself both moved and aroused by Rachel's strength and simple beauty, his honor demands that he uphold a blood vow he made long before he ever set eyes on her.

MCKENNA'S BRIDE

Caitlin McKenna defied her family to marry her sweetheart, Shane, on the eve of his departure to America. But years passed, with no word from Shane for Caitlin to join him. Now, after eight years, a letter comes. But the main who greets Caitlin in Missouri is a stranger—a tall, rugged cowboy utterly different from the lad she married. And, as Caitlin soon discovers, he is a man with a past that includes a son by another woman.

Published by The Ballantine Publishing Group.
Available at your local bookstore.

Coming in Summer 2000 . . .

THE IRISH ROGUE
By Judith E. French

Anne Davis is in terrible trouble. Jilted by the English wastrel who got her with child, Anne must find a husband at once, and she is willing to trade her fortune for a man's—any man's—name and protection rather than force her unborn child to bear the stigma of illegitimacy.

Michael O'Ryan fled Ireland to escape the hangman's noose when he was falsely accused of murder. Determined to succeed in a country filled with immigrants willing to work for slave wages, Michael must find a way to raise funds in order to bring his widowed sister and her four children to America.

When Anne becomes lost in the streets of Baltimore and is attacked by a mugger, Michael impulsively comes to her rescue. The ill-matched pair quickly enters into a marriage of convenience and soon discovers that the passion ignited between them is anything but convenient.

Published by The Ballantine Publishing Group.
Available at your local bookstore.